Repercussion

Repercussion

L.A. Rae

© 2024 Ethereal Fox Publications

Repercussion

Copyright © 2024 Ethereal Fox Publications

All rights reserved. Except as permitted under the U.S. Copyright Act of 1976, no part of this publication may be reproduced, stored in a retrieval system, or transmitted in any form or by any means electronic, mechanical, photocopying, recording, or otherwise without the written permission of the publisher.

Cover art by Jade Merien

ISBN (Paperback): 979-8-9863633-2-5

For Shauntel, without whom I'd have never believed
in myself enough to get this far. Thank you.

In loving memory of the beagle crew: Penny,
Pumpkin, and Peaches.

PROLOGUE
DEFIANT DAUGHTER OF VENGEANCE

A piercing scream tore through the air, vibrating my eardrums at such a pitch that it hurt. The noise did not sound in the least bit human, just pure anguish in vocal form. The pain in my throat acted as confirmation that it was indeed my voice echoing in the forest, but I did not recognize it. My lower register had somehow reached notes I didn't think possible as my shattering heart screeched into the void of despair. Even the sirens might have held their breath and shed a tear had they heard my sorrow.

"Lykos!" The word fell desperately from my lips as tears poured from my eyes. For a moment my brain stuttered, amazed that I could still form syllables, but then my chest suddenly constricted until I couldn't grasp a proper breath. Her name repeated off my lips but no sound came forth. It was as if something inside of me had shattered beyond even my heart. The spot in my torso where Hades' hand had disappeared remained whole, though the essence he'd left within burned white hot. A piece of Lykos' soul was now forever a part of me.

Meanwhile, where his hand had entered Lykos, a gaping wound was left behind and blood spilled out of her, soaking the earth - and in turn myself as I lay over her. This was not how it was meant to play out.

He was supposed to merely take a bit of her and put it within me, a small bit of the cadmean vixen's essence - unable to be captured by death.

"You wore it." A whisper of a voice croaked out below me, focusing my panicking mind for only a split second.

Her dying words seemed just out of reach as my world crumbled around me, yet somehow I responded, the words choked with sobs and barely discernible in my scrambled brain.

"Of course I did. I love you." Whispered, screamed, I couldn't even register my own thoughts well enough to know which method the words escaped me. Everything was dissolving.

The blood beneath me should have been hot, but I could feel nothing as the numbness spread. My hands shook and my body began to panic as my lungs tried and failed to pull in air until I was gasping - caught between sobs and desperate gulps of air. Everything hurt and I began to claw at my neck with blood soaked hands, still crouched over my love's lifeless body, the color in her skin still fresh but the signs of life completely gone. Her cerulean eyes stared up at me, the smile she'd died with now gone as her muscles went slack.

Time escaped me, the air growing stale as the warmth of her light dissipated and the cold hand of death stilled the forest around us in homage. The wind may have blown, but the trees didn't dare rustle, nor did the living creatures pipe up with a single noise. Silence swallowed the world up until the only sounds were the beating of my broken heart and the rattling of my lungs as my body forced stuttered breaths.

The numbness that spread through my body finally reached my mind and just as suddenly as the hysterics had begun, they finally stopped. It was like my mind had snuffed out the fire and left me in the dark. I took another deep and shaky breath as my survival instincts kicked in and refused to let me just suffocate. My eyes were burning now, every blink bringing fire to them as they tried and failed to produce more tears. I'd bitten the inside of my mouth and lips, the tangy, coppery taste of blood registering only moments before the scent of it did. I looked down and saw only crimson. Only crimson and a glint of teal and purple?

"No. No. No. No." Jolting upright, I tried to wipe the blood off but I only made it worse. The carved kitsune that hung from my neck was splattered and now smeared red where I had unconsciously grabbed it when Lykos had noticed it. My beautiful vixen, whose love consumed me like a wildfire and grounded me like roots. This token of our love was all I'd have beyond memories and deep in my soul I knew that would not be enough. Staying alive and living were two different things and I knew which I would be doing without her. That she would reincarnate didn't matter, she would do so at the Fates' leisure and I couldn't wait that long.

The hairs on my arms stood up as I felt a presence at my back, the chill of apprehension somehow permeating through the fog in my brain. Unthinking, I lashed out violently, only to have my arms caught by strong hands that swirled with shadow. Recognition made my momentum leave me, my legs giving out at the knees, hitting the earth with a hard smack that would smart later. The hands released me to let me crumble to the ground as my breathing grew more erratic in a new wave of panic. I was hyperventilating, but I could do nothing to calm myself.

"Breathe child, you must breathe. Look at me." The voice was lovely and sweet, but in the same way a rose was - absolutely appealing until you were pricked by its thorns and made to cry. In that moment I could care less for the thorns I knew lay hidden beneath the leaves, desperate for comfort, my heart reached out for the warmth of family. For my mother Nemesis.

"Look at me." She repeated the words and the inflection in her tone suggested it hadn't been just the one repetition.

Surely I tried to obey her, but I was sinking and could not figure out which way was up. I was drowning, flailing uselessly in a crimson sea, desperately searching for the blue lights that had always guided me home.

"Nyx." Hands grasped my face none too gently, the tone of voice now more severe than sympathetic. The pain forced me to focus, my eyes locking onto my mother's until I took a deep breath, mimicking her motions.

"Yes child, breathe. Calm yourself." She seemed satisfied once my lungs expanded fully, the pain of the act causing me to wince, but her fierce gaze bid me to keep at it until a smile finally graced her taut face.

Nemesis crouched down and hugged me from the side, gently securing my arms in case I began to spiral and flail again. Her words were soft, perhaps even nurturing, but she was not the mother who had ever comforted my wounds. Despite my need for motherly warmth, somewhere in the back of my mind a voice was none-too-gently reminding me of thorns. Nemesis had always been the one who had scolded my carelessness or sheer stupidity, uncaring of how badly it hurt to clean wounds with strong spirits and salve.

"Come back Nyx. Do not fall apart. It is not the end, she will return to you." Nemesis did not whisper, her words were not a caress, they merely stated fact in an almost annoyed tone.

Desperation undoubtedly flooded my eyes as an idea swarmed my brain, ignoring the still prodding warning blaring in the back of my skull.

"Yes, bring her back. Please mother, bring her back. She wasn't supposed to die. Hades, he lied." My words almost slurred together in their haste, my hands clinging to her arms pathetically. At that moment I was every bit an ignorant child seeking her mother's ability to solve any troubles I had. This however, was not a scraped knee or an angry chimera pup, though there was no doubt in my heart or soul that she could solve this problem too.

"I know my child, I arrived just in time to see her fall. I am sorry, but you know I cannot bring her back. She will be reborn in another lifetime, when none know her face, as a child." Nemesis' tone was that of a mother tired of being asked a question she knew her child already had the answer for.

Oh yes, the cycle Lykos would endure had been described to us, in vague detail, the moment my mother knew I wouldn't relinquish my love for her. She had been trying to use it as a tactic to pull us apart, but it had only made us more determined to find a way to stay together. This however, wasn't how that was meant to go. There had to be some way. None would know she had died - there were no other witnesses. Surely there was no harm in guiding her back to this body instead of some new one in the distant future.

"I cannot wait that long!" The words ached, my lungs were on fire and my mouth tasted like death, every breath attempting to strangle me.

"You must." Her words were an impatient sigh that made me want to scream. For all the love my mother was capable of, her long life had left her far more prone to coldness than warmth. She loved in her own way, but it was one that left much to be desired, especially in moments such as this.

"NO!" I shoved her away from me, finding a strength I wasn't convinced was my own. What good was it to have a goddess for a mother if she could do nothing to help you? How vehemently she had protested our union, was this lack of intervention a sort of revenge for my defiance? Suddenly her previous words registered more clearly in my mind and my jaw clenched. Surely she wouldn't have.

"Why didn't you stop him?" My vision narrowed as my brows furrowed in a barely contained burst of dread and rage.

She didn't hesitate but her tongue clucked disapprovingly in my direction, as if to question my audacity.

"I couldn't." Plain and simple, no emotion in the tones.

The lie stopped me cold, for if nothing else my mother had always been an honest woman. For her to lie to me now, at this moment was a twist to the knife already carving out my chest.

"I know damn well that you have the power." There was no familiarity in my voice, the venom dripping from my words foreign to my own ears.

"Why didn't you stop him?" One last chance for honesty. My gaze caught the subtle breath she took, a mild shutter present.

"The Fates forbade my interference. In order for her to be born when they need her, she had to die tonight." She at least had the good sense to avoid my eyes, for if looks could have killed, the small bit of shame on her face would not have protected her from my glare.

To hear her utter those words was the final blow, a fatal strike to a bond frayed at every edge. That truth, it was just one more slice into my heart, another fracture to my soul. How many pieces could I be shredded into before I lost my shape altogether? What mother chose to tear their child apart instead of the world? The answer was simple - one who feared the repercussions -but how could she make that choice for me?

"So instead you decided to come watch the show as I lost the love of my life?!" Spit flew from my lips, the bloody froth flecking crimson across her clothes. She pretended not to notice.

"Let's not be dramatic now. You may one day be reunited and until then you can live your life. It seems that Hades did at least keep his part of the bargain, that was-" she said, before I cut her off.

"The reason you came? To make sure he made me immortal before killing her?" I hissed.

No, that wasn't why she was here at all.

She seemed confused as to why I was mad, her lips pulling down into that frown of disappointment that seemed to plague her only when I was around. "Well yes, that is the main reason I came - to make sure you were not harmed. The price to keep me from interfering was your safety and the completion of   the   ritual."

Anger replaced my sorrow and burned white hot where the piece of Lykos' soul now rested. The price to keep her from interfering? The pieces were clicking together like a child's wooden puzzle. Hades had said he owed a debt, could that debt have been to my own mother? The world narrowed and a single truth shone bright like a lighthouse through a storm.

"How dare you." My words were a whisper, my rage simmering beneath the surface, ready to boil and burst, but she heard them.

"I have only ever wanted what was best for you." Nemesis was an intimidating Goddess for any who had not grown up at her knee, but in this moment she looked small - unsure.

"You do not get to choose what is best for me. You don't get to have a hand in *any* part of my life anymore." There were things that could be forgiven in time, but this would take quite a lot of lifetimes before I even considered it.

"Don't be ridiculous Nyx." Panic, then disbelief crossed her features, her lips parting as if to say more, but I had had enough and sorrow propelled me forward.

"I never am, mother. I have done nothing but try to exceed your expectations but none of that means anything so long as I love her. I see that now," I shouted.

"Please Nyx, I just want you to be able to live a normal life." She stepped back just a hair, subtle but enough that I knew I had the upper hand.

"Thanks to you, my life will *never* be normal. Don't you see that? What child of a god is ever allowed a complacent life? So guess what, now you get to watch from the shadows because I do not want to see you again. Do you understand me? If I get even a whisper of your presence I will let out every drop of blood in me just to rid myself of our connection. You will have no tether to the human world and you too will have to suffer the wait of time until Lykos is reborn."

"You wouldn't do that to Medusa." She scoffed slightly, but with her words she only gave me more fuel for the fire.

"She will know what caused it, once she hears what happened here. Do you think I'm the one she will blame when she knows the truth? Think very hard about your next actions, mother. Mom would forgive me her heartache, but I wonder if she would be so eager to forgive you?"

Medusa had been trying for years to get my dear mother Nemesis to stop meddling in the affairs of the Fates and the other gods, but she always had to have her hand in it. This would be the last straw for my infinitely patient and loving mom.

"Fine. I will leave you to your sulking. You know how to find me when you come to your senses, but one day I hope you will see that this was all ever for you my child." She managed to puff out her chest indignantly - now more goddess than mother.

"No, it's all been for you - but no more. I hope you enjoy the show. Its about damn time the Gods were reminded that there are repercussions for fucking people over. Hades will know my vengeance when it arrives in a river of blood." Tears were starting to rise in my eyes once more, the words practically choked out as I turned my back and knelt back down beside Lykos.

"Do not do anything foolish Nyx, you are not the only one who lives with the consequences." She huffed the words, her footsteps light and then gone.
"Goodbye mother."

Chapter One
Stalking the Enemy

Three days' travel was enough to convince me that a nice little cabin in the woods was far more my style than a crowded village. Although my heart sank to have left Lykos behind, the peace and quiet of the wilds soothed an itch I hadn't been able to pinpoint, even out scouting. Here there was a freedom that couldn't be obtained when coexisting in a mass. The wilds did not judge and out here the world was honest about its intentions - eat or be eaten, survival of the fittest. The dark part of me thrived off the adrenaline of a hunt, of heading into the fray not knowing what would await you, having to adapt to whatever lurked around the corner.

The breeze was crisp, drifting in and out of the wooded areas in gusts that made the spring leaves rustle above. The dry tinder of the forest floor crunched beneath my feet with a satisfying sound I would have to be careful of, but enjoyed while I could. Only the first part of the trek could afford to be noisy, but thankfully a recent rain soon muffled my steps once I'd reached the base of the mountains.

There were amazons from the coastal villages whose retreat needed to be secured, but that didn't mean they needed to slow me down. I had no intention of pausing their trek with pleasantries, a sense of security would only put them more at risk. I could not babysit their entire journey, nor would I backtrack before it was time to head home. The deer trails were not the easiest to follow, but they would grant me passage parallel to the main path. From a position out of the way, I was less likely to be slowed down with wary greetings and more likely to avoid stumbling on the enemy unawares.

The first of the fleeing amazons I spotted were well worn, their faces masks of despair and not a one even noticed when I skirted around them to follow the tracks left in their wake. After studying their progress through the signs left in the earth, I slipped back into the thicker brush just in time to avoid the next traveler.

Unsurprisingly there were no enemy forces tailing the first batch, only a few stragglers and one particularly skittish horse who jumped out of his skin any time the wind brushed him. The poor brute had suffered more than he was likely to recover from, perhaps more so than the haggard woman who had all but tied herself into the saddle to stay astride.

They would be the village's problem, I was not equipped to soothe their wounds or calm their nerves. An escort I was not.

Wedged between a large tree trunk and some rock, I awoke a few days later with the sun warming my skin and a silence in the woods that instantly alerted me to something moving in. A scout had been sent ahead of a far more alert and diligent group of amazons. The young man, whose keen eyes couldn't quite figure out what he was missing, stared into the space I occupied. A smirk pulled my lips as he came close to spotting me, only to be distracted by a skittering squirrel. When he looked back, I was already on the move again, forcibly stifling a yawn. Whether he slowed his pace or turned back to caution his fellows, I didn't know, moving far more quickly than his tired body would allow him.

The group he preceded was much larger than the first group but also incredibly quiet for coastline dwellers. Perhaps it was because they were so used to the whipping winds of the coastline that they now tread so carefully, their ears hyper-sensitive to the noise they were creating in the silence of the forest. Their adrenaline was still high, assuring me that this group was the one I'd been looking for, the last of the coastline refugees.

They were still stained red from injuries, the blood not yet browned with time. With any luck there would be no festering, but they had a while yet to travel and weren't in the best of condition. The tangy taste of fear mingled with a steady stench of sweat and dirt, the perfect environment to create infection.

Laughter danced silently within my chest even as I scrunched my nose with distaste. I had never been able to taste the air before, but after my convergence with Lykos, my senses had become more sensitive. It was odd to have acquired new skills without even recognizing it. Perhaps I'd learn to appreciate it, but today my heightened sense of smell was not exactly something I was grateful for. It did at least aid me in my mission.

Even if they hadn't left tracks akin to a stampeding herd, their smell lingered in the air, pointing me in the right direction. For a moment I considered attempting to cover their trail a bit, but with as large as this group was, it would have surely been a waste of energy to even try. Once they had passed by, I waited a half hour and then rose from my shady hiding spot and pressed on.

My movements were now staggered, a sense of foreboding creeping up my spine as the forest seemed to hold its breath. Any time there was a gap in birdsong or squirrel chatter my feet halted, eyes scouring the trail and woods as far as possible before proceeding. After a solid hour and a half of movement, the caw of crows rang out, their screeches sounding indignant as they flew past towards the mountain. My muscles twitched with anticipation as I crouched in between two trees whose limbs bowed low to the earth, creating a crossing of shadows that swallowed me up.

My prey would arrive just as surely as the wind blew, I merely needed to be patient now.

Hyper aware in anticipation, time moved by like molasses as I chomped away at the bit, ready to turn my static energy into something more productive. It took a great deal of effort to center myself, slow and deep breaths calmed my mind enough to channel my energy into focus but did nothing to ease the tension in my back. My patience was waning and my skin was beginning to itch from a multitude of bug bites when, as if I had summoned them with magic through sheer force of will, the enemy finally arrived.

Their steps weren't loud, but their gaits were clunky, though I couldn't figure out why until they came into view. The small group was made up of burly men with faces full of hair that had perhaps been groomed at one point, but had since grown wild like their eyes. Their thick bodies were misleading with a soft layer of fat barely obscuring rippling muscles. Leather armor adorned their vitals, back with metal plating that shone at the joints. They had large axes strapped to their backs and swords at their hips to offer versatile fighting that I had no doubt they were capable of.

A few of them had taken blows to their legs, which were the least protected. Their injuries hadn't slowed them much, they had simply taken pieces of cloth and tied it to them to stem the bleeding and provide support. That the wounded had joined the others in chasing after the retreating amazons was both absurd and impressive. One had to have respect for their enemy, though it would do nothing to stay my hand, I would be quicker with my finishing blow because of it.

They stayed bunched together, the worst off of the group keeping to the middle much as you'd expect from defensive prey animals. These few would be the most dangerous simply because they seemed the least threatening. The tactic was smart and misleading - one might assume that those in the middle were easy pickings and try to take them out before the others and get themselves surrounded in the meantime. Even worse would be to disregard them completely, assuming a wounded animal had less fight in it than a healthy one was how many a hunter found themselves on the losing end, hurt and hungry for their efforts.

The earth shifted beneath my feet with a silence that only an unnatural creature such as myself could manage. My mother's shadow magic hushed the world, causing even the snap of a twig underfoot to be as silent as sand falling. These warriors were no fools and I would not treat them as such, to do so would only delay my return home. The wilds were comforting but I was missing my lover's arms. It was time to cut off the diseased flesh so the wound could heal and I could get back.

Eight men; three in the middle and five surrounding. Easy enough.

Reaching down to the earth I grasped a handful of rocks, adjusting them in my hand so that they were easy to maneuver. Carefully I peered through the brush and roughly calculated the strength I'd need to send them across the clearing the men were starting to fill. Admittedly my arm wasn't the best, but thankfully precision wasn't necessary, strength alone would suffice well enough for what was needed. Half a dozen rocks left my hand one after another as I lurched them high above the men to the opposite side of where I hid. Their descent wasn't noticed, the soft tapping of their fall proceeding in a way that mimicked something trying to sneak through the brush towards their rear.

Although the sound wasn't loud enough to hint at anything large, likely to be mistaken for a squirrel rather than a human, it was enough to make them pause. The men immediately stopped their trespass, heads swiveling towards the sound, their breath held in anticipation of a trap, only they were looking in the wrong direction. It wasn't much, but it was a small window of opportunity I wouldn't let pass me by.

There was no sound upon my lips nor grunt from my lungs. With a precision that had been drilled into me by lifetimes of fighting and tracking, my feet and body moved with a fluid unity that created only a whisper of sound. My sword remained sheathed across my back, preventing any noise when running. This type of attack required a much more subtle approach which called for a pair of particularly long knives. Their blades were sharp and curved halfway down their length, not quite as strong of an angle as a scythe, but pretty close to a miniature version in appearance. Outnumbered and outsized by well triple the amount, I needed to even the odds as quickly as possible and that would require me to be up close and personal.

Dancing along the outside of their tightened circle, my blades sang as they hit flesh and bone and sliced across both. Their curved edges glided through the soft stuff and over the hard in a smooth motion that allowed my body to twirl away and then back close for the next without even a pause for breath. A whirlwind of blood splatter slung through the air as four men fell, unable to scream out as they grasped the gaping wounds across their throats.

In different circumstances I might have given them a more honorable match, but today was not that. Today their cruelty and ferociousness was well known and met with the same. I'd not waste my own life or those I was meant to protect for the sake of being able to say I killed them nobly. So long as it was a quick death, my soul could handle the stain.

The rest were quick to pinpoint me, the shuffling of their brethren instantly putting them on high alert. Now the true fight was on.

As predicted, the men in the middle were the true threat as they pulled short swords out of their sheaths and lunged as if they weren't wounded at all. The last outer man reared back his fist and only just missed a solid blow to my head. 'Only just' being a touch too close for comfort, but more than enough room for me to react.

My blade lurched forward as I twisted away from the giant fist, crimson raining across my face as it sliced through veins and tendons then got stuck wedged in bone. The left handed man screamed out in rage as he ignored the lost blade jutting out of his arm, letting it finally clatter to the earth as he continued to swing on me. Tough bastard barely even flinched.

Best leave him for last if I could help it, he needed my full attention.

Dancing away I drew my sword, meeting two of the three short swords as they bore down on me. The third swiped low, trying for my legs and I couldn't help but smirk. These boys were very well trained indeed. They kept me moving as they worked together, attempting to wear me down so that they might take advantage of an opening. If I hadn't lived the life I had, their method would have surely worked, much like wolves who ran a moose til it couldn't fight back.

Unfortunately for them, although I wasn't half as strong as I once was, I was not anything close to what they were used to fighting. After dancing around the clearing long enough to have drawn up a sweat, I was done playing.

They came at me one after another but with every attempt they made to strike me, I learned a little more about how they moved and how they could be countered. By the third round of their cycle I had taken a few shallow slices, but I was able to do more than just block, their bodies showing proof of how quickly my sharp blade could bite back.

Blocking with my knife I struck out with my free hand, my fingernails shifting into stone claws that caught the man closest to me off guard long enough for me to lodge them halfway into his chest. I kicked the injured brute away without releasing my hold on his flesh, causing a spray of gore to soak us all as he fell backwards to the earth. His shriek of pain hurt my ears and caused his buddies to stutter in their step.

The left handed man who I'd struck earlier was unbothered, his movement in my peripheral vision was faster than expected. In the brief moment that I was occupied, he barreled through his companions, striking my ribcage with jarring strength before he stepped back out of reach. If he hadn't been bleeding out this whole time I might have been worse for wear. Thankfully, I was certain nothing had cracked, but it hurt enough to piss me off.

That was when the darkness within crept out.

"Playtime is over boys."

The words were the first I'd uttered in days, barely audible, but I saw their bodies shuttered as the venom in my notes seeped into their pores. Who knew what I truly looked like to them in that moment, but more than one less favorable adjective had been used to describe me in the past. Whatever curse they might have uttered never reached my ears, but I saw the surprise and terror that gleamed across their eyes, their jaws clenching.

My wings burst from my back as I hopped backwards, dropping my knife and drawing my sword instead. The blade moved in an arc that forced their short swords to slide down the sharpened edge as they tried to converge all at once. My arm was not strong enough to pull their weapons from them with such a maneuver, but I didn't need it to be. As they attempted to recover my wings curved around in front of me, then arched outwards, the bone protrusions at their tips acting like daggers as they sliced their way through flesh.

My wings were not capable of true flight, but they could act as extra weapons when the occasion called for it.

The first of the remaining three fell when the bone protrusion of my wing darted underneath his jaw. The appendage arched upward and lifted him from his feet, his body flailing for only a moment before ceasing all twitching. His death was quick, if very wet sounding.

When his friend snarled and lunged, I was ready, my wings dropping so that they were out of the way just in time for him to swing at empty air. Ducking beneath the blow I dropped my sword on the ground and rose instead with bare hands. Chest to chest with my enemy he now had no room to move in defense, off balance and stumbling backwards, he realized his mistake too late. My hands reached up and grabbed his head, claws digging in for grip. With wings pulled in tight I twisted in place, bending my knees so that I could twirl with just enough precise force and motion to snap the neck.

One more to go.

Last but certainly not least was the brute whose arm I had sliced and whose fist had bruised my ribs. His left side was covered in blood he had leaked throughout this whole engagement, adrenaline making him oblivious to its effect. He had grown pale and despite his bravado, his footsteps were unsteady.

"You really should have tied that off, you know." A cruel grin pulled my lips towards my brows as I stepped away from his fallen brethren and faced him full on.

He groaned as he stepped forward, but as he did so he seemed to think better of it and paused, foot halfway raised. He stepped back as he took stock of the deep gash in his arm, as if he had finally registered my words. A deep rumbling laugh shook the air between us until it consumed the entire area.

"Oh shit. Yea, spose I ought to have huh?" He more crashed, than sat upon the earth, a scrutinous look upon his face as he peered down at his body.

"You might have given me a run for my money if you had." There was no doubt in my mind I'd have won against him in a fair fight, but if he hadn't been bleeding out the group might have managed to do some permanent damage.

"Cocky bitch aren't you? Doesn't matter anyways. You might stand a chance against us, but the rest of them? Heh, my god will eat them for breakfast." He idly waved with his bleeding arm, the strength draining from him quickly now that his adrenaline was wearing off.

"What makes you so sure?" I stayed a distance from him, smart enough to know that even in this state he was dangerous.

"They aren't killers. They fight hard, I'll give them that - but they still fight with honor and that won't do shit against my kin. We were born to kill in the name of our god. You really think these people stand a chance?" He laughed deep in his chest until it became a cough that seized him and shook his great body.

"Don't just sit there and watch - you're not a coward, let me die like a warrior," he seethed.

Whether or not he deserved it made no difference, there was something deep in my bones that ached to finish the fight on my own terms. There was a darkness within that haunted my soul, a soft echoing of my name that spurred me on even before his words had finished on his lips.

"First tell me the god I send you home to and why he bids you to attack the amazons?" My jaw clenched as I waited for his response.

"My god is one of vengeance, your amazons must have pissed someone off. Now, send me home; the Valkyrie will carry me to the halls of Valhalla and there Vidar will praise my strength until I fight once again." He said the words with reverence, his heart wholly committed to words he must have spoken often.

My blade sank into his chest, dirt and blood mingled in what would have been a festering wound had it not been a lethal one. A smile pulled weakly at his lips before his body went slack, the weight of his mass pulling him from the metal, crashing awkwardly backward onto the earth.

My hands shook with adrenaline as I scooped up my other weapons, their metallic surfaces dingy now with blood and gore. My body ached, a lack of use showing in the way my muscles strained. Amazons were tough sparring partners, but these vikings were double their size and strength. It was no wonder they had been able to take so much land so quickly.

What would the death tally be in the end? Even worse, how would my dear vixen fair when faced with such losses, with failing to protect all those she loved? We wouldn't be able to save them all and although I could live with just saving those who meant the most to me, I doubted she could. Her heart had been given a chance to heal with every reincarnated life, so that she remained beautiful and light within. When I slept as a gargoyle, waiting for her return, my memories followed, darkening the world around me.

A trip to the cold stream nearby did nothing to lighten my mood, the cold turning me sour towards everything, most especially the solitude that suddenly swarmed in around me. There were so few options ahead and my soul knew where Lykos' heart would lead us. Fear wormed its way in, the future threatening to drown all the happiness I'd accumulated in the short span of my reawakening. There seemed to never be a reprieve, at least not for me and Lykos. When would it be our turn to just exist and enjoy life again?

Necessity forced me to swallow down my emotions. I still had a job to do, somewhere I needed to get back to. With the better part of the blood and gore scrubbed from my goosebumped skin, I let the wind dry me off as I headed back the way I came, certain that if others came along, their dead brethren would take precedence over a chase. All I needed now was to get back to the village and my lover's warmth. More than just the cold water had left me chilled to the bone.

CHAPTER TWO
LOVE IS THE COLOR BLUE

Da Duh Da Duh Da Duh Da Duh.

The sound of my heart beating in my ears set the rhythm of my stride as I tore through the forest. Night had long since settled, but unlike the Amazons who had passed ahead of me, the darkness of a no moon night did little to hinder my progress. The sky was alight with stars and although they provided no visibility, they were a comfort when I looked up, carefully mapping my progress when the canopy was sparse enough. The constellations had always been a double-edged sword, but one I never failed to fall upon when times grew hard and the night long.

As I ran, the world's vibrations -as well as those from my lightly treading, bare feet - helped me to see everything more clearly. Reading vibrations was subtle, like water parting ever so slightly for a pebble in shallow water. There was a kind of static to every living thing, their energy tangible to the sensitive. If you weren't looking for it you might never notice, but once you learned to see the subtleties, the world became even more amazing to look upon and much safer to tread through.

Humans were perhaps the least sensitive of beasts, so I was grateful for what my mother Medusa had passed on to me. It had taken years to hone the skill into something useful and I was still just a novice compared to the way she perceived the world.

The air was still cool, warmer spring weather had refused to settle in, even when the dreary fog that remained on the mountain had dispersed and the days grew longer. It didn't bode well and everything inside of me screamed that the world was amiss - something was about to change. I could feel it in the earth's miniscule tremors and the way the shadows refused to retreat.

As if that weren't enough, the presence of the Vikings solidified just how much our way of life was headed towards an end. That a god was part of the equation made it even worse.

Our continent was small and had lain forgotten for centuries thanks to the God Poseidon. Although the Greek Gods had long left this plane, their influence had remained longest here. The Amazons had kept Artemis' magic alive in their lands, which I was certain had been blessed even before they had arrived here. The Centaurs, who now spoke of their lands slowly becoming divided from the continent by the sea, had kept Poseidon's favor. It was this which had kept us safe for so long, but as was the case with most things- it faded with time if it wasn't fed.

The sea creatures which had patrolled our world had finally been defeated or fled, the vikings and their new gods proving too much for those blessed with minimal magic. It hadn't taken them long to make their presence known and although the Amazons were warriors, most had never seen true battle. I might have envied them, had they not now faced an enemy they had no chance of defeating.

The vikings were brutal, reminding me every bit of the roman gladiators who had been forced to train day and night for the sole purpose of earning glory in death - either their opponent's or their own. The thought sent a shiver down my spine and made my rhythm speed up. Oh how I had tried and tried to run away from those ghosts. To see their shadow in a new threat unnerved one part of me and fed a darker piece.

Shaking myself as I almost stumbled into a tree, I focused once more on my surroundings. No more vikings had pursued further, for now. All that was left for the immediate future was to get back home to Lykos. The Queen wouldn't be thrilled at what I had to report, but I wouldn't sugar coat the reality; any time we had left was a gift from an enemy who already knew they had won. It was one thing to fight invaders, it was another to face an enemy strengthened by their god.

Generally I was not one to admit when an enemy had the upper hand, there was always a way to turn the tide, but it was not just my life on the line. Lykos was a part of those who might face this enemy head on and I was not about to take risks where she was concerned. Our Amazon family might hold out for a while, but we simply did not have the numbers or experience to compare. Lykos and I would even the odds, but even we could be overrun and defeated. Not to mention I knew without a doubt Lykos would put herself at risk to save her friends; which meant I would be forced to do the same.

As much as I adored our friends, it did not compare to what I held in my heart for Lykos and I simply couldn't handle losing her yet again. Her reincarnation had always been inevitable, but the pain of loss and waiting had never gotten easier - no matter how many times I suffered it. Even if she would no longer die a true death, now that our magic had merged and given her a gorgon's ability to sleep as stone, it was too soon to feel that absence again.

I'd rather see the world burn than have to live without her.

Sure, I'd wade in the blood of our enemies before I took on the whole world, but I would not mislead the Queen when I let her know what would await us if it came down to that - and what decisions I'd make if forced to do so. Twenty, or even a hundred, versus one wouldn't matter if Lykos was that one.

Shadows danced alongside me as I quickened my pace, trying in vain to outrun the fears that were always just on my heels. These were the only moments I let them get close, when I was alone and could turn them into something productive. My muscles screamed in protest but I ignored them, the pain merely letting me know I was still alive, still here amongst the living. Staying still wasn't an option, not this time.

When I finally found the mountain path that would take me back to the amazon village I called home, I sat for a moment to catch my breath. The ground was hard and cold, but the tickle of grass was comforting in ways I couldn't put into words. It reminded me of days long past, of innocence and youth. The first time I'd dared to show affection towards Lykos had been in a field of grass dotted with wildflowers. I hadn't even realized I'd done it until I felt the pressure of her hand holding mine back.

A smile pulled at my lips, a warmth blossoming in my chest that would keep me warm through the coldest of winters. Love. I didn't care what I faced so long as I carried her love with me. She was my one weakness and my greatest strength.

With my breath caught and a cozy memory for company I made my way up the steep paths until I finally reached the village and a very anxious shifter. Immediately the lovely homecoming I'd imagined in my head went out the window. Lykos' wind blown hair was tied back, her clothes still dusty from stable work and her characteristic smirk no where to be seen. Whether the scouts had made a detour to let her know the others had made it back without me, or she'd sought them out herself I couldn't tell. What I *could* tell was that she was not happy.

"You said you'd be back a week ago!" The undercurrent of a growl was unmistakable, her lush lips straight lined in a look she had long ago perfected to show her cross mood.

"Ah so argue first, affection later then?" My brow quirked, though there would be no answer to the question. Not so long as her mood remained sour.

She growled low in her throat, a conflicting mix of emotions pulling her face in different directions to the point it made me want to giggle. I barely managed to contain my amusement to a mere smirk as I watched the corner of her lip twitching as she tried to wrangle it.

"I've been worried. No one had even seen you!" The glare she caught me in held a cold fire I'd long learned to dance in, the flame composed of a fear born of love more than anger.

"That's rather the point my darling Lykos. You realize most women would just be happy their partner made it home safe, right?" Although I'd have likely been the same, I deeply wanted to skip the scolding and just be held.

She rolled her eyes and huffed, her shoulders shifting backwards uncomfortably as I tried and failed to stifle my smile. Just being to lay eyes on her made my soul warm from within, any irritation I'd possessed dissolving into the wind, my aching body ignored.

"Most women's partners aren't infuriatingly good at communicating except when you need them to do so the most." She sighed, the worry furrowing her brow genuine enough to make me wince.

"They didn't see me because I was doing my job and making sure no one followed them. I also told you I *hoped* to be back that soon, but not to write it in stone. It's nice to see you though, so please come here and let me breathe you in, even if you do it angrily."

She crossed her arms over her chest in protest as I walked towards her with mine wide open. Ignoring her huff, for I saw the longing in her eyes, I wrapped myself around her, my wings preventing the world from seeing us as I leaned my forehead against hers.

"I'm sorry I worried you, my love. You know I would never do so intentionally."

The tense muscles in her back relaxed a bit and finally, after an acceptable few moments of pouting, she breathed out and slid her arms around my waist. Pressing my face against her hair, I breathed in her earthy scent, a foxy musk tainting the edges. A chill ran along my back and electricity through my limbs as she nuzzled into my neck, her lips grazing my jawline as she drew a deep quivering breath.

"You smell like blood and sweat." She murmured against my skin, the vibrations tickling and turning me on all in one breath. It never failed to amaze me just how she affected me; able to unravel me without saying anything at all, though when she did it kicked it up a few levels.

"Well my dear Vixen, perhaps you can help me to wash off the scent in the hot springs? That would be far more pleasant than the freezing stream I had available after the skirmish and my muscles would certainly stand to benefit from a soak."

She nodded and kissed my shoulder, though I felt her sharp teeth as she nipped me before stepping back. The silent reprimand was taken without complaint, there were far worse things she could do to punish me.

"I'm still mad at you." Her attempted scowl still looked more of a pout.

"You can be mad all you like, so long as it's at my side. I have missed you." The ache in my chest tightened, attesting to my words. It wasn't that I could not live without her - my body had proven it could and would - it was that life was richer with her there beside me.

"The queen will want to see you." Despite her words she grasped my hand and led the way towards the caves behind the village that housed the natural hot springs. Whichever Amazon had discovered it and chose to build around it was an absolute genius whom I would praise until the end of my days.

"She can come find me if she wishes, but I daresay she may live to regret what she finds if I'm in for a punishment." I waggled my brows for emphasis, hoping it was enough to break the tension.

A devilish grin finally split her lips and revealed that foxy smile I loved most. For a moment she forgot she was mad, her eyes lighting up as she squeezed my hand gently. My tired body practically had to trot to keep up with her quick, short strides.

The village was still bustling even late in the afternoon. There were over a hundred new Amazons within the village. All of them were sisters, like those I'd seen on the trails, seeking refuge from the attacking vikings along the coastline. It had taken a while, but when one of the strongest villages had fallen, the rest had finally come to their senses and reluctantly abandoned the coast. The mountains were far more easily defended, though I wasn't sure how long that would deter the enemy. With any luck the fallen vikings would at least delay the enemy enough to give the queen time to plan the amazon's next move.

We dodged around groups of people, strangers quickly darted aside while those who knew us waved and smiled with knowing eyes. The hot springs were at the rear of the village, in caverns that had naturally formed ages ago. Their warmth was a saving grace in winter and a soothing treat for sore muscles year round.

As soon as we entered the caverns I felt myself relax as the warmth surrounded me. Happily I was led to our favorite spot, the one where I had first seen her bare and embarrassed in this life. It seemed like only yesterday and forever ago all at once. Our lives had always been interwoven but each life was new in what it brought us.

As we moved forward I felt the shift in her demeanor when she became shy and was forever amused that such a confident fox could be so undone by nothing more than intimacy.

She wasn't the only one.

My heart began to triple its beat as I felt her eyes on me. The tiny hairs along my arm rising with apprehension that made my muscles tense. I could tell a predator was watching, but I wanted nothing more than to be caught and devoured like only she could. Unfortunately, her skittish nature had not slipped away just yet. Her memories were roughly put together and although she had accepted her feelings were true, in this life our romance was still new.

Anything fast would spook her, so I restrained myself and we took things slow.

I withdrew my wings as they took up far too much of the limited space. With them once again beneath my skin, I crossed my arms to pull my top off and watched as Lykos nervously took me in. Her fingers were tapping at her ribs, their rhythm erratic. I could see her chest rise and fall quicker, causing my skin to ripple with goosebumps. Undoing the clasp on my skirt was easy and I quickly stepped out of my undergarments, letting them fall on top of the pile of my things. Carefully I stepped backwards into the warm waters, momentarily distracted as the warmth reached through to my bones.

"Oh my Goddess, I missed this." I had to break eye contact as I moved backwards into the deeper part of the small pool, all the while my fox stood hovering near the edge. I couldn't help but laugh when I dipped underneath and rose back to find her still standing there fidgeting awkwardly as she waited for me to rise.

"If this show is for me, might you move your arms so I get the full effect? " I asked.

She managed to smirk then, gaining a bit more confidence in her stance as she moved her hands to her hips.

"I was beginning to think you were looking forward to the water more than me." Lykos said, pouting the whole time.

Shrugging I replied, "Eh, you run a close second."

I couldn't help the giggles that poured out of me when her face scrunched up in a look that made it clear she didn't think I'd have the audacity to say such a thing. Thankfully for me, she retaliated only with a splash of water to my face as she walked in.

"We will see who is a close second come tonight when you're begging me for attention." She retorted with all the sass of a fox.

Kneeling, I pushed my lips into a pout with my hands out in front of me - a pitiful display of remorse. She turned away from me, purposely putting her nose to the sky, her butt cheeks bouncing from the quick motion. Suddenly all play was forgotten as the heat in my core lit up and scorched my insides.

Reaching my hands out, I gently grabbed her hips before sliding my arms around her, starting at the dimples in her back and kissing my way up to her shoulder. I could feel her trying to resist and smiled against her skin. I kissed up her jaw until I could whisper in her ear.

"You are all I could ever want in this world and I'd watch the whole thing burn if it meant an eternity with you." I said, softly.

She turned in my arms and looked into my violet eyes, her cerulean blues an ocean I would drown in if she let me.

"Nothing needs burning down tonight Nyx, but it is nice to hear it. I missed you." She replied with a sigh.

The admonition cost her a bit of pride every single time, but she was getting better at expressing her feelings aloud. It made my lips curl into a smile I could feel rise into my eyes and brow. Leaning in close I waited, breathing her in before she closed the miniscule gap between our lips. She was everything wild in the world, earthy and delicious, nourishment and starvation all at once. As soon as I tasted her, the rest of the world disappeared. The air was cold compared to the hot water, so I pulled her down with me into the depths, erasing the mottling from our skin.

"I missed you too, though in truth I am exhausted. Would you be horribly disappointed if tonight was just kisses and cuddles?"

She nuzzled my neck as I sat back against the rocky ledge, her legs straddling me in a way that made my skin tingle. For all that I would have loved to devour her from top to bottom, I hadn't slept in two days and the hot waters were already making my eyelids droop.

She laughed and replied, "Horribly disappointed, no. Amused that the woman with all the libido is turning down sex? Absolutely. Come, let me wash that mess you've made of your beautiful hair."

There were lots of kisses in between, but Lykos never took it further, her hands instead working the soap into my long hair and fingering out the knots and bits of debris until my locks were straight and clean. Eventually the soothing motions had me drifting off so badly she had me lean over the edge with my arms and head on the rock so I wouldn't accidentally try to drown myself.

My bliss was interrupted when a cough woke me from a doze and I jerked back hard enough that Lykos snarled - likely having dodged a headbutt. My eyes refused to focus for a moment, but the voice was one I recognized immediately as one of the Queen's messengers.

"Sorry for the intrusion ladies, but the Queen wishes to have your report Nyx." She stood rigid as she spoke, tension emanating off her.

Perhaps it was merely her annoyance at having to track me down like an errant foal, but she could have benefitted from a relaxing soak. There was a long pause as we all waited in silence, until finally my patience broke.

"Are you going to take it to her or will she be joining us in the bath? Or better yet, should I stroll out naked into the night and give her the report as I am?" I asked sharply.

The edge in my voice couldn't be helped. There was nothing worse than being woken from a nap with business that could absolutely wait. The queen had undoubtedly already spoken to those whose ass I had been covering anyways. Two days awake and on edge was enough to spoil even the best of tempers.

The messenger had the humility to look embarrassed and from the corner of my eye I could just see the way Lykos' lips twitched, trying to suppress a snicker of laughter. Thankfully she curtailed it into something that could be mistaken for a snarl, instead of ruining my attempts at intimidation.

The messenger stuttered, "S-sorry. I'll let her know you will see to it as soon as you are finished with your bath."

The woman gave a slight nod then darted back the way she came, walking swiftly until the echoes of her feet increased to a jog. Sound was weird in the tunnels, sometimes carrying along the corridors and other times disappearing almost before the ear could register it. There were also spots where the water dripped in some hidden crevice no one could find, offering a steady cadence. We avoided those areas, my poor vixen unable to bear the repetitive sound for long before she became as agitated as a horse plagued by biting flies.

A sigh slipped off my lips, not merely from exhaustion but for all the pieces of ourselves we had lost along the years. What would this newest venture cost us? It was that inquiry that had made it hard to sit still long enough to even rest these past few weeks.

Lykos' hands returned and gently massaged my traps before slipping around to hug me from behind. In her grasp I felt all the comfort of love and all the nervousness of someone who didn't know what was coming. She knew for me to lose my patience meant something was amiss, mere exhaustion would have simply had me ignore the woman.

"Suppose it's time to share the bad news. She won't be sleeping any better tonight for having heard it, that's for sure. Though perhaps that is a little bit of revenge for my having not slept for two." I muttered with a huff.

"Is it truly so bad?" Lykos asked softly. The wince didn't make it to her face but I could hear it in the tightness of her voice. She was not a coward, merely worried for her people. Lykos was no fool, she had seen the injuries and heard the stories from the refugees and knew the dangers of what might come.

"Nothing you and I haven't lived through, but for them?" I vaguely gestured to the air, too tired to mince words and never wanting to with her. "The few seasoned warriors amongst them may hold for a day or two, but the rest?"

My hand fluttered across my face as I elaborated, "Even those whose labors nourish the earth must one day join it again. Let us all be so lucky as to find it peacefully in the arms of a lover, or in the glory of fighting for those we love. Death is but a stepping stone, the underworld a second chance."

My words were from another lifetime, meant to soothe my broken heart and shattered mind. They offered comfort to many, though they'd done nothing for me back then, no matter how much I had tried to believe my own words.

"How is it that you can make something so morbidly dark, poetic?" She asked, a warm breath tickling my neck. "It's absurd how much hotter it makes you."

She nibbled my shoulder, releasing a bit of her own tension by doing so.

Laughter forced its way through my chest as the bitter truth flavored my mouth, "My dear Vixen, never forget whose child I am. Between Nemesis' vengeance and the Fate's maneuvering I doubt there is very much I haven't had a hand in or been witness to. The only way you get through that with any ounce of sanity is a twisted sense of humor and a bitterly poetic heart."

There was a shift in the air, a stillness that I had meant to prevent and failed.

"There is a lot you haven't shared with me, isn't there?" Lykos asked, her voice soft, the question cautious but curious.

I shrugged, a heavy breath leaving my lips as I turned to face her, my hands sliding up her arms to frame her face. Those endless depths of blue had become my sanctuary even as they held me prisoner. Unable to break away, I attempted to be as gentle as possible with my words.

"Depends on what scale you're using. We both have lived lives without the other, I am certain you've kept plenty from me, either for your own sake or mine, it is not worth dredging through."

She grumbled, "Likely only because I cannot remember them."

Her argument was valid, but also irrelevant. Whether she remembered them or not, they held no sway over this life or what I felt for her. Still, she had scrunched her nose up in that particular fashion that meant I was not getting off the hook so easily. Lykos despised any sort of dismissal and leaned in harder for my attempts.

I responded with a groan, "Mine are memories I wish I couldn't recall. I do not regret the decisions I've made, but not all of them have been pretty. There are many sections of my life that are drenched in crimson. You need not be soaked in it too."

She held my hands between us, unrelenting in her gaze, knowing full well that the moment she broke our stare I'd have the strength to stray from the conversation.

"It wouldn't make a difference, not now." She was prompted.

I knew she wanted me to share, to allow her to see into that part of my life I'd consciously kept from her, but now was not the time. I wasn't ready. Who knew if I ever would be.

"If that is true, then neither will not knowing." Barely a whisper now, my words trickled out with an exhaustion far surpassing the last week's events. Lifetimes of sadness drenched the vowels.

She grumbled low in her chest, having been caught at a standstill. She nodded slightly, a temporary acceptance. I had won this battle, but the war was far from over. It pained me to think she felt slighted by it, but truly, what good would it do to trudge through a bloody past? Especially the ones whose start were marked by the loss of her? She need not carry any guilt. I wished she would never know, but my optimism wasn't so deluded as that.

"I suppose it's time to go see the Queen. Will you accompany me?" I asked hopefully. Her presence was a balm to all my ailments and annoyances, but I prepared myself for a rejection; her temper was just as stubborn as she was.

Instead, she smirked and the tension between us disappeared. I could have dropped to my knees then and pledged my undying soul to her. For every reason I could think of that made me unworthy of her love, she made me endlessly grateful she did so anyways.

"Oh, want me to share in the misery eh?" Her voice was musical, teasing and all I could have ever wished to listen to.

"Absolutely, how else will I manage?" I asked with a grin.

Poorly was the answer.

"I can think of a few ways, though I doubt the Queen would appreciate it." Her grin was toothy, her fox shining through.

"I do *try* not to find more trouble than what already chases me, unlike you." I said, scolding her playfully.

She snorted in response.

Rising out of the water I just managed to curb the smirk that pulled at my lips as I watched her blue eyes follow me, her lower lip falling enough that her mouth gaped a bit. It was hard not to go back to her and nibble that pouty lip, but alas duty before pleasure. I missed the heat immediately, but it only lasted so long as it took for me to get clothed again. Lykos slipped her hand into mine and my body once again heated from within. Truly a lifetime of that alone was worth every questionable deed I'd committed and every drop of blood that stained my soul.

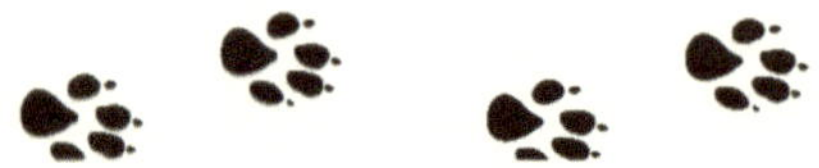

The Queen looked mildly annoyed when we entered. Her face was pulled into a frown, the wrinkles between her brows furrowed more deeply than what was usual. Lykos' hands tightened into fists, her anxiety sensitive to tense situations. Although I didn't know for sure, I assumed it was merely that queen anticipated my news. Afterall, the scouts would have described it to her long before I showed back up.

The queen gestured towards the meeting table, drawing the attention of all in the room. The council had been called in, but extra seats had been obtained so that we would not be left standing. There were two chairs, which made me smirk, the presumption that

Lykos would be alongside me was not at all an offensive one.

She addressed me directly, "I do apologize for pulling you away from a well deserved break, we will make this quick."

The Queen's eyes flitted across to her council women and they all nodded slightly. They were still dressed and stained with the day's work, obviously having pulled from tasks which had lasted later than was usual. That knowledge did little to soothe my annoyance at being interrupted, though I managed to quell the temptation to make a snarky remark.

Rhea, who was the oldest woman at the table and was once one of the Fates of Time, smiled gently at Lykos before turning a knowing gaze at me. She gestured for us to sit with a shooing motion of her hands.

"Do not mince words dear, tell us what you saw." She said, her eagerness barely contained.

There was a sudden shift in the room, a subtle unified holding of breath by all in attendance. The calm silence was eerie, my skin growing itchy with discomfort. At my side Lykos' hand drifted to her side, her fingers dancing up and down her ribcage. She hadn't asked for more details than what I had given, perhaps she could see the truth on my face without the words off my lips, but now she was nervous. A pang of regret jabbed my heart as I readied myself to confirm bad news. She had lost enough already, yet I knew more was to come. Placing a hand upon her leg, I jumped right to the truth of it.

"The vikings have taken the coastline. Some pursued, but are no longer a threat. It won't be long before they make their move north to us. Our time here is running out. The group today confirmed they act with the blessing of one of their gods, Vidar." I said, concise and with as little emotion as could be afforded.

The words felt heavy, as bad news often did, but the certainty of it made it worse. People had come and gone from the earth, disappearing like smoke on the wind time and time again. Those who remembered the amazons would tell their tale, but one day they would be stories no one believed. Thus was the nature of humans - to create, destroy, and forget.

The warrior at the table rubbed her forehead just below a scar that pushed her hairline back a bit. She was one of the few amongst them that had lived through true battle, though it had not been with the amazons. I suspected she was not born in our land, a subtle accent just enough to set her apart, but had never cared enough to ask since she often kept to herself.

"Can we withstand them?" The warrior asked. Her voice didn't carry much hope for my answer.

"If even half of our warriors were blooded, then we might hold out for a while, but from what I've seen? No. The enemy is vicious and worse than that - they are organized and well trained. The pathways here will slow them, but I would be lying if I said we had a chance of winning against them. Your next moves must focus on survival."

Their faces only changed minutely, more like my words were a confirmation than a surprise. The cold hard truth was that there was nowhere for them to go, no neighbor to flee to and no far away place to seek refuge. The continent was not large by any map's comparison and the amazons had never sailed the sea. What survival might look like, if it was even possible to obtain, was questionable.

The scholarly councilwoman, whose name I had never caught, nodded solemnly.

"We had feared as much. Our sisters along the coast have fought off pirates of all sorts - for them to fall is no small thing." She said softly, her fingers steepled in front of her.

"Will we flee then?" Lykos asked, her voice soft. The words held little emotion, but her fingers tapped away, confirmation of her worry.

It pained me to think she might have to endure heartache once more. She remembered the pain of distant losses and the heartbreak of those from this lifetime, but they were mere echoes of what I remembered. All our lifetimes of struggles were clear in my memories.

"There is nowhere for us to flee. The lands to the west will not welcome us even without the Mad King. We have been cut off, which is perhaps what was intended all along." The scholarly woman replied.

Lykos growled and I couldn't help but give her thigh a gentle squeeze. She turned her head to look at me, the cerulean blue bright, despite the way her lips pulled slightly into a frown. A sigh fell from my lungs, the sight not unfamiliar. We had lived many lives and lost more friends than I could count. It never mattered how hard we tried - we could never save them all.

The former Fate addressed me. "Nyx, perhaps you might try and reach your mother. Her power may no longer reach us, but information on the enemy might change the way things look."

Rhea's voice held an edge, her chilling eyes seeing the world through a lens none of us could understand. I was hesitant to agree, but I knew the difference between a suggestion and a demand. There was no point in refusing, she'd find a way to move me as she wished anyways. For all that I had come to see her as a friend, I still hated the way she manipulated those around her, if only because I was included.

"Very well, I can go tomorrow." I replied, trying to keep the exasperation from my voice. "Do keep your expectations low, even if I reach her the odds of her knowing anything useful are low."

The thought of having to trudge up to the temple and attempt to call my mother was not an exciting prospect, especially after having been on the move for over a week. That we had what most would deem a 'rocky' relationship on the best of days didn't help either.

"Perhaps our newest arrivals will have more information about this god Vidar. I will speak with them tonight. Now, go and get some rest." Rhea's words were spoken as if they were law, but I didn't try to make enemies out of allies, so I looked to the Queen for her approval before rising to my feet.

The Queen nodded her head, a hand waving us off. Any planning on their part would not include us and for that I was grateful. Lykos paused, as if she might ask something more. Reaching out I gave her hand a light squeeze, prompting her to follow me back to our home. There would be no answers tonight.

Chapter Three
Blissful Silence

Everything was too loud.

The muffled mutterings of dozens of people speaking at once clogged my ears with a buzz of noise much like a swarm of flies. Volumes varied, occasionally meshing cohesively, but mostly the sounds jarred against one another. Footsteps acted as an off key bass line, the snort and huff of a horse messing up the already off-rhythm beat. Winter clothes shuffled against bodies in a way that made my teeth ache, the pressure giving me a headache. Pottery occasionally broke, the strike of the blacksmith's hammer rang out and coughs scattered about like the plague. Winter had refused to leave the vulnerable alone and their orchestra of wet noises made me cringe the most.

The world sang a beautifully chaotic song all around me but all I could focus on was the cacophony of people. The noisy resonance of people living their day to day lives was almost torture. It was as if each sound struck me physically until I was black and blue. How had I ever dwelled in the big cities of Greece and stayed sane? One could argue that perhaps I hadn't kept my sanity, but that had truly been lifetimes ago so perhaps I was simply less sensitive then.

Living in the wilderness had fine tuned my senses to nature and now they were being forced to readapt to a space congested with humans. The peace and quiet of our return trip after defeating Tereus had been shattered like a sheet of ice upon rock. Well before the sun rose the Amazons began their day, including my love who had resumed working at the stables, and far into the night did the women congregate.

This became even more so the case when the weather had begun to warm, though 'warm' was perhaps too generous as winter seemed to be clinging on desperately well past her time. The only thing that really proved the season had changed was the sun, which now lingered in the sky longer. Large fires were built late and people sang and danced long after supper, ale and liquor passed around until all were boisterous for life. None seemed to care if their neighbors were kept up far past a decent hour, they used every ounce of their spare time to enjoy the life they'd been granted.

It was easy to understand why and I was not without sympathy.

An impending doom lay at their doorstep, ever just a soft knock away from ripping their happiness away. Winter had kept them safe enough, as the attacks from the vikings had dwindled when the frigid seas bid them to depart, but already the coastline's waters were smoothing out and forgiving the previous year's trespass. A half a season's reprieve did nothing to soften the reality of what was coming.

I was reluctant to bear a grudge toward them for their celebrations, the efforts to raise their morale were, after all, admirable. I merely cringed at the noise of it all. With scout rotations, there were always fresh bodies to fill the seats taken by those who finally resolved to sleep. The cycle of noise, therefore, was never-ending.

Even before I had slept a gargoyle's rest, I had lived in relative solitude. Solitude began with my mothers, who wished to raise me away from the other gods whose influence they deemed less than ideal. Then, it came by choice. In every life losing Lykos had become harder and harder until I finally lost interest in keeping up with any relationships afterwards. My heart could not bear the pain and in the silence I found a haunting sort of peace.

It would not be easy to adjust. Though if the vikings had their way, adjusting wouldn't even be an option.

When Lykos reawoke me from my gargoyle state and brought me down from the mountain, I had hid away as much as I could. Headaches had often threatened to split my skull in two when I dared to stay too long, dying to catch Lykos' eye just once. Now that she actively sought me out, I gave in to the need to escape the social gatherings much more often.

Thankfully, scouting was an excellent excuse and Xalia, who had recovered enough to take to the trails again, was equally appreciative of the peace and quiet when I joined her rounds. The arrows she had taken had done permanent damage to one of her shoulders, but only so much that she couldn't hold a bow taut for long. In an emergency she could shoot the enemy, but nothing needing a long hold was feasible. Her swordsmanship had not suffered at all and so her pride remained intact; she had confessed to being a poor shot prior anyways.

She was perhaps the only Amazon I had formed a solid friendship with. Serah and Onya were wonderful, but they were Lykos' friends - where Xalia and, somehow, Camilla had become mine. The latter was quite reluctantly. When the Mad King's people captured a group of amazons, I traded myself for their freedom. That had apparently won Camilla's respect and as such her friendship - whether I wanted it or not. It hadn't mattered how often I assured her the motive was purely selfish, she refused to budge and a small part of me was glad for it.

Xalia and I had spent many mornings in comfortable silence, but it was quickly apparent today would not be one of them. The tall amazon had been buzzing with energy, but whatever she wanted to say would be on her own time and not simply when I asked. She was stubborn that way, which only ever made me smirk for how much she and Lykos truly were alike. Ironic, considering their start.

We leaned against the trunk of the same tree as we took a break, a sigh escaping my lips as a cool breeze tickled my face. I breathed in deep, trying to ignore the echo of an absent pain. My body had healed far too quickly, causing it to cling to the memory of a pain that should have still been there. I could still see the look of devastation that had lain upon Lykos' face as she pulled herself free of the weapon jutting through us both, to turn and look at me. Our blood had poured out of wounds created by that single weapon, our magic mixing and somehow creating something new between us that I doubt even the Fates had foreseen. Stone had taken me, but she found me in the ether between life and death and we had returned whole and permanently changed.

My mind wandered for a moment, refocusing only when Xalia's presence stirred. I only just managed not to giggle when I saw Xalia breathe in deeply, as I had, and regret it. The only difference between us was that her wounds were still visible, the scarring fresh and pink against her suntanned skin. Two peas in a pod it would seem.

A second deep breath came a bit more easily. The crispness of winter still lingered in the air, despite the change in season. There was a strange tinge to its taste and a bad sense of foreboding, as if this temporary calm would lead to a torrential storm. There was no heaviness in the clouds, nor static in the air, but the energy felt off. I couldn't place exactly what it was that made me feel that way, but it was enough to leave me on edge and in need of a distraction.

"I don't understand how those who stay in the village all day stand it. It's so loud." Perhaps if I started a casual conversation Xalia would build up the courage to say what was on her mind, plus who else could I speak to about this?

"Well, not everyone has as good of hearing as you Nyx. Honestly I think a good handful of them are nearly deaf. I suppose the noise is a comfort to others. I've had a fair number of recruited scouts change their mind after a few days of nothing but the woods for company. They said they couldn't handle the quiet."

Xalia stretched herself out, her arms propped behind her head with minimal cringing as she settled back once more. Her dark hair had been pulled back into a ponytail, but she had left two strands free to frame her face. Anyone close to her knew it was because Serah had a knack for tugging the strands loose if she didn't. The spritely healer had practically squealed when she first saw Xalia do it of her own accord. Lykos had stuck her tongue out at me and forbid me to alter her hair style - not remembering it was a comment I'd made lifetimes ago that had started her wearing it loose.

"Hmm. I think that's the case with Lykos, not that she would admit it. She still hasn't told me quite everything about the time she spent imprisoned, but when it's too quiet at night she asks me to hum or sing so that she can sleep. It might not seem strange, but I've never known her to need it before."

Blood tinged my lips as my teeth split their surface, an anxious habit that soothed the heartbreak I felt knowing I wasn't there to help her. We had gotten into some tight spots together, but imprisonment had rarely occurred and when it did it had usually been together and was always very short lived. Xalia and Serah had been kind enough to let me in on some of what my dear love could not bring herself to revisit yet, but I knew even their descriptions barely scratched the surface of what was Lykos' reality in that time.

"That must be so weird, to have known so many different versions of her. Do you ever worry you won't like the newest one?" Xalia's eyes were closed, but that didn't take away from the expressions that passed across her face, her brows furrowed with curious intent, but also some other worry she couldn't find words for.

"I daresay she's known just as many variations of myself. It's more like getting to know a friend after years apart, rather than someone new altogether. Even when together, we change over the years, it is hardly any different. I worry more that she won't like what she sees in me than my being displeased with who she is. I think I've changed far more than she has over the years."

To say it aloud made it ever more real. Lykos had varied in her lives, but to me she had been consistent in her ways, so much so I could usually predict her movements. It made me wonder how her memories of me looked when merged together. Did she even recognize one version from the others? It was a question I would never be brave enough to ask of her.

"Do you ever miss the way it was in other lives?" Xalia's eyes peered over at me now, somehow sensing the rabbit hole I'd fallen into. Her expressions, which were naturally more severe, softened just a hair.

I couldn't help but laugh out loud, though there was very little humor in the notes.

"Oh there are times, sure. Usually just after the Fates hand us a giant pile of shit to trudge through. Those moments quickly pass though. I have the memories to revisit, but none ever compare to the here and now. There are enough lives I'd rather leave in the past, such as those where I was far more monster than woman. I'd rather not revisit even the best of those previous lives if it meant I had to relive the bad parts again."

A sigh escaped my lips, red had run through my hands so many times I'd lost count. It was by becoming a monster I learned to see the world through a clearer lens, but often I wondered at the cost. There were pieces of myself I would never retrieve and I did my best not to dwell on what that meant for the here and now version of who I was. To look back and see where I started was a task too daunting to do, except in moments of desperation when I might lose those innocent pieces that made my heart whole.

"Every life came with its own trials and very few of them had extended periods of peace. The truth is, the Fates have had a hand in our lives since the very beginning and I'm the reason Lykos got dragged into any of it. We haven't in a single life, lived to what regular humans consider old age, even back when we were capable of it."

Xalia took a long, slow breath, paused, then let it out with a flustered shrug. Finding nothing else to say she smiled at me in a pained way that I knew all too well. It was the face of a friend who didn't know how to help, despite wanting to.

"Well, at least now you don't have to age at all." Xalia retorted with a shrug.

Bless her, she tried and that was enough.

"Watching those around you wither and die is far harder, I assure you." I replied dryly.

The message was dark, but my words were light and airy, nothing to hold close but instead meant to be whisked away by the slightest breeze. It was the truth, for although people chased immortality, it truly was mortality itself which made a human life so precious.

"Suppose that is what we don't really appreciate about death. That it is a definite end to one life before the next begins. To be honest, your life sounds exhausting." She replied with a smirk.

I couldn't help but laugh.

Xalia was one of the few amongst the Amazons who just got it. She had seen battle and death and knew a small bit of what I carried with me. I imagined the queen would have understood as well, but I wasn't about to rub elbows with a leader. I had learned a long time ago, that was how you got volunteered for shit you didn't want to do.

"Oh it most definitely has been. There is a reason Gods say the greatest gift of man is their mortality. Though it's a backhanded compliment, since they have no problem snuffing out a mortal life, it is still true. The shortness of life gives one an appreciation that gets lost without an end. Even the cruelest of the gods were once kind and loving. At least that is what the few who still care say."

"We all have our roles to play I guess." There was a subtle tone shift, one that made me think she might finally be getting to what was bothering her. She was digging her heels into the earth, small craters left in the wake of her nervous movement. Her gaze shifted from the ground to the sky, as if trying to chase down her own thoughts.

"I hope you've been cast in a role you want." An elbow to her ribs made her jump slightly, but when she faced me she was glowing. It made my heart warm to see her so full of hope.

"I am happy now. Serah completes me in a way I didn't dream could exist."

Xalia's usually serious face was soft with the thought of her love. The edges of her eyes crinkled and her lips pulled up with an endless bounty of love and happiness. I imagined my own looked much the same when I thought of Lykos.

"What about you? Now that Lykos remembers, is life what you wanted?" She pivoted, her face flushing red with embarrassment as I smiled knowingly back at her.

Oh if only that question were ever as simple as that.

"Her memory was never what I needed for life to be what I wished. I've spent lifetimes loving her and hoping I was still someone she could fall in love with. All I've ever dreamed of was never having to lose her again. If I can finally live my life without the fear of living it alone, then perhaps it can be."

If it couldn't I would certainly tear the world apart to try and make it so.

"That's what I want, to spend every day with Serah, knowing that when we die it will be together, hopefully of old age." She took a deep breath and I could tell she was finally getting around to whatever she was holding in her chest. I nodded slightly, encouraging her if she were to look.

"She's asked me to marry her." She said in one exhaled breath, as if puffing out all the courage she had with it.

I laughed simply because it was the last thing I had expected. Xalia looked concerned and I hastened to soothe any perceived insult.

"That is wonderful Xalia, surely you've said yes?" My lips pulled my cheeks back as my own smile refused to be tamed.

"I have, but we aren't sure if now is the time to do it. There are battles happening along the shore, with fleeing amazons arriving every week. Come late spring we will undoubtedly have enemies at our gates. It seems selfish to want to celebrate." Although she hung her head ever so slightly, she was still beaming with happiness.

"Nonsense. This is exactly the kind of thing the village needs. Nothing rallies a family together like something to celebrate. Love is hard to find and even tougher to keep, it is worth the fuss when someone we love finds their forever." Grasping her hand I gave it a slight squeeze of encouragement.

"Are you sure it is not selfish?" She was genuinely concerned, her lips pulled into the slightest frown as she contemplated.

"Why must selfishness be so bad? There are a great many wonderful things that have come from a person's selfish actions. Almost everything I've done in all my lives has been for myself or Lykos. People might assume and perceive the actions as selfless or brave, but why else do we do anything except for the want of something for ourselves?"

When she didn't quite look convinced I shook my head and pulled her hand into both of mine, clasping it firmly between them and giving it a gentle jostle.

"Even most people's desire to be heroic or selfless is at its root selfish - for how many would choose it if it weren't recognized as a good thing?"

She seemed to consider that, a sigh falling from her lips as she scrunched her face in quiet contemplation. Every moment of happiness was worth celebrating, especially when you might be living on borrowed time, but the choice was not mine to make. Still, it was obvious she wanted to shout from mountain tops, her body was buzzing with excited energy.

"Besides, I doubt the Queen would let you skip a public wedding even if you wanted. I'm fairly certain the council has been betting on when you two would do it and the Queen is your biggest supporter." She looked up at me and I couldn't help but give her a playful wink.

Xalia laughed at that, her face finally relaxing as her lips curled into a soft but beautiful smile. It was almost like she was scared to show the world just how happy she was inside.

"Well then, I think we will just have to give the village an excuse to get drunk then."

A toothy grin pulled my lips up, a sharp canine grazing the soft flesh so that a tinge of metallic touched my tongue. There wasn't an Amazon alive that I'd encountered who couldn't match, if not outdrink a full grown man. What else was there to do all winter?

"I can't remember the last time I went to a wedding. I avoided them for such a long time."

The thought escaped my lips before I could contain it, but she did me the courtesy of not asking why. Xalia was good at knowing when to ask, when to leave it and when to simply take my words for the end of the conversation.

"Best hurry back then, go find Serah and give the news to the Queen. I'll bet they will have everything ready in less than a week. Long enough for me to recover enough to enjoy the festivities."

"Are you staying out here?" She rose to her feet and dusted her pants off, the fur shaking free of the debris easily.

"Yes, I think I'll enjoy the quiet a bit longer, then head out to the shrine to try and reach my mother. Lykos will still be at the stables for a few more hours anyways."

She grinned, pausing before heading back down the trail towards home.

"Thank you, Nyx."

With a nod and a wave I shooed her off. Despite the potential dangers ahead, my thoughts threatened to overwhelm my mind, not with fears of what might come, but with memories of a life lived long ago.

CHAPTER FOUR
WASTE NOT; WANT NOT

There was nothing but silence as I sat in the center of the empty temple, surrounded by debris and dust. What was once a beautiful place of worship and communion with the goddess Nemesis, was now reduced to stone remnants held together by tree roots and luck. There was an irony to it that had given me the giggles on more than one occasion. How ridiculous it was, that I related to something inanimate, but I too was the result of someone's love for a goddess, preserved with stone and anchored by perseverance.

Looking around at the scarred walls and broken foundation, I could see my own inner chambers, worn away more and more with every life I lived. The tapestries on the walls were faded, dust and dirt laying so thickly upon the surfaces that there was no telling what lay beneath. Books that had been left sprawled open long ago had lost their inked words, water having leaked in and spoiled the parchment pages. The amazons had spent three days chiseling away at the sealed door, only to be met with remnants that hardly held any memories of what once was.

It was going to take a lot of luck to make this work.

The weather had shifted and winter had finally broken, but with its retreat came the threats we had tried to push from thought. Tereus' death just a season prior had left the throne empty and although none were heartbroken from it, it left the seat of power up for grabs and more than one snubbed debtor to come calling for it. There was only one thing that had kept the remaining Greeks safe from outside conquerors and that had been Poseidon's rule of the sea. The viking attacks along the coast were as clear an indication as any that he no longer held his reign and more trouble would be finding us soon enough.

That alone brought me once again to the ruins of this temple, seeking information and a way to connect with my mother. She hardly ever seemed drawn to me, probably because I was far more Gorgon now than goddess, but I had to try. At least I had some of my beloved's magic coursing through my veins now, that would strengthen the connection.

Readying myself for the effort of such a connection, my distracted mind almost missed the sound of footsteps behind me. Their quiet tapping jolted my body and mind all at once so that I spun around on instinct. Rhea stood behind me, an odd almost elated smile stretching her face. The former Fate had played a part in my life for as long as I could remember and it had taken a long while to accept that fact as inevitable. No matter how I had tried to manipulate my fate, it somehow twisted me to its will anyways.

The woman was a menace early in our cycle, but eventually became a rather tempestuous ally. Lykos' magic allowed her to reincarnate, but it was with no memories and only a vague magical tug from our bond to pull her along. Rhea was handy in speeding up that reunion once she was of proper age, allowing me to sleep in my gargoyle state until Lykos was near. Unfortunately, she only did so to speed along her and her sister's plans.

The duality of her nature was never lost on me, though these last few lives she'd become more friend than foe. Now that mine and Lykos' magic was sealed in blood and tied to our souls, death would no longer part us or steal memories - making our relationship with the Fate feel balanced for the first time ever.

"Rhea, are you alright?" I asked, taking in her too wide smile and eyes that looked more manic than observant.

"I am perfect, I will soon return to my sisters." Rhea's voice sounded detached, like she was speaking underwater. Her posture was tall and proud, her pristine, almost sheer, dress dragging the earth behind her.

"I thought your sisters left this plane when the loom was broken?" The hairs along my arm began to stand on end - something was off.

"Oh they did, but they were not left to live out their peace. Finally, all the blocks have been set in place and there is no more to do. The end of Gods and Goddesses will soon arrive, everything us Fates have worked towards for centuries will be realized. We could not have done it without you and Lykos. Our catalyst for change." Her reply was airy, her hands drawing arcs in the air as she spoke.

She continued, "There will be decisions for you to make soon, but your choices will no longer affect our future. No matter what happens now, we will be free and the reign of Gods on this world will end."

Her eyes watched me, but it felt as if they were seeing through me, her pupils shifting between constricted and relaxed. There was a glossy sheen to them, though the lighting in the temple was beyond poor.

"End of Gods? What do you mean? There are new Gods even now, encroaching on this last piece of the world they have been denied by Poseidon's monsters." My voice contained my concern, trying to make sense of her words.

Unlike Rhea, my timelines were too numerous for me to see as one whole. The bigger picture had always eluded me until it was too late to change course.

Rhea's response was not reassuring.

"These will be the last. We have seen it, we have assured it. With every stroke of history upon parchment we touched the threads of lives just enough to send a ripple through the future until there were no other possibilities but one -Ragnarok."

Rhea's eyes were lit up, her smile twisting in a way I had only seen on the war weary victorious.

"You have got to be kidding if you think the cycle of Gods and Goddesses can be destroyed." Had I not tried for years just to take down a single God and failed? How could they all be felled at once?

Laughing, Rhea replied, "Why do you think it took this long, dear? There was work to be done, which is why we had Lykos killed that first time. It was us who whispered the idea into Nemesis' ear, hinting that her wife's gorgon magic was your salvation. It was our bargain with your mothers that made Medusa agree to it. Those seemingly small things sent ripples into the future that slowly moved the pieces into place. It has been a laborious thing, guaranteeing Ragnorok's success, but the result shall be phenomenal."

Admittedly, I should have been far more concerned with her claim to destroying the gods and my own role in it, but instead I latched onto what was closest to my heart. Taking a deep breath to steady myself, I let my exhale turn into a sigh, my annoyance uncontained.

"What bargain?" Carefully I posed the question, sucking back the venom in my words so that she would not simply ignore me.

Rhea's lips peeled back to show her teeth as she smiled.

"Surely you know that even Goddesses cannot bear children with one another without magic. Who but the Fates can allow new threads to be weaved? We needed our catalyst and they desired a child. Fair trade." She waved a dismissive hand in the air, as if I was being tedious.

"Surely you did not simply pluck a fresh thread and will it into my mother to create me?" There was surely a limit to their power of life and death, there had to be a balance. If there wasn't, perhaps they truly could bring about the end of the gods.

Rhea made a tsking sound as she replied, "You are not naive Nyx, you know well the power the Fates have always held."

"Why did my mother not create me as she had Lykos?" There was so much I should have known and my ignorance rubbed me raw in the worst of places.

"Your mother did not put herself into Lykos, only her magic. Since she was not created from flesh and blood, but instead stardust and magic, it allowed us a champion of our own -through Nemesis, untethered to the limitations of what we could do with a mortal."

She actually cackled then and for the first time in a long time I saw her as she had once been; a terrifying creature working outside the laws of nature and gods alike.

"All these years and that is truly all you see us as? Pieces on a gameboard to be moved and discarded at a whim?" I asked, venom beginning to creep back into my tone.

"Do not sound so put off my dear. We too have suffered manipulation and for far longer than your short life. There was no way out unless we made it and that required a few extra pieces on the board. Our future was bleak until we decided to change it. You too have benefitted from our work, remember," she replied.

Rhea had begun to walk around the small room, her steps far more graceful than her age should have permitted. The bottom of her dress billowed about her legs, yet never seemed to impede her steps.

"Not so much as I have suffered from it," I growled. "I will not play your stupid games, nor any of my mother's - not any more. " My patience leaked from my pores and evaporated into the air, anger flaring into my words despite how empty they felt in my mouth.

"It's a bit too late for hindsight dear. At this point in the game, it doesn't matter what you do, nothing can change what will happen in the end. We have seen it. The side you choose now does not affect the outcome for us. By all means, do as you please," she laughed.

"All the bloodshed, the death - it was all so you could change the future, but what of all the destruction you left in your wake?" I asked, knowing my part in it all.

How many of the wars I'd fought had been created at their behest? Death was a part of life, but just how much of the blood on my hands was their subtle doing?

"Well, history was never written in ink my dear. Blood has washed the past away each and every time it has changed. Do not pretend you'd have stayed clean had we not interfered - we both know the truth in your heart. For all that Lykos has been painted the villain in most of her histories, it is you whom people should have feared most. Remember dear, the Fates see all - even events that left no survivors to tell the tales." The humor left her voice, the edges now sharp in warning.

What could I say to that? A denial rose upon my lips and died there, the bitter taste of a lie filling my mouth. Would things have truly been different? Lykos would have been Nemesis' champion either way. Wouldn't that have led me down the exact same road?

It did not matter. I could not change the past and letting it haunt me would do no good for any of us now. Instead I clung to the relief of knowing the fates were done toying with us. Perhaps there was a chance that Lykos might be spared any further staining upon her soul, even if I had little hope for my own.

"What is Ragnarok?" Knowing thy enemy was the first rule when dealing with impending doom, so why not take advantage of the woman's talkative mood.

"Self-sabotage, as it turns out. Civil war amongst the Norse gods. Take care that you are not one of the casualties, I always did like you dear. That is why I'm here to help!" she said ominously as she drew a blade from some hidden place in her bosom.

She moved in front of the small pedestal as she continued, "You'll need strong blood to reach your mothers, let me give you one last gift - small penance if you will, for all the misery we pushed your way. Goodbye Nyx and good luck. I hope you succeed."

Her laugh was a horrendous cackling sort of thing that started soft and rose like a wave to fill every crevice of the small room. It grew until my ears throbbed, my hands clamping against my head in an attempt to dull it. When it suddenly died, I only managed to get a yelp halfway up my throat before a warm wash of hot liquid squirted across my face.

One last gurgling chuckle fell from Rhea's lips, her bloodied knife grasped firmly in her hand as she dropped to her knees. The thick scent of spilled life filled my nostrils, my stomach growling in yearning as the odd side effects of my gorgon blood rose to the surface. A small part of me wondered if that too was the Fates' doing.

Too late to ask now.

The floor pooled with deep crimson blood, the coppery tang in my mouth accented with a strong dose of magic that tasted almost fruity. I couldn't see the threads of magic like Lykos could, but I could feel it as if it had tangible weight. A blanket of it layered itself over me, tickling my senses until a sneeze ripped its way out of me. As the old woman's body crumpled across the floor, her life gone in mere minutes, a groan fell from my lips.

"What. The. Fuck." Emphasizing every word somehow helped me to process what had happened in those quick moments. A lifetime of manipulation masquerading as guidance flashed across my mind's eye. The result was a strange emptiness.

My empathy for the friend I thought she had become was consumed by a wicked sense of vengeful satisfaction for the enemy she had more often been. She had used us to somehow bring about the end of gods and that had once again put us in a position to lose everything we loved once more.

A stress headache began to pulsate just behind my eyes, causing my hands to reflexively rise to my face. Regret flooded me as I felt the warm blood beneath my palms, now smeared down my face like war paint. The scent of it was nauseating, my breakfast churning uncomfortably in my stomach as I kneeled down to steady myself.

This day had started out so promising too.

Sweat beaded across my forehead as my frustration peaked, the insanity of it all gathering in me like a fire waiting to catch and explode. Drawing in a deep breath I attempted to calm myself before I lost control. Afterall, what good would it do? I could flail and throw things, curse the ocean for the waves of bad luck I'd been sent, but the energy would be wasted. There was a solution here somewhere, but I wouldn't find it by throwing a tantrum.

"Well, since you provided the means I might as well use it. Goddess knows I could use some fucking clarity."

Rising to my feet, I carefully edged around the puddles of blood to the dias just behind Rhea's fallen body. Blood magic would work whether it was neat or messy, so at least there was that small mercy. Sitting upon the stone seat with my back to the offering bowl, I drew my wrist to my lips, draggin a sharp canine across the thin skin. With such a large offering on the floor already, my own blood was mostly symbolic, but I let a few drops fall, mixing with Rhea's.

A deep breath calmed my mind and kept my breath from staggering as I swallowed down the lingering urge to scream and curse the world. The magic in the air shifted, awaiting direction.

"Mother, we need to speak." I whispered the words, for they were not just for myself, but instead a call into the ether. I could only hope that it was enough for her to slip through the planes and reach me. Now that she had no power here, it would not be an easy feat.

Time passed slowly. The air was dank, the dust tickling my nose and threatening to send me into a coughing fit if I breathed too deeply. Patience was thankfully where I had learned to excel, my mind traveling within to a place where the sun's traversing of the sky meant nothing as I listened only to the shadows of thought whispering within.

It was there that she reached me.

Her presence behind my closed eyelids was subtle, a soft encroachment of my personal space, just a gentle nudge to let me know she was there. I didn't dare open my eyes. The shadows that surrounded me, warm and tangible like arms, would disperse the moment I searched for them.

How long had it been since I had beheld my mothers in the flesh?

Too long.

A wave of sorrow washed upon me as my heart reminded me how much I had missed them.

"We don't have long my daughter, it is only another's power that allows me this." Her voice sounded troubled, wary. "Whose blood have you used for this? There is a strange vibration to it."

"Rhea decided to depart this plane the old fashioned way and left a mess behind for my benefit. So she claimed, at least." She couldn't see my shrug, but surely she heard it.

"That old crone is a menace. Her and her sisters. Be wary, my child, even gone, her gifts always come with a sharp edge. They would see everything burnt to the ground." Her voice was strained in a way I couldn't remember hearing before.

"She was quite certain they had succeeded already, at least as far as the gods are concerned. What do you know?" I asked.

"The world has moved on, but the Fates still play their games. Poseidon's monsters have finally fallen and the Norse people -the vikings- will return soon, spurred by the sisters who they now call the Norn." Nemesis spoke with a quiet confidence.

"Yes, I have already seen the damage the vikings can do. Though with this latest development," I casually waved my hand behind me to the dead woman she likely couldn't see, "I suppose there is no need to guess at just how right I am about the trouble coming our way."

"The end of the world if the Norn are to be believed and these gods do believe them. You will be caught in the middle if you are not careful. Their Gods and Goddesses have allowed those of us who did not attempt subterfuge to remain in their realm, but that is all. My powers will no longer reach you or Lykos and the Norn have let your names slip more than once."

My mother's words were tight, their tone holding a familiar edge.

"Why should that matter?" I asked. "Rhea said what I do will not change the outcome."

Scoffing, Nemesis retorted, "The outcome, no - but the survivors, yes. Or at least that is what they have whispered in a few ears."

A sigh accompanied my reply. "I suppose those ears don't belong to the lesser, more peaceful of the gods either."

"Hah, when has your luck ever been that good? They may leave you be, but some may seek you out if they can, if only to tempt the odds in their favor. Do not trust any of them."

I rolled my eyes, even with my lids closed.

"Do I ever trust strange Gods?"

My mother laughed, the musical notes dancing across my memory and striking me in the core. There had been a time when our house had been filled with the sound, happiness filling every room to the brim. A part of me wondered if that too might have remained if not for the Fates' meddling.

"Are you safe?" It was hard to keep the worry from my voice. Our relationship had been tenuous at best for a long time, but I loved her no less for it. If war waged within the ranks of the Norse gods then outsiders would likely be forced to earn their place, putting my mother in danger.

"Yes. Hel, the Goddess of Death has welcomed us into her home as a courtesy to your grandmother."

My heart skipped a beat.

"Us?" A strange mix of hope and fear tumbled together in my heart. There was only one person she'd pair herself with as an 'us' or 'we'.

"Yes my dear daughter, Medusa is with me." Her tone was hesitant, her words slow so that I would grasp some meaning hidden in their depths, but they were also happy. My heart soared for a moment, then that hidden meaning hit me. Medusa was in the underworld; there was only one thing that could mean.

Emotion rose up and crashed down upon me, though I knew now was not the time to process it all. Pain laced through my heart like I'd been stabbed by a serrated blade. I had not known, had not had the time to seek her out. When had she died? How? The questions were like fire in my throat, scorching the flesh as they desperately failed to crawl out of my mouth.

"The ocean will no longer seclude you, it is only a matter of when the Vikings arrive in true force." Nemesis' voice wavered with worry.

"They already have," I croaked. "We are no strangers to war, Lykos and I will persevere."

By all the gods it was hard to swallow down the storm of emotions raging within. My mind was struggling to focus on the task at hand.

"Your amazons won't. They have not lived during the times of wars raged by gods."

She must have felt my struggle, my helplessness, as she hurriedly continued.

"It may be the way of the world Nyx, but it does not have to be their end. Artemis has earned a place alongside the Goddess Freya and has convinced her to bring the Amazons into the ranks of her Valkyrie. The only problem is, to do so they must pass through the land of the dead."

A scoff of laughter slipped past my lips before I could catch it.

I continued for her, "Which the living aren't meant to do. So of course, she needs me to cross the planes and somehow get them through without losing their lives and becoming one of the dead. That certainly sounds like a walk through a flower filled meadow."

How on earth was I supposed to manage that? Why would I even try? What did I owe any of them to put myself and Lykos at risk for what sounded impossible? Didn't she just tell me not to trust the Norse gods?

An annoying tingle rose up my spine as I remembered just who it was I spoke to. It became quite clear then, what the answers to my questions would be.

"Mother," I asked, "why does she think I would do this for her?"

"She doesn't. Artemis remembers you well enough to know you would not simply do it for her out of kindness. Instead she suspects you will do it to spare Lykos the pain of losing yet another family."

It was a low blow that sent fury through my body, way deep into my bones. My eyes remained closed, but I could feel my arms shaking with a rage that bubbled inside. She had some nerve, both of them did.

"Some audacity you've got saying that to me." My voice was gravely in my ears.

"I know she has no right to ask, but it is no less true. Your lover-"

"My *wife*." I practically shouted, my words cold as ice in winter.

Nemesis would not dare lessen what Lykos was to me, not ever again. Lykos and I may not have spoken of it in this life, but every life before we had renewed the vows taken so long ago. She would never be anything less to me.

There was a subtle cough before she continued.

"Your wife stands to lose everything, except you, if the vikings reach them. Could you truly face her knowing you could have prevented it?" Nemesis asked.

If she weren't already there I'd have cursed her name and damned her to the underworld. The onslaught of mixed emotions ravaging my soul were becoming increasingly hard to hold back. I needed this conversation to wrap up soon or else I risked absolutely losing my shit.

"How can I reach Hel's realm?" Swallowing my emotions best I could, the words came out clipped and precise.

"There are tears in the world, portals, that will lead you to a tree called Yggdrasil. This tree is home to many portals which lead all across the world, but also to different realms. Most of the ones to other realms have been blocked off or destroyed by Odin, but the underworld's remains. Helheim is what the Norse call it," she stated plainly.

"Got a map handy by chance?" My sneer bled into my words, the shadows that wrapped around me recoiling ever so slightly.

"Artemis will send a guide. You will find us here in Helheim and be welcomed by its Goddess. She asks only one favor for the safe passage of any whom you bring through."

That didn't sound like it was too good to be true at all.

"What favor might that be?" I asked.

"I'm sorry Nyx, but I do not know." She sounded distant, as if she had stepped away from me.

"Welcomed in the Land of the Dead, the one place I've avoided my entire life, to do a favor for a goddess I've never met. Sounds perfect," I grumbled.

That they assumed I would agree only added fuel to my simmering outrage, which reminded me of another issue I needed addressed.

"According to Rhea, thanks to the deal you and mom made, Lykos and I are the pawns they used to cause all this, care to elaborate?" I asked, annoyed.

There was a heavy sigh, a tiredness she would not express in words, then silence. The voice that finally responded was not that of Nemesis and all my anger slipped away.

"Now is not the time, sweetling. We have much to explain when we are reunited and even more we have tried to make up for, but know it was all done out of love. You, of all creatures in this world, know best what love does to one's perspective."

Her voice was like honey soothing a wound I didn't know had begun to fester and burn. I knew that voice before I knew anything else in the world. This was Medusa; my loving mother whose magic was all that made being parted from Lykos bearable in every life I had lived. My heart swelled with love almost as much as it broke to know I would not find her amongst the living any longer. Her love had always been unconditional and the only thing that saved my soul when the darkness threatened to overtake it.

"You're right." I admitted, reluctantly. "I will focus on the trouble at hand and find you when I can. Tell Artemis I will see that her people are allowed to rejoin her, but I cannot promise it will be enough. We will keep an eye out for her guide."

My voice cracked, tears crept from my eyes as my heart lurched in my chest. Oh how I had missed her. Desperately I tried to regain myself, to keep my voice steady, but the smile in her words told me she knew how I was struggling.

"Remember my dear girl, you are a Gorgon and we do not suffer fools- mortal or otherwise," Medusa whispered.

There was something in her tone that caught me off guard, the hissing notes of her snake nature adding venom to the words, drawing a smirk to my lips as the dangerous tone filled my soul. I could hear the pride in her voice even as her presence ghosted across my cheeks, an ethereal hand gently wiping my tears away.

"We must leave you now, I love you my darling Nyxia. Make us proud," Medusa said, a smile in her voice as she used my given name.

The connection dissipated, the warm touch of magic replaced with the chill of the temple's shadows and the scent of blood. The sudden disconnect left me feeling empty, the love that spilled over dwindling away until I was almost certain I had dreamt it all up.

Opening my eyes rid me of that delusion quite quickly.

Everything rushed over me at once and the scream that tore from my lungs was a mixture of anger and anguish. It took a while for the hot tears to stop and the shaking of my body to calm enough for me to gain my legs again. When it all settled, I was resolute.

Careful not to disturb the pooling blood or splatter, I retreated from the confines of the once grand structure, a grimace pulling my face at the mess I left behind. The idea that any would believe Rhea had taken her own life was absurd.

Even if I told them what had truly happened, would they believe me? Was it worth the risk? With what was coming, I needed them to trust me.

Rhea was known to disappear for days on end so none would go searching for her immediately. On the off chance they did, this was surely the last place they would think to look. Yet, there was something within me that sickened at the thought of lying to the queen. There were many lines I had crossed without pause, but this was different. This wouldn't merely be a betrayal of their trust, but of Lykos' too. They were her family, betraying them would equate to her as well.

"Not as if they can afford not to believe me anyway." I muttered as I made my way back towards the trail home, decision made.

The walk back seemed much longer, the elation of Xalia's news having dissipated like dew on a summer day. The urgency of the situation pushed my pace to a near jog, but my feet felt heavy and off balance. The urge to scream again, or punch something rose within, but I just kept walking, muttering to myself as I tried to make heads and tails of the thoughts running circles in my mind.

"Why not just tell us and prepare the Amazons to meet this new threat? Surely Rhea did not intend to sacrifice their lives. A whole group of people she has lived with for years, would that not be too far? No, I suppose it's not that hard to believe, it wouldn't be the first time. My own hands have created just as much loss, afterall. Rhea has lived far longer than I, she has surely moved far past regret and morality."

To place myself alongside the Fates seemed a bit dramatic, but had I not also chosen to walk the blurred edges of morality more often than not? Were we so different, making choices solely to accomplish a life we desired for ourselves? Would my life have been different if they had not played such a strong hand in it? Some days I wondered.

"How could my mothers make a deal with the Fates? They were the ones who always told me how cunning and deceitful they can be. Is that how they learned in the first place? Why is it always us? Why can the world's wars and bloodshed not leave us out of it for once? When was the last time we truly knew times of peace when we could just *be*!"

My words leapt from my lips like a raging fire, reaching into the sky desperate to relinquish the turmoil flickering within. Years of frustration bubbled to the surface and here in the wilderness, alone, I let myself drop the mask of calm disinterest and thoroughly lose my shit. Pausing in the middle of the wooded path, I screamed and cursed my lungs out until there was nothing left but a whisper - a promise.

"I will tear those Fates apart if I get my hands on them. I don't care if it makes a difference or not in their scheming, I will not be toyed with anymore. First though, I must do what I can to save our friends."

Walking was the only way to regain my calm as I tried to mull through all the information and possibilities that lay before me. As long as my feet were moving my brain would do the same. I couldn't stop moving, couldn't settle, couldn't sit and let the world pass by me without my knowing.

Except that's exactly what happened.

Pausing in stride, my thoughts sputtered as if someone had tapped my shoulder ever so gently to get my attention. A dark recognition settled over me, my mind had been spiraling. There was only ever darkness waiting at the end of that path. Blinking a few times, my eyes regained focus on the world around me, a sigh of relief falling from my lips.

"At least I didn't stray off the path."

What had felt like a few moments of meandering was actually half of the day and probably no small amount of sanity alongside it.

The rest of the way home was traversed with full consciousness. Although there were more people in the village, the bustle of activity made it much easier to pass through unnoticed. The path I'd chosen to return to my cabin was close enough to the kitchens that no one would think twice about the blood splattered across my clothing - they'd merely assume I'd brought home a kill and made a mess of dressing it.

A quick scrub in the wash bin and a change of clothes was enough to clear the evidence of Rhea's end, even if the image lay painted on the backs of my eyelids. I longed to collapse in bed and forget about the latter part of my day, unfortunately, there was no time to waste in regards to what I had learned.

A sharp knock on the door caused my body to flinch back, my hand halfway extended to open it. To my surprise, and discomfort, I found the queen waiting on the other side as I finally reached out and wedged it open.

"Might I have a word Nyx?" She was kind enough to make it a question but I was under no delusion of choice. She allowed me to get away with quite a bit, but there was no mistaking my welcome had limits we'd both rather not reach.

"Of course Queen." Purposefully there was no possession before the title. She was a queen whom I respected, but she was not mine. Never again would I submit to the rule of another and there would be no illusion of such between us.

"I do hate the way that title sounds on the tongue, but I suppose there is no getting around it. What else is there to call me that would sound better?" She grimaced playfully, but it looked forced. Her brow was furrowed and the lines around her eyes were tight with worry.

"Perhaps your name, though that might lead to some confusion amongst guests and slip ups among the younger generations." My shrug was as nonchalant as I could muster, which wasn't very. Tension caused my muscles to stiffen, the stress of what I was about to convey settling there.

"Indeed. The title brings with it a lot of power, but also a horrid amount of responsibility. Such is what has brought me to you today. I know you went to the temple today and I wish to hear your news if there is any, but first you need to hear mine." She sounded as exhausted as I felt and looked as if she had aged overnight.

Stepping backwards I waved her in and motioned to the table where we each took a seat at opposing ends. We were not friends and I was not an Amazon to be commanded, so we sat as close to equals as was possible.

"Nyx, you have all the age and experience to surpass my station so I will not quietly tiptoe around what I need to say and I suspect you will be as welcome to that as any."

Nodding my encouragement, I kept silent, far too curious to delay her with words.

"You and Lykos must leave. Before you react I need you to hear why." She held her hands up to stay whatever temper she perceived I would have.

I took a deep breath, one that made my lip quiver slightly from the tumult of emotions that flooded through me. Most of all it was heartbreak, not for myself but for Lykos. She had just found her new home and family, only to face something new that threatened to tear it away. This news would not sit well with her short temper or sensitive heart. As much as I might be able to say no, Lykos would not have such luxury, even if she wanted to.

Once I told her of the bargain, Lykos would have no problem departing, though a small part of me wished she would. If the Queen had discussed this with her already though? I held my anger tight to my chest, hoping she would give me a reason to extinguish it.

"Do continue." A practiced calm filled my voice, though my toes curled and unfurled beneath the table as my emotions fought for top position. Was it possible she already knew, or was this something else entirely?

"Rhea came and spoke with me this morning, before she left. Her spies have reported that Tereus has become the pet of the Norse's god Vidar, their god of vengeance. He cannot stray from his hawk form, but he guides the God and it will take no time for him to lead his reinforcements across the river."

"What of the centaur? Do we need to alert them of the danger?"

"The centaurs have pledged to the one they call Nerthus for protection, though they were sworn to speak no more but her name. They are protected, but we are not."

My first thought went to Onya and her partner. Lykos' best friend had only been with the amazons a few years and her partner only a couple of months.

Although there was a chance she'd choose the option we offered, if there was a safer option it seemed prudent for them to take it. Even if them leaving would break Lykos' heart.

That it was Tereus helping the enemy hardly surprised me. Aries' son had always found a way to try and gain power and a god of vengeance seemed perfectly ironic enough to fit.

"Leave it to that pest to find a new host so quickly," I muttered. "What else did Rhea say?"

The Queen gave me an odd, measured look, then sighed. Her hands rubbed her cheeks as she did so, drawing the color back into them.

"She told me she was leaving us." She purposely met my gaze and nodded ever so slightly as if to reassure me I had heard correctly.

Perhaps I wouldn't have to describe what had happened so precisely afterall.

The queen continued, "She said her role here was finished and that if the chance came to save the amazons, she hoped I took it, for there would only be one. I asked her what she meant, of course, but she said I'd know it when it showed itself and that the world would be changing. A war amongst gods was at our feet and when the smoke cleared, if we chose correctly, a new world would await us - but we would be the last of our people either way."

"Never one to mince words, was she?" I'd have scoffed if it had been appropriate before a queen.

"Not when it was important." She raised a brow at me, her eyes searching my face for something.

"You aren't surprised by what I've told you, so you must have been successful. What has your mother conveyed?" She asked, hope in her eyes as she met my gaze.

"She told me what must be done to save the Amazons, but I have no clue how long it will take and we are short on time. Artemis has fought for you to get a new home, but you must fight for yourselves as well. Prove that you are the warriors she has claimed you are and with any luck I'll manage to secure safe passage for you all to join her."

"Rhea was right." The queen held her hands together, her gaze looking upon me with a glimmer of hope that made me vastly uncomfortable.

"Her most annoying quality." As the queen stared me down I felt the throbbing of a new headache start up in my temples.

"I knew the chance we had as soon as I saw it. You dance between two worlds and are the bridge between them. When I saw you return today, I heard a whisper on the breeze which sounded so much like our beloved Goddess. 'Have Faith' she said."

"Funny how they find ways to talk to you when they want to, but never when you need them isn't it?" There was no stopping my eyes from rolling to the back of my head. Artemis couldn't speak to her own people all this time, but the second I was coaxed into helping she had to whisper in the wind and take the credit.

There was a long silence as she soaked in the information, her eyes glossy with unshed tears, though I pretended not to notice.

"We ask too much of you Nyx-" she started.

I raised my hand, stopping her from continuing.

"As it turns out, I haven't been asked, not once, to do the things I'm about to have to do. Instead I have been *told* what I must do - but know that if it weren't for Lykos, I'd have told them all to kiss my solid stone ass."

There was no malice in my words, the venom controlled so that it didn't slip past my lips, though my irritation at the world roiled within my core. Artemis, Hel, the queen, and even my mother - none considered the cost to myself or Lykos for all they had planned.

To my great surprise, the queen laughed. It was a strange thing, sad at the edges but filled with a dark humor all the same. She smiled broadly, as if the weight of the world were no longer upon her shoulders.

"I will be forever grateful for her, though I would not begrudge you had you told us all to do so anyways. Life is not fair in what it demands of us regular mortals and you Nyx...Rhea did share with me some of what the Fates put you through. Just know that although your reasons may be your own, the deed still has selfless results all the same."

Her words made me wish I had swallowed my own that morning when I'd said the same thing to Xalia. The world had a cruel way of biting me in the ass with my own damn teeth.

A sigh escaped us both as we rose, but there was nothing more to say to one another. She paused, turning to face me before reaching out her arm. Without hesitation I wrapped my hand around the high end of her forearm in a warrior's clasp. Her eyes met mine and I felt the sorrow pouring through them, but also the gratitude.

"Thank you Nyx," she whispered.

"Don't thank me yet Queen, I have to succeed and make it back first."

Hopefully with time to spare.

She nodded as she replied, "When you do, I hope I am still alive to give you a proper one then. If

I am not, find me in the underworld and tell me all about it, I will hold no grievance if you fail trying."

It was then I truly saw the queen. Her age, her wisdom, and the horrible reality that she knew it would take me far longer to succeed in my task than what was needed to keep everyone alive. The sad truth was, many Amazons would likely die before the end. Selfishly, I hoped that it would not be anyone we loved, for what was the point of it all just to lose those we were trying to save.

She left me alone in my hut with only my thoughts and the puzzle of how best to break the news to Lykos. I knew she would not falter, not if it meant saving her friends, but she was far more sensitive than she would admit and I knew it was going to break her heart.

CHAPTER FIVE
WEDDING DAY JITTERS

Something was wrong, I could sense it the moment she walked into our home. Lykos walked in and closed the door, leaning her head against it, as if the whole world was weighing upon her. There was no point in asking her what was the matter, she'd just sigh and shrug until the words to express herself came to her, which was rarely in the moment she was feeling them. Instead, my feet purposely tapped the floor loudly enough for her to hear my footsteps as I approached her from behind. Slowly sliding my arms around her, my hands met just above her breast as I leaned forward to embrace her loosely, giving her the opportunity to break away if she wanted to.

She didn't. She leaned back into my arms, her head resting against my shoulder so that I could breathe in the scent of horses from her wavy hair. Kissing the side of her head, I could feel her relax into my strength. It took a while, as it usually did, but eventually she took a deep breath and cocked her head so that she could see my face. Her eyes were swimming, but she blinked steadily.

"When do we leave?" Her voice was tired, but there was no judgment, no anger, only resignation.

"How did you know we were leaving?" My first guess would have been the queen, but surely she would have told me if her intentions were to go to Lykos as well.

"Apparently someone sent us a guide in the form of a Lynx. Needless to say the horses were *not* happy. Prince might've killed the poor beast, but thankfully it spoke up quickly enough." She looked as if she might have laughed had the situation been different, a weird mix of amusement and regret mingling across her face.

"Well, I had hoped to tell you myself, but I suppose at least the subject can be broached easily now. Where is the cat waiting for us?" That Artemis had gotten the feline to us so quickly was a bit disturbing.

Lykos' nose scrunched up as she replied, "He said - and this is a direct quote, - 'since you obviously aren't the one in charge, tell the other we leave in four days, I'll be waiting on the northern trail.' I'm trying not to take that personally, but I'm also thinking I may be a dog person."

A laugh fell from my lips as I leaned forward to gently kiss her cheek.

"Oh, trying are you? Would you rather lead this charge my love? I will happily give you the reins of whatever chaos we are about to embark on," I teased.

She tilted her head back, offering her neck for a continued spackling of light kisses. Her flesh was salty and mildly dusty from the day's work.

"I'm not volunteering for anything until I know more. What have you gotten us into now?" Her tone was playful, but her body screamed tension, the muscles in her back flexing against me.

She turned around in my arms and I couldn't help but lower my lips to hers. She met me in the middle, the touch gentle and sweet but also questioning. I tested the waters for a moment, then delved into their depths. She sighed as if she had been waiting forever and I melted against her. A light moan slipped from my chest as the heat from her body made me more aware of the bits and parts of me that were sensitive and growing equally warm. Every caress was a gentle reassurance I couldn't live without and everything I needed to get me through all that came next.

As I deepened our kiss I breathed her in, hating that this might be the last peaceful evening we had together. My tongue tasted her lips and found her willing to explore, if only for a few moments. We let ourselves be distracted, knowing all too well what the future might hold. Eventually we had to resurface and as we broke apart, breathing heavily for the shallow breaths we had taken in our fervor, we pressed our foreheads against one another. Her words were just a whisper.

"How bad is it?" The sag in her shoulders told me more than her words.

"I'm sure in hindsight it'll look worse." A soft smirk pulled my lips, thankful when my words achieved their purpose.

She chuckled, the sound deep in her chest. It could have easily turned into a growl of mischief if the circumstances had been different. My arms remained wrapped around her, offering support as she leaned into me.

"Alright then, ruin my night." Her sigh was heavy, all the weight of the world pressing in around her.

"Only if you promise to make mine afterwards." Gently my hand guided her chin so that she had to look up at me.

A coy smirk pulled at her lips then, all the love in the world reflected back at me in twin pools of cerulean. She nodded her agreement, a quiet promise between lovers. We would make the most of our home's luxuries, but first I had to tear a world we'd barely found again, apart.

Thankfully, she took it much better for having been warned the news was coming.

"Finally we are rid of one set of gods, just to get pestered by a new batch. What luck," she growled.

There was little argument to be had against that statement.

"Artemis has fought for her people, for your people Lykos. If this is what you want to do, I will see it through with you. But, if you'd rather stay here and take our chances in battle - I will rise or fall with you - always." A part of me hoped she'd choose the latter, battle was far easier to plan for than the unknown.

"We have to at least try, if there is a chance to save them. I know gods can't be trusted, that they've fucked us as much as helped, but I have to try." Her eyes were watery, her emotions usually hidden from the world as best she could manage, but by the goddess she was so beautiful when she let herself be vulnerable.

"I couldn't do this without you," she whispered, clear and heartfelt.

"I know," I answered in turn.

My laughter echoed against our walls as she slapped my arm, her playful growl rising in her throat, the one I loved for the way it pulled her lips up into an adorable twitch. As much as I loved her vulnerability, I couldn't stand to see her so sad. She leaned in against my chest and nuzzled close until I wrapped her up tight in my arms.

"Do you know who this lynx is?" Her words were barely audible, muffled against my shirt.

"A friend of Artemis, I suspect. We are to do a favor for the goddess of death, Hel, in exchange for safe passage for any we bring. Freya will take them in after that. The cat will show us the way to Helheim and from there we will find out what favor is asked of us. Knowing our luck it won't be anything easy, nor will it go as smoothly as it sounds."

"It's a gamble." She tapped my chest with her fingers for emphasis.

"Only if we play by the rules." I replied, a smirk gracing my lips as she pulled back and glared at me.

"I remember now why I never play against you," she sneered, nose crinkling in a way that reminded me of her kitsune form.

She was so adorable.

Teasingly I countered, "Only because you are a sore loser."

"You are an infuriatingly smug winner," she snorted, indignant.

"One day you will know what that feels like, my Vixen."

She smiled then and took me by surprise with her next words, "That was the day you said yes."

The energy shifted, my heart leaping into my throat and swelling to the point I couldn't breathe for a long moment. Her ocean eyes were bright, the love reflected there seeming to make them glow. Closing the gap she'd put between us, the warmth of her body reached past our clothing, the pressure of our bodies a comfort I'd never outgrow.

Most of her major memories had returned, but there were still a lot of gaps along spans of different lives lived. Her tracking of the time lines was messy and although it was understandable, a few key items she'd forgotten had hit hard. I wasn't sure which 'yes' she was referring to, but I didn't care - a win was a win. If I pretended it was the one that meant the most, who was there to judge me? I would give myself this small victory and let my heart swell with the love pouring off my love.

"Let us enjoy the comforts of home while we have them, yes? I'll be hard pressed to say no to a romp in the wilds, but I do prefer the cleanliness and warmth of a bed."

Lykos laughed, her voice always like music to my ears, weaving a song that would forever stay on repeat in my head. Leaning down, my lips pressed a kiss to her forehead as I breathed in the wildness of her scent, forever a mix of wildflowers and forest. Beneath the layer of horse dust, her hair smelled of lavender, the flowers crushed into the soap she'd been using lately. There was a comfort in the way her hands went around my waist, their grip firm and demanding in their own way.

She turned her face up towards me and I peppered more kisses along her cheekbone, then down to her jaw. Her breath caught when I nipped ever so gently just behind her ear as I worked my way along the side of her neck. Fingers dug into my sides as I licked her exposed collar bone. Her soft groans of enjoyment stoked the embers in my core until the heat rose within and a fire blazed there.

Moving us towards the bed, she took the opportunity to find my lips, her tongue tracing unseen lines to gain entry. As I let her in, my world imploded, consuming us in that singular moment where nothing else mattered. What could have been a sweet exploration turned into a desperate race to extinguish the blazes rising within us, to quench a thirst we didn't realize we'd had until we were close to dying from it.

In one moment we were standing and in the next I had stripped her of her wraps and held her pressed against our bed, her wild eyes alive with need and want. Her hands worked my own clothes off as needed, but I didn't bother to pause. I craved her like the desert craved rain, the impending doom of the vikings only spurring my actions as I sought to show her all the ways I loved her, all the ways I was consumed by her.

I kissed, licked and nipped every inch of her flesh, my hands massaging her breast until my mouth found its way to them. Lykos' moans were a mix of growls and yips, her animal every bit a part of her soul as I was. Her hands sought to give back the bounty I lay at her feet but more often than not they could do no more than hold on as she bucked beneath me, desperately trying to earn friction against my hips.

Sucking on her nipples, I grinned up at her, dodging her attempts to satiate the need for pressure against her core.

"Patience is a virtue my love." My muttered words blew softly across her wet flesh, puckering her nipples to hard points.

"A virtue that will kill me, if you don't succeed first." She whined, her face a pout mixed with pleasure as I emphasized her words with a pinch to the nipple my mouth wasn't on. Oh how I wanted to give in to my urges, to care only for the end result and fuck her hard and fast until she screamed my name, but I had so much more to tell her first.

In every press of my lips I whispered unspoken words. *I adore you.* Every playful nip uttered a painful confession. *I am nothing without you.* Every lick of skin screamed truths. *I want you, I need you.*

Working my way down to her most sacred of places, I tried to convey everything that words just couldn't quite cover. A vast and endless stream of knowledge was left written on her body in only love, but here at her center she would know my soul at its purest.

Her deep, guttural moan as I breathed upon the folds of her lower lips almost broke me. Close enough to smell her wetness, it'd have been so easy to dive into the ocean that lay within and drown, but I too had to be patient. I had to tell her everything and give her my heart, yes, but also my soul in painstaking measures. She was the goddess I sacrificed to, a supplicant at her altar.

She bucked the moment my tongue touched her flesh, my grip tightening to brace her hips, willing her to still. When she settled I helped her brace, the long strokes of my tongue starting low and rising until they circled her clit and then slid between her inner folds to do it again. Slow and steady, resisting the urge to devour, I moved my mouth so that she could not speed up the rhythm, though she tried - boy did she try. Her whimpers of pleasure had me dripping before she finally murmured words I could never disobey.

"Nyx, please love, finish me."

Innocent enough, but they held far too much meaning. I didn't let my mind go to the darker end of that spectrum, my arousal far too high to do anything but give in.

My tongue moved to her clit and stayed, two fingers rubbing down into her wetness before diving deep inside her core. My admonitions of love would finish in these less than gentle of motions. She cried out in surprise and moaned deep, her hand grasping my hair painfully, the heat of it searing through me like a jolt and giving me pleasure in turn.

I might have drowned or suffocated and died happy as she pinned my face to her pussy, my fingers curled to hit those wonderful inner ridges as my arm pumped them in and out. The walls began to tighten even as I lost room for air, but I would not move. Let me suffocate in her and die blissful, my own core burning with a need that powered my thrusts until both our bodies were moving on the bed. Tighter and tighter her core squeezed until with a nip against her clit I sent her over the edge, spiraling into the abyss, my name screamed like a desperate plea for salvation - which I would give to her over and over before the night was out.

Dreadfully needy, my clit pounded between my legs, sending jolts through my core and into my heart. I was desperate to fill the years of solitude, of missing her, with every scrap of affirmation I could get. Fear prevented me from asking for it, so I did not dare speak of my needs. I could not risk pushing her too far too fast, but by the gods did I crave her.

Her wild eyes fluttered for a few moments as she recovered, but she did not forget me. She pulled me up to her, immediately consuming my lips with her own, tasting herself there and growling with satisfaction.

"Mine" she said, though her voice never touched the air. It was all I craved and more, to look into her eyes and see that bit of possession in their depths. If

only she knew that I had been hers from our first kiss and had been no one else's for as long as I had lived and well beyond what our lives would become. There was no part of me that was not consumed by her.

"I love you Nyx." Her words sounded shy but her eyes were hungry. It always amused me how she could be both shy and bold all at once. Her own feelings often scared her, but she had tried to overcome that fear. Just like the foxes in the wild she was ever so tempted to dart first and ask questions later. Fleeing only to come closer.

Her confidence waned at times, embarrassment winning out, but in these moments, she found the answers she wanted and the strength to give me mine. It was when it all became too deep that I feared her faltering, for where would that leave us? Where would that leave me? I couldn't let her get spooked, the one time she had turned away before had nearly killed me.

"I love you my Vixen, but what I need now are not words, but actions." I offered her a coy, toothy grin which she mirrored back at me. The moment was saved, shifted to a more sultry tone that she knew how to handle. She was not as patient as I, but in these moments I was ever thankful for that. Pleasuring her wound me up tighter than I could have handled were she to move at the teasing pace I had for her. Even as I felt the pounding of need in my clit and the delicious jolts of lightning in our kisses, I relished the lingering emotion in her eyes.

Lykos' hands explored my body fervently, as if she had been starved of food and I was a feast. She used her entire body to set my skin alight, fire racing across my flesh until I thought I might sweat from need. Her own still wet center pressed against me, our moans coexisting as her lips slid against my clit. Half sitting up, she continued while my mouth sought salvation with hers. Above all else I loved kissing, every breath shared a cherished thing that fed my soul. Her mouth muffled my moans as she slid her hand along my stomach, tickling my abs until they slipped into my wetness and deep into my core.

She used our position to her advantage, her knees pressed under my buttocks so that her hips helped her hand to thrust. All I could do was hold onto the colors of the world as it exploded behind my eyelids.

Climax came too quickly to truly satisfy. Thankfully, she refused to relent when I peaked, her pressing ministrations throwing me off the edge I had been clinging to until every inch of my body buzzed. Her name fell off my lips like the prayer it was, hers the only name that might offer salvation for my soul and all I had done to get back into her arms.

When we were finally exhausted hours later, covered in sweat and salty to the taste, we collapsed into each other. Sleep came only when she was pressed into my chest, our arms wrapped around one another and our legs interwoven, her outermost thrown over my hip in the way I loved best.

Sleep found me quickly.

The next day the queen called everyone together. There was a nervous silence as she explained the plan to join Artemis, declaring that any who wished to seek salvation elsewhere would be given provisions and horses to do so. This perhaps, more than anything else, allowed the severity of the situation to sink in. There would be no more sweeping it under a rug, pretending the attacks would trickle off and eventually find them living in peace again.

The queen outlined what would be expected to start preparations for the inevitable strike from the Viking reinforcements. They would meet their enemy on familiar ground, but take advantage of the natural barriers they had been given. The mountain paths would slow the enemy and allow them to defend in the narrowed channels leading up to the village.

She was careful to keep her words upbeat and hopeful, but the somber looks in the crowd proved that none were oblivious to the odds of success. The goal was to hold the enemy back as long as possible, to protect the weak and wounded and ultimately hope Lykos and I succeeded in time to procure an escape.

To save morale, the queen had spoken to Xalia and Serah, who agreed to combine their wedding with their seasonal celebration honoring Artemis and thanking Persephone. A wedding was as generous a gift to their goddess as they could provide, all things considered and quite fitting since they now had confirmation that she still felt their love.

Despite my opinions on the futility of worshiping the gods, the amazon's relationship with their goddess did seem to be paying off. There was genuine love and beauty between Artemis and her subjects, a rare thing indeed.

All too familiar with the Gods' ability to give absolutely no care in the world for their followers, Artemis' dedication was quite the surprise. Faith was a powerful thing amongst mortals, but it could cripple them and make them compliant if they weren't careful. Too often had I heard the words 'if so and so God wills it', as if any of them paid that close attention to their followers.

Some were kind and generous with their faithful, but that was far and few inbetween. Sure, they had relied on them, taken their gifts and made their appearances, but most had no true love for their mortals. It was like a herd of cattle that the farmer needed but only cared about so far as they provided meat and milk.

The village barely slept, but two days later they were ready for the ceremonies.

The Amazons did not decorate the village except where the marriage ceremony would take place, but the details were stunning. Dried vines were used as rope, sectioning off places for the ceremony, while fabrics hung in bundled swoops, billowing in the breeze. Hardy late winter blooms had been gathered into bouquets, while wild grasses had been tied up and shaped into an array of flourishes.

They built bonfires using wood soaked in fragrant oils and herbs, the likes of which would keep the aroma pleasant even when the air grew stagnant with sweat and spirits. Hunters brought in fresh deer to be smoked days prior so that the savory smell filled the village, making my mouth water every time I walked through a gust of it. There were many extra mouths to feed, so it only encouraged the level of feasting which would be done. A large portion of the coastal amazons would be leaving, but they had been encouraged to enjoy the festivities first.

Lykos had already been chased out of the kitchen at least half a dozen times over the last couple of days trying to snag a sample piece. She was quick, but not nearly as smooth as the fox she shifted into. The last time she tried I had mercy on her and let her have a taste of the thick slice I'd grabbed during her scolding. The look on her face had been pure outrage followed by bliss. The kiss I received as my own reward was well worth it, if a bit more greasy than I preferred.

She left our bed before dawn, heading to the stables to visit with Prince and get her chores done before taking her place alongside Serah as she and Onya helped her prepare. She'd groaned about not being allowed the morning off, especially since she was about to leave to save them all. Onya had soothed her over with another sampling of deer meat snagged from the kitchens and a promise that she'd have some dried meat set aside for our journey.

Xalia's sister and mother were helping her get ready, much to my great relief. I was certain she'd have made me help just as a form of friendly torture if they hadn't jumped at the opportunity. Camilla on the other hand had pouted profusely until she'd been asked, which left me to my own devices undisturbed and unharassed for the majority of the day.

The previous two days had been spent making sure we were ready for whatever lay ahead of us and dreading that final moment when we would have to say our goodbyes. Exhaustion pulled at my lids while nerves made my body restless and the combination created a poor attitude around me.

To combat both, I meandered throughout the village, taking in all that could be absorbed through sight, sound and taste until the sun began to drop in the sky. As the wedding time drew nearer, my mind drifted to the past, reflecting back upon the beauty of weddings long past. There was a bitter sweetness to it all. When the noise of the day shifted and things seemed ready to get underway, I made my way towards the back of the ceremonial area.

Taller than most of the Amazons and having no desire to be jostled by the tight crowd when things got emotional, I settled in towards the back along the outer edge. Looking out into the large outcropping beyond the trees, I studied all that had been done as the rest of the village trickled into place. It was clear just how much work had been done in such a short time.

The center area that was usually used to address the village for ceremonies or simple announcements had changed. The square platform had been replaced with a tiered round one. The backdrop of the couple would be a marvelous circle made of young saplings and vines that had been weaved together. One side was decorated with beautiful white flowers at the center and blooms with bluish purple petals beneath it. They were flowers of healing and took up half the arch to represent Serah.

The other side was decorated with the fluffy white ends of pampas grass that grew on the lower part of the mountainside. Threaded around them was a carefully managed weave of red roses, a symbol of a warrior's life - beautiful but dangerous. Since warriors were brought into life through bloodshed and often left the same way, they deemed red as the best suited hue. That side would represent Xalia.

The temperamental weather was cooperating, the sky clear and bright. The day should have been warmer, but the sunbeams' warmth barely seemed to touch the skin. The mountain was still clinging to winter. With so many bodies close together, I was grateful for the coolness, but there was an unnatural feel to it that set my nerves on end.

It didn't take long before the trickle of people became a stream as everyone finished their duties. The sound of voices started as a soft murmur, growing as the hour grew later until it became a loud buzz that made my ears ring and my skin itch. The soft throbbing of a headache was sure to follow.

By the time those closest to the brides had gathered, a group of amazons with stringed instruments had begun a beautiful melody. The soft tune reminded me of the wind through hollow reeds along the shore of a long forgotten lake. A ceremony of my own, held in secret long ago filled my mind. As the memory wrapped around me, a soft warmth spread through my chest, calming my nerves.

A gentle brush of fingers along my arm made me practically jump out of my skin. Lykos' giggle danced in my ears as I jerked forward before spinning to face her. A broad smile showed off her teeth in a foxy manner that I loved.

Endlessly amused to have caught me off guard, she prodded gently, "Miles away already? Surely weddings aren't *that* boring."

All I could do was smile, the bright blue of her eyes drawing me in like a bug to fire. They were more alive than I had seen in weeks, worry of the future having loomed like a storm cloud, especially these past few days. Today they vibrantly hopeful and happy, as if nothing on earth could spoil her good mood.

"Is Serah ready?" The words barely rose from my lips as my lungs caught, my eyes taking her in fully, devouring every morsel of beauty.

Lykos' hair was pulled up and twisted into place, a few 'too short to be tamed' waves dancing across her shoulders. Her lips were stained dark with berry juice and she wore a top that was decorated with beads and bones along the neckline. The top plunged far deeper than anything else I'd seen her wear in this lifetime, the curve of her breast just visible at the edges. Her skirt was not as revealing, but it was kept open at one side so that her left leg was out of it just as much as in it. After an extended winter with barely an inch of skin exposed during the day, she was a treat for my love hungry eyes.

"She was squirming so much we could barely get her dressed, so I'd say that's a solid yes," she laughed, her grin broad.

Seemingly oblivious to my stare, she continued, "You won't believe how beautiful she looks. I spotted Xalia on the way here too. I never knew she could look so friendly!"

A chuckle fell from my lips, her and Xalia had a notoriously rough start to their friendship, though it was on the healthier side of things now.

Just as I was about to respond, silence enveloped the area as everyone quieted down. As the music grew louder, we all held our breath in anticipation.

The wedding was beginning.

Xalia was the first to walk down the aisle, its border marked with slender tree limbs and scattered with petals of red and white. Her outfit was nothing unique in its design, but it had been dyed from its natural tan to a saturated black. Her long locks had been loosened from their braids, the waves tight and lovely at the back, while a batch had been re-braided and weaved together on the top to create a mock crown. Her sharp angled face was terse, surely from nerves, but her lips twitched as she tried to control her smile. Even from a distance, she radiated joy.

The happiness around Xalia was nothing compared to the energy that thrived in Serah the moment she drew near. The healer was always high spirited and happy, but she practically glowed from head to toe. If I hadn't known better and the times had been different, I'd have sworn she was a goddess for the way her light spread to those around her. That everyone looked at her with adoration didn't hurt the image either.

The color had been pulled from her outfit, the cream hues a beautiful contrast against the slight caramel of her skin. Her usually messy and spiky blonde hair had been wrangled with salve, the waves creating movement all the way to the front where her bangs arched above her eyebrow. Flowers had been stuck into it, the tiny little blossoms accentuating her look but taking nothing from her natural beauty. She was the embodiment of bliss.

From where we stood I couldn't hear the rites they repeated back to each other, but Lykos and I had heard them practice plenty, as they had spent every spare moment with us after the announcement of our departure. As they spoke in tones I could hear, my hand reached out and grasped Lykos', my gaze diverted from the two brides to her. The hushed murmuring, filled with tear soaked happiness, took me back to a time I doubted she would recall. A moment from our first life together before I was a gargoyle.

Applause erupted around me, startling me in place. Lost, walking down memory lane, the ceremony had wrapped up without me realizing. Laughing, Lykos squeezed my hand gently. Her cerulean gaze met mine, their depths pulling me in instantly.

"What?" She asked softly, her brow raised and her head slightly tilted. My cheeks tightened as a smile formed, a sigh filled with love falling from my lips, though I couldn't bring myself to tell her all that lay behind it.

"Just admiring the most beautiful woman here." I whispered, breathless.

Lykos rolled her eyes, but her lips curled at the corner and her cheeks grew pink with a blush. Tiptoeing, for our height difference was significant, she placed her hands upon my chest, her lips pressing lightly against my own. The kiss was gentle and sweet and every ounce of tenderness my heart needed.

Leaning forward, my forehead pressed against hers as the rest of the world faded away for just another moment. When I opened my eyes again, the amazons had all spread out, readying for a night of fun and feasting. A final celebration before their entire lives turned upside down.

Onya, Lykos' best friend amongst the village, waved us over to one of the smaller bonfires. She offered a plate of meats and dried fruits, though the only thing I went for was the skin of fermented fruit juice. I wasn't alone in my intent to drink away my worries either; it was practically all you could smell. A cacophony of chatter enveloped the village. People spoke of how beautiful the ceremony had been and debated how late they could stay up without suffering through their work tomorrow.

Although there was joy in their faces, the magnitude of what lay ahead never truly dissipated. There was a quiet tension just beneath every surface.

Serah and Xalia eventually settled around our fire, their happiness contagious as pure bliss lit their faces. With hands interlocked, they gazed at each other in a way that had me almost envious. There had been a time Lykos and I had been in their shoes.

It didn't take long for the Amazons to begin dancing to the sound of drums and stringed instruments. This was the high before the fall and no matter how many times I had lived through it, there was still a hollow pit of dread in my stomach. Whether she sensed my unease or merely was enjoying the night, Lykos didn't stray far from my side. The constant contact between us was perhaps the only thing keeping me grounded.

The music shifted and the newly wedded rose, beckoning all the couples to join the dance. Lykos' energy buzzed. I watched her watching them and couldn't help but smile as she grinned wide, sharing their joy. Memories of nights spent dancing and then falling into bed together made my lips curl into a smile, my chest blossoming with blooms nurtured by adoration.

"Would you like to dance?" Standing, I offered my hand out to her, the space between us vast and minuscule all at once as I waited.

"Are you sure? I don't know this one." She glanced around, ever a skittish fox despite how eager she looked..

"When it comes to you, always. Don't worry my Vixen, I will lead. This one can't be much different than those we know, the steps are passed down through the ages, after all."

The tempo changed as I tugged her forward, our bodies pressing close as I wrapped an arm around her waist. The movements were like the ebb and flow of the ocean, a pushing and pulling of lovers entangled in a net of affection. Our steps were off a bit here and there, but we eventually got the overall rhythm and followed suit as couples turned and twirled, weaving amongst each other in a circle that shrunk and then grew. It was like we were the breathing earth, inhaling and exhaling with the rolls of thunder created by the stomping of feet.

Soon the heat of the fires and our own moving bodies created a sheen of sweat across our skin. Gazing at my beautiful fox glistening in the firelight, I felt complete. The soft waves of her hair bounced gently around her face. Joy poured from her, lighting up her eyes and creating a surge of energy around her I could have lived off of for years. Moments such as these kept me grounded when I was lost in the chaos of the world, and threatened to drown me when cast out into the ocean without her.

Oh how life had honed that double-edged sword to perfection.

Lykos' brows raised in question, my movement having suddenly ceased without my noticing. My hands shook and I couldn't pin down the exact cause, though my mind conjured quite a few options. My beautiful fox smiled and I practically melted into her arms as she drew me in close.

"Let's get out of here." She whispered, the notes pure mischief.

I could deny her nothing.

Giggling like children, we fled the firelight as if we might get in trouble were we caught. Stealing kisses behind trees and huts, we paused just long enough to snag a breath and take off to the next shadowy spot. When we finally burst into our shared home I collapsed onto the bed in a fit of laughter. I felt crazed, the night swallowing us in a warm embrace as we quickly stripped off our clothes, entangled like some deep sea creature. We were all limbs with no concept of what was up or down. The world shrank to that one moment and for a while we forgot that the fate of all those around us rested on our shoulders.

What a way to end a wedding.

Chapter Six
Freezing Tits and Tantrums

Despite the bliss of the night before, our spirits were poor when we rose the next morning. Lykos words were shorter than her temper, her dislike of waking early only adding to her mood. Understanding only made it marginally more bearable. For Lykos, it all felt too much like running away.

Unable to bring myself to try and coax her out of her mood, we prepped in silence. To tempt her into better spirits felt like manipulation, so I let her feel it, hoping my presence would be enough comfort.

We both knew that we could easily turn the tide in any mortal battle, but when it came to fighting against gods, the survival of friends caught in the crossfire became much more tricky. Leaving now felt like a betrayal, but it was their only hope of survival.

A sigh slipped from my lips as we walked in silence to the only trail that crossed the river this high in the mountains. The northern trail was part of the scouts' patrol, but it was the least traveled. As promised, the Lynx was perched at the start of the trail, mottled coat blending into the rock almost perfectly. The only thing that really gave him away was the slow blinking of his eyes and the long tufts of black hair that waved atop his ears when the breeze gusted.

"Lead us into a trap or attack us yourself and I promise to wear you as a cautionary tale to any who would dare cross me similarly. Got it?" I warned, Lykos' growl backing me up just behind.

The beast practically rolled its eyes as he gave a soft growl, but between the two actions I caught the slight dip of his head. It was likely as much of an acknowledgement as one was going to get from a Goddess' pet cat. Turning my back to the beast, I faced Lykos. This was it, every step from here on out would either save or doom everyone we knew and loved amongst the amazons.

Lykos' face was set in an emotionless expression she used when she was trying to ignore her feelings. Lifting my hand, I caressed a piece of hair away from her face, letting my thumb graze her cheek. She leaned into the touch, her facade falling away just the slightest bit.

"Don't worry my love, we will do what needs to be done to keep them safe."

She nodded and lifted her hand to my own, grabbing it and pressing a kiss to my palm. Such a small gesture, yet it always made my knees weak. She smiled ever so slightly before turning towards our guide.

"Alright puss, let's get this show on the road, time's a wastin'." She shook her body as if physically shaking loose the despair I knew sat just beneath the surface.

The cat stood up and stretched his body out, bobbed tail straight up as he bowed low in the front, yawning as if he had been bored. Without another word between us, we set off down the trail eventually veering off onto a path neither of us had known existed. Perhaps it hadn't before the lynx appeared, Gods had their ways, afterall.

The trek was uneventful and tiresome. The cold weather should have been breaking, even this high, but as we trudged through the remnants of snow, my body grew ever colder. Each day should have drawn us nearer a scrap of warmth, but I was slowly forced to accept that I was doomed to my misery of being cold.

The overrun trail we had switched to a day back guided us until we reached the dividing river. Lykos' lips curled in a quiet sneer, perhaps remembering her chilling drop into its waters further south, less than a year prior. The top was still frozen, but there was a subtle sound of water flowing beneath it. Here the river traded width for depth, making me question its soundness.

The Lynx gave no indication of worry, his heavy paws lightly thumping across the ice as he tread across, sitting proudly upon arrival on the other side. The spoiled cat puffed out his chest and yawned widely before looking across at us with slow, expectant blinks.

Grumbling, I glanced at Lykos, "He definitely acts like the pampered pet of a Goddess. We are significantly heavier, do you think it'll hold?"

Before I could stop her, she took a fist and slammed it upon the ice several times and then shrugged as she shook the pain off.

"No cracks," she replied, "so it should hold - as long as we don't linger."

As if I had any intention of lingering in the middle of a frozen river.

"I'll slide our packs just in case. Best not to take unnecessary risks by making ourselves heavier." A shiver ran down my spine at the thought of falling through.

Motioning for her to go on ahead, I slid our bags across a few yards south of where she started. Of the three of us, I was the heavier and I would not risk weakening the ice before Lykos went. She almost slipped a couple of times, but caught herself easily enough, making it to the other side with a triumphant grin.

Channeling my magic through my body, my leathery wings broke through the skin on my back, slipping through the flaps I had cut out from my clothing for that purpose. Just in case.

"Here goes nothing." I muttered to myself as I cautiously started out across the ice.

My boots slid on a couple of slick spots, but my wings were held out wide, maintaining my balance as I skated in place. The ice held. A few yards from the opposite bank I lowered my wings, confident that the surface beneath me would not give so near the shallows.

Foolish me.

A crackling rose from beneath my extended foot, halting my step. Dread filled my body as I waited, praying the silence lasted, my breath held in anticipation. A groan came from behind me as my weight shifted back. My heart leapt into my throat as I waited for it to dissipate. Time slowed as I took a deep breath, eyes focused on the ice, my ears deaf to what Lykos was yelling in front of me. Ever so slowly I slid my back foot forward just a hair.

Thunder rumbled below me, accentuated by the very distinct cracks that were now spider webbing their way out from my foot. My wings spread wide, but they were not meant for gaining altitude. One more giant rumble and the ground beneath me gave way.

"FUCK!"

A shock of cold rushed up my legs as they slipped into the icy waters, shards of ice slicing through my pants and jabbing into the flesh of my hips. Instinctively my wings arched out, the sharp points anchoring into the more solid blocks of ice around me as my arms strained to hold me up out of the rushing river hidden below. It took no time at all for my legs to go numb, the cold causing my muscles to tense with painful shivers that made it hard to breathe.

My legs tried to tread water, but the rushing waters were relentless, my height a distinct disadvantage. Twisting my hips to the side, my toes caught on a rock, giving me just enough purchase to claw my way forward. A groan of pain fell from my lips as my fingers were sliced, desperately seeking purchase on the slick surface.

Just as my foot was about to slip from the rock beneath, the sound of claws skittered towards me. Golden red fur immediately enveloped me, as a mildly painful bite on my shoulder dragged me forward. Within moments my body was towed across the remaining stretch of ice and up the embankment, the painful grip on my shoulder instantly disappearing.

The lynx's scratchy laughter moved from just to the side to further away, a sharp snap of teeth ringing out in warning. There was no energy to spare for glaring at the beast as my body used every ounce to try and warm my soaked extremities. My body convulsed with the effort, my hands fumbling to try and remove the freezing articles of cloth.

My beautiful vixen whined, the warmth of her furred body enveloping me as she lowered herself to the earth behind me. The many tails of her kitsune form curled around in front, creating a cocoon of sorts. Her soft whines were filled with worry, her muzzle nudging me softly as she sniffed out my wounds and offered a warm lick to clean the blood.

"I'll be okay, my love, just help me get warm again."

Hidden in the depths of her tails and fur I struggled to remove my wet clothes, the deerskin pants clinging to me like a second skin even when dry. When I finally had them off Lykos moved a tail just enough for me to grab my bag and disappear beneath her fur once more. Thankfully my spare pants were fur-lined and much warmer than the discarded pair beside me. It would be much more pleasant to end up too warm than stay wet and cold.

It took a little while before the shivers finally ceased, but when they did a sigh of relief escaped me as the muscles along my back finally loosened. Sitting comfortably against Lykos' side, the bristly parts of her fur started to get itchy, which in itself was a good sign - I could feel properly again.

"So, are you going to apologize?" Lykos' laughter made her entire body shake.

"For what?" I asked, genuinely confused.

"For calling my tails useless," she snickered.

A groan fell from my lips, my hand instinctively rising to rub between my eyes.

"Seriously?"

"Yes."

"Lykos, there is no reason for you to have nine tails, no matter how beautiful, or warm they are."

Lykos shoved her nose under the tips of her tails, her head precariously close to my own, bright blue eyes staring into my soul. She blinked slowly, her ears flicked back in what I knew to be her 'serious' face.

Slowly, she retorted, "So says the flightless gargoyle." The tension in her stomach proved just how hard she was trying not to laugh.

Silence.

"Oh you asshole!" I yelled, playfully smacking her side as she finally gave in to her laughter.

Her whole body shook as she unfurled from around me. My beautiful kitsune got to her feet and pranced around me, her horse sized fox form distracting me from the cold. The tail tips were as dark as shadows, matching the tips of her ears and legs, a stark contrast to the golden red of her body and warm cream of her underbelly. She was a lank thing, but muscled well enough to carry a person on her back with ease.

"Are you warm enough?" She finally asked, ears swiveling between myself and the lynx who was growling irritiably.

My ability to understand Lykos had started with reading her body language, then grew from experience. It was strange to simply hear her words as if they were spoken aloud, the result of my skills and the magic that bound us working together. Although more seamless, it was also a bit unnerving and made me wonder if it had changed at all from her end.

"It'll have to do. Let me wrap my wounds and we can go." I sighed.

She tossed her head back towards her rear, but I shook my head to decline the offer of a ride. Who knew what we were getting ourselves into, best she was unhindered by my weight. Movement would warm me up faster anyways.

By the time we made it to the base of the cliff where Tereus had jumped, my body was comfortably warm beneath my furs and the stiffness in my muscles had worked itself out, but a chill still ran down my spine.

Lykos was forced to shift back into her human form as we followed the lynx. She grasped my hand as we continued up a few narrow outcroppings of rock until we reached the place where Tereus' stolen body had splattered across the mountainside.

Winter preserved what was left, but the scavengers had made quick work of the free meal. Little more than bones remained and I was certain a few of those were missing too. Lykos' grip tightened as we peered up the mountain, my free hand instinctively going to my chest. Although the wound had healed near instantly when our magic combined, I could feel the ache of memory.

On rainy days especially, it would throb, leaving me with a mixed set of emotions I preferred to avoid. The magicked spear had made it clean through Lykos and kept going until my own body stopped its progress. Not that the damage wasn't done at that point. The squelching sound of her removing herself from the wood shaft so that she could embrace me still haunted my dreams.

The irony of Tereus' attempt to kill us for good, actually making us immortal still made me chuckle sometimes. Not today though. Today we looked at our past and cringed, knowing our future might be just as bleak. Lykos squeezed my hand before pressing her free one atop the one at my chest.

"You're right. We have survived worse than vikings." She murmured, gentle tugging me away from the painful memories.

We followed the cat as he skirted around Tereus' remains, taking a few sniffs before edging along a goat path to the right. If his chuffing noises meant anything, Lykos kept it to herself.

The rocky and narrow path ended where a large boulder had lodged itself between a cluster of very determined trees and the cliffside. The tree roots were a tangled mess of desperation, holding firm in their precarity. There was a space between the rock and the mountain, though it was nothing short of a squeeze.

The Lynx paused, motioning towards the gap with a bob of his head. Approaching cautiously, I did a double take as my eyes caught a slight shimmer in the air. It was as if there were a mirage, much like you'd see in the desert. Lykos cocked her head as she walked up beside me, a skeptical brow raised.

"Think it's safe?" She grabbed a loose rock and tossed it, flinching slightly when it disappeared into thin air. The arms on her hair stood on end, making her look like she'd rubbed against a wool blanket.

"I think he is going to show us." I stated, turning to meet the cat's gaze unrelentingly.

The lynx scoffed, or at least that's what the weird rasping noise he made sounded like as he raised his bobbed tail and pranced through the space. As soon as his whiskers touched the surface it rippled and opened up like water parted by rocks. He stepped through halfway so that he looked creepily disembodied and then backed up to show us he was still intact before walking all the way through.

"Well, we can't be outdone by a cat now can we?" I asked, nudging Lykos with my elbow. She huffed, her hands rubbing her armchairs down before she followed me through.

Whatever I had anticipated, it certainly wasn't to feel a cold draft before walking out onto the broad side of a tree's branch. The luminescence of the smooth bark took me by surprise, my eyes instinctively squinting in defense. The shifting hues swirled with a magical pulse that made the air feel thick and cold all at once. From the branch we stood on hundreds of other shoots diverted off, creating a chaotic weave of glowing wood. Once my eyes had adjusted it was easy to spot the lynx, who stood waiting impatiently for us to get ourselves together.

Lykos spun in place, my nerves jolting as she meandered dreadfully close to the edge, trying to take it all in. Her face was filled with awe as she twirled back to the center, allowing me to breathe again.

"It's so beautiful." She whispered as I stepped up beside her and slipped my fingers into her own. She squeezed lightly before simply holding my hand back, unaware that she'd sent my heart into my throat.

As I calmed, my head swiveled around as we slowly followed the impatient cat, pausing unconsciously here and there to study one of the many portals scattered along the branches. On the other side our portal had made the world look like a sheet of fabric, its shimmering form a tear right in the middle, but here they were different. When I looked back, our portal looked like a doorway, its frame engraved with intricate designs, perhaps even a language of some sort.

"I wonder how many worlds this tree connects." There was no hiding the awe in my voice.

The lynx made a rumbling noise, but the only creature I could understand enough to put words to was Lykos. Cocking my head, I peered in her direction, a brow raised in question - just the same as she often did to me. She rolled her eyes as I continued to look at her expectantly.

"Do I look like I speak cat?" She grumbled, a glare following the lynx.

Smirking, I bumped her shoulder, my brain instantly conjuring the best way to tease her.

"You've got no problem using that tongue to speak to mine." I whispered, leaning close so that my breath might tickle her neck.

My reward came in the form of her face, which turned scarlett, though she couldn't hide the slight smirk that tilted her lips before she growled.

Lykos hated that she could, in fact, understand magical creatures other than Prince. I was fairly certain it started with her run in with a talking squirrel. The little guy had followed her around non-stop, causing her to stay in a bad mood for weeks. The situation was only made worse by his apparent attention issues, often never finishing one thought before the next chattered out his mouth. It had driven her crazy.

"He says that this is Yggdrasil, the tree of life. It connects all nine worlds, though few have seen them all." She muttered grumpily.

Looking around it was apparent that each world must have tons of different 'tears' throughout their realms, as there were certainly more than nine doorways in our vicinity alone.

We walked for what seemed like an hour, though the scenery all seemed to blur after a while. The glow had begun to make me nauseous by the time the lynx finally found what he was looking for and stopped in front of a doorway that was surrounded by weird vines that twisted upon themselves. Their leaves were half way wilted, as if frozen in time.

"Where does this lead?" My hand paused in mid-air as the impulse to caress the barrier overtook me.

"He says it leads to Helheim and the Goddess Hel." She replied, her eyes studying the doorway as the Lynx made more growling noises, though she didn't elaborate further.

"Will he escort us in?" Even as the words left my lips I knew he was telling the truth, something in the air felt familiar and comforting. A mix of emotions followed that realization; alarm and a prickly sensation warning me I was forgetting something I should know.

"No, he claims this is as far as he was instructed to lead us. Good riddance too, I'm tired of looking at his asshole." She offered a toothy snarl, her eyes glaring at the beast.

The lynx sneezed, though I was unsure if it was from amusement or insult, before trotting off and disappearing through a different gateway.

"I bet that one leads back to either Artemis or Freya. I wonder where the rest go." My voice was a whisper as I gently released Lykos' hand.

Consciously I refocused on the world around me, ignoring the subtle doorway ahead of us that led to the one place in the world no one sought to go. It seemed so familiar. The pull was almost tangible, cold like death yet warm like sunshine on a fresh spring day. My chest twisted in conflict, my magic reacting to something beyond the doorway in a way that made me nervous. Taking a deep breath I tried to soothe myself, quietly counting a few deep breaths before turning and pointedly investigating our surroundings.

Curiously I approached another gateway that stood a few feet back from the direction we had come from. I hadn't noticed it until we passed it, but the shimmering texture seemed a bit different.

As I leaned forward, my body was pressed by cold air, just as it had been before. It was so dark I wasn't sure my head had made it through until the sound of sweeping filled my ears. As my eyes adjusted a huge sweeping tail of black and gray pummeled towards me. Jerking back, the cold washed over me briefly before I stumbled backwards out of the portal.

"Fuck that was close!" My breath came out in puffs as my lungs caught up with my panic.

"What?" Lykos' expression was more curious than concerned.

"Almost got sideswiped by a wolf tail thicker than your fox after a bath. Don't think the other end of it knew I was there, but that is not the way I wanna go out." A few extra steps backward assured I wouldn't repeat that mistake.

"You mean you don't wanna die buried in stinky wolf fur?" she chuckled, obviously amused.

"No thanks, fox fur is bad enough," I retorted.

My laughter rang out around us as she searched and failed to find something to throw at me.

"That's just rude." She turned her head away from me, nose pointed to the sky, indignant.

"Don't worry my love, I've got no problems dying buried beneath you, I just want it to be without fur and you sitting on my face." Reaching out gently, my fingers danced across her arm, gently scratching my way up the neck and to her jaw, her skin prickling with goosebumps in response.

She choked on air at the words her skin flushing scarlet as the arousal of my gentle touch became overridden by embarrassment - the exact desired reaction. The look on her face when she managed to recover filled me with mirth. Bursting out into laughter, my body doubled over as the humor overwhelmed me. Each breath was ragged as my muscles clenched around my ribs, the giggles unrelenting.

"I swear Nyx you are going to kill me from a lethal mix of embarrassment and arousal one day." She swatted at my head, easily able to reach it now that I was bent in half.

"Oh please," I managed to chuckled, "neither of those will kill you my love, not so long as I am around to ease the latter at least."

A wink set her face to scarlet once more, despite the fact that we were completely alone and she was not at all a timid woman. It was amazing, seeing how I could still affect her so thoroughly. She finally rolled her eyes and then her shoulders, physically shaking off her discomfort best she could.

"Well, let's go meet this Goddess and see if we can find your mothers. No point in delaying, lest the former come seeking us out instead."

Lykos was always surprising me, suddenly becoming the voice of reason.

Sighing, I responded, "Something tells me it wouldn't take long for her to find us. The Gods usually have eyes everywhere in and around their realms."

Which was even more annoying considering their lack of action to defend their people most days. That we were trekking willingly into the realm of one I'd never met was a bit disconcerting, but necessary.

Stepping forth through the gate, the air around us shifted. It was as if a thick fog had rolled over us, despite our view being clear as a cloudless full moon night. An odd familiarity fell over me, chill bumps running across my skin because of it. The air was close and the sound of footsteps seemed muffled where one might expect them to echo. We walked in an open space with high cliffs surrounding us, the way ahead nothing more than a narrow ridge of extended rock that created a bridge.

There was a tightness in my chest as I took extra care to step more softly. The steep drop on either side of the walkway gave me little comfort, even without this horrid sense that something was off. Glancing back at Lykos, I could see her blue eyes darting to and fro, as if searching for an enemy she could sense but not see. She growled low in her throat, sticking close, just a few steps behind me.

That was all the reassurance I needed that something was wrong.

A noise caught my attention, starting as a whisper, almost like a sharp breeze whistling through a small tunnel. The high pitch grew in volume until it was an ear piercing screech. The sound was so loud and distracting I almost didn't notice the shuffling stomp of feet approaching us. A clamor of metal on bone buzzed alongside the drum-like beat, magic practically vibrating in the air. Seeking out the source, I looked ahead, across the bridge, a sharp breath of surprise slipping from my lips.

The sight that met my gaze was one of the most disturbing I'd seen.

Every degree of decay was present in the undead army that shambled its way towards us. Their spirits clung to their bones, the shadows of their former selves cast off their backs or above their heads in a sickly green hue, as if they couldn't keep up with their reanimated bodies. The rattle of bones added to the music of the whistle and the stomp of feet, creating a strange and deadly symphony. I could almost imagine someone in the distance adding a melancholy string instrument to the mix. A few chills went up my spine and then ran back down, an instinctual warning causing me to turn just in time to barely dodge the sharp end of an obsidian sword.

Everything went silent just as the blade split the air, pushing a slight breeze against my face. The speed of its travel created a swooshing sound, the onyx blade seeming to absorb the unnatural light cast upon it from the underworld's strange sky, making it hard to track. I had only a few seconds to take in the wielder before a second swing arched towards me. Twisting away with a groan, I crouched down so that I could propel myself forward.

"Lykos!" I called out, fear creeping into my tones as I searched where she had been and found nothing. "Where is she?!" I demanded, eyes narrowed as I glared at my attacker, venom dripping from each syllable.

The mystery woman before me smirked, her face split between healthy pinkish tones and gray, dead flesh that was mottled. She was tall, her bodice covered in a black dress that seemed purposely tattered at its ends. The loose strips of sheer fabric billowed as she moved, loose enough to be comfortable but fitted enough to show the subtle curve of her body. She was alluring in a strange way that made my stomach twist.

This must be the Goddess of Death.

The acknowledgement made a whisper of familiarity fall upon me, the creaking laughter of the Fates echoing in the back of my mind, drawing a growl of displeasure from my lips. It was hard not to pick up Lykos' habits.

My weight shifted from one foot to the other. I stood vulnerable in an unfamiliar space with a woman who may or may not be my enemy. It was hard to trust a goddess, no matter whose she was, or what she ruled over.

Lykos' disappearance gnawed at my heart, desperately urging me to turn away and check every nook and cranny, to peer over the edges and call her name. She was capable, strong and resourceful, but that didn't stop my heart from leaping at the thought of any harm coming to her. I had to resist the urge. One of the first things Lykos had taught me was to never turn your back on a predator and the woman before me was certainly no deer.

With no word of warning, the woman struck out again, but this time I was ready. Lunging forward, I ducked beneath the blade as she sidestepped to avoid my collision. Her feet seemed to barely lift from the earth, her grace that of a dancer's. As she moved her sword twirled back and around at her side, then in front of her as she circled me like a cat stalking its prey.

I would be no one's prey.

She grinned, as if she could read my mind and was laughing. With a twirl that was surely just for show, the goddess of death fast stepped to my left and then last minute changed direction, swinging her blade in a downward arc toward my shoulder. Ducking my head to dodge under the blade, I twisted alongside her sword arm, rising on the outside.

The jarring pain of impact rippled up my arm as my elbow slammed down into hers. My left leg took my weight as I dropped, right leg sweeping out to take her legs from her. Despite my timing, she used the force and momentum of my actions to roll forward, popping up with her sword already swinging back around.

She moved with an expert's elegance, but I was no mere novice.

With Medusa's past, my mothers had spared nothing to make sure I was trained and capable of taking on any who might challenge me. In the beginning of my training there had been an easy air around my betters, they did not fear my blade or temper. That changed swiftly when history marked me in the books. When I had come across them again, there had been tension in the air that had made me smile with pride.

It was that familiar feeling of easiness that annoyed me. She regarded me as a pup playing with a big dog. The way she moved around, toying with me, made it very clear she was not threatened. Her confidence stated clearly that if she had wanted me dead, I'd have been hers the second I walked through the gate.

This was nothing more than a test; a cat toying with a meal it never planned to consume. No matter how much I resented the assumption, it was best not to change her mind, especially when I still had no clue where Lykos was.

Stepping back and then forward for every swing that she took, I attempted to drive her as much as I let her direct me. The army of dead stood blocking my passage, a threat all on their own, but I was far more concerned with the edges of my would-be arena. Anytime she tried to direct me toward the edge it forced me to charge forward or dart off to the side. My wings were always a safety measure, but gliding to safety would mean admitting to being outmatched.

I couldn't do that, nor could I leave Lykos. She had to be here, somewhere.

As we moved, Hel said not a word. She drove me until I was panting and couldn't recall how long I had been dodging the edge of her sword. The dance only stopped when my step stuttered for the briefest of moments, just long enough to feel the sting of her blade across my cheek.

The strike was barely a graze, but it was enough to draw blood and that seemed good enough to prove whatever point she was trying to make. As we stood there with our eyes locked, a cold chill once again fell around me. The sensation overwhelmed me as a stray wisp of fog moved in. Despite myself, my eyes darted downward when I felt the brush of a tendril winding up my leg. When I looked back up, I was no longer in Hel.

Chapter Seven
Helheim's Fog of Regrets

My hands began to shake as the hush of the moment changed into a growing hum. The sound reminded me of bees until it rose in volume and took a more volatile form. Cheers from a huge crowd roared all around me, the sound deafening as it coiled around a part of me I thought long buried.

My blurry vision slowly cleared, revealing stone walls that surrounded me. The stacked blocks towered over me, the bench-like seats that rose from them all filled with Roman spectators awaiting the bloody massacre promised to them.

My hands began to shake, sweat rising along my flesh, gathering at my brow and slowly trickling down my face. The sweat had nothing to do with the heat that usually accompanied the gladiator ring. A mix of fear and apprehension consumed me as my mind reeled. I stood not in the present, but several lifetimes ago, in the past. My mind was split, a searing pain etching through my head as my present day consciousness fought for control and lost.

My blood pumped harder, sending adrenaline through my body and causing my breath to quicken. Fear and excitement mixed together as the thrill of the battle to come twisted inside and strangled a piece of my soul. Disgust for everything filled my mouth. I hated them all, hated myself, and I hated those blasted Fates for leading Lykos and I into a trap.

"Why am I back here? What are you trying to do? Torture me? Where is Lykos!?"My words resonated loudly, though I never felt my lips move. My mind was being torn apart, trying desperately to claw to the forefront.

Hel whispered, "No dear, you have done that to yourself quite well enough. Do not fear for your partner, she is safe and will be waiting for you at the end. Focus now on what you must relive, fighting will only delay the inevitable."

Desperation filled my voice and I hated myself for it.

"Then why?!" I screamed.

"There is something here you must face," she replied, her tone barely sympathetic. "No one can escape this trial to pass through my lands. I do not choose - I merely act as a witness for those with immortal blood."

I hissed in reply, "Where there are witnesses, there is judgment."

My fear and panic, which usually remained so well contained, burst free from my every pore. It was not the battle I knew was coming that had me shaking though, it was the aftermath of it. This was the only life that had broken me in ways I had yet to recover from. I did not want to live it again.

"So it will be, though not from me. First you must face what lies ahead, or be stuck here for eternity," she responded, this time more gently.

The sensation of a hand ghosting across my side made me jump - a quick image, a memory from that blasted dream snaking its way across my mind. Why had I dreamt of her? There was no time to dwell on it as the memory took over and my body no longer responded to my conscious mind. I had lost the struggle, my mind now fully submerged.

The shouts became impatient as the heat rose around me. It wouldn't be much longer now. As soon as the horn sounded, this nightmare would begin. Survival was all I needed, then we would be free.

My feet started sinking in the sand, a moisture lay beneath that I didn't dare inspect. These arenas were not known for their polite discussions. Here you either destroyed yourself to live, or you died in the path of someone else's destruction. Either way, you never left the same way you entered, if you left at all.

"Whatever gods are listening, please no more animals," I prayed quietly.

The only creatures treated with respect here were the horses that kept gladiators alive, but even they didn't always make it out. I had far less qualms about the killing of humans who were trying to kill me, than animals trying desperately to survive. Especially since most of the humans didn't simply try to kill you - they had to put on a show as well.

My neck cracked as my head swiveled around to look across the arena, my stomaching dropping as I realized what lay scattered around me. The day prior's carnage had not been cleared away, the reflection in the mirror becoming even more hideous in today's light. All around me lay evidence of the monster I had become.

Dead amazons, stripped of their dignity and dressed in barely anything, lay in whatever manner they had fallen. How they'd gotten so many was a question I hadn't had the heart to ask. Though it wouldn't have mattered, their honor had been soiled the moment they'd been thrown into the ring. They'd died trying to live, just as I had killed to do the same. All I could hope for now was that their goddess would find a way to retrieve their souls, since their bodies would never make it home.

The goddess Artemis had protected her people as much as she could, but the Amazons were exotic warriors to the Roman empire and the wealthy enjoyed watching them be 'put in their place' almost as much as they loved the pure brutality of a blood bath. In every life I had lived Artemis' people had been allies, their connection to my mother Medusa was always a precious thing to me. At least it had been. This life, this arena, had ruined every good thing I'd held close to my heart.

The far side of the arena grew quiet, the silence spreading as everyone, including myself, held their breath to see what it was I would be facing this time. The strange sound of snake scales rubbing against one another slowly carried across the arena and my stomach went cold. I would know that sound anywhere. A flash of sand colored scales was all the confirmation I needed, but my eyes couldn't look away as they lifted the gate.

The world around me held its breath in anticipation, the unknown exciting and terrifying to them. They sat at the edge of their chairs, curious to see what beast lay in the cage beyond their sight, oblivious to how cruel this game had just become.

Emotion overwhelmed me and my stomach lurched, vomit burning its way up my throat and spewing out as I fell to my knees. A huge, vastly oversized snake moved into the sun, her body coiling upon itself in fear as she blinked slowly, her tongue tasting the world around her. She was starved to the point her sides dipped in and her face was gaunt, but my dear sister in everything except blood stood before me with eyes that didn't recognize me.

Medusa had the ability to create shifters much like herself, saving women from a fate worse than death by giving them a new one. They had always been my sisters, even if the only thing we shared was Medusa's magic and love.

"Oxia, my beautiful sister. What have they done to you?" My words were swallowed by the crowd but she dipped her head curiously as she shifted her body so that she moved sideways towards me.

The smell of my mother Medusa's gorgon magic still wafted strong enough for me to catch, but it was faint enough for me to know that Oxia hadn't seen her human form in too long. She was lost to this world, in mind if not quite body.

The announcer yelled out, "A snake made for the gods, ladies and gentleman!"

"Please, no," I whispered, desperately trying to hold back tears.

She raised her head, tongue darting out slowly to taste the air as she arched her neck back. The crowd began to yell as I stood back up and stared into eyes that were too wild and yet just as broken. There was no recognition there, but for a brief moment the world stood still, I remembered the loving woman she had once been and she basked in the sunlight pouring into the arena.

The horn blared and all that brittle stillness shattered.

The sidewinder lurched forward, her body coiling sideways while her head traveled straight at me. The motion appeared slow at first, but I knew from experience that it was all just a trick of the light. Even in her weakened state, there was no way I could outrun her. My options were limited, if they had kept her healthy I wouldn't have a chance of winning, but in this state, I just had to be smarter.

With the taste of bile fresh on my tongue and sweat making my skin stick, I cursed my misfortunes and dug in deep for everything that drove me to survive. Lykos and freedom were but a match away, I had to win, had to live. Tears could not be afforded now, so I shoved my emotions down, grabbed the blades strapped to my back and charged forward.

She wasn't Oxia anymore.

The distance between us disappeared. Once she was close enough I leapt forward to dive over the thick girth of the snake's body. A gust of wind hit my back as she struck out just behind me, the rattle at the end of her tail vibrating as she reared back for another attempt.

Rolling upon impact, the momentum lurched me towards her tail, my blade seeking scales as I ran along her length towards a wall. Silently I prayed to my mother for forgiveness, though I knew there would be no redemption for what I would have to do next. How could there be?

My blades found the hard scales and struggled to slip past their armored surface, but just at the base where the rattles were, lay a weak point. The large snake screamed in pain as one of my blades hit their mark, slicing deep. The smell of my mother's magic hit me harder than her tail, which jerked away just to whip back into me. The impact felt like running into a wall full force, the world blurring around me, air whooshed by as I flew backwards.

As I hit the ground my lungs emptied, my body unresponsive as I tried desperately to gasp in air. My body throbbed from head to toe and my vision spotted. As soon as I was able to draw in a deep breath I rolled over onto my hands and knees, the world spinning as I desperately tried to track the snake's position.

She was gone.

True fear enveloped me. Blinking repeatedly in an attempt to cast away my splotchy vision, I searched the arena for a snake that was way too large to just disappear out of thin air. The only thing that caught my eye was a blood trail that ended abruptly at a dip in the sand. Two and two added up almost too late.

"SHIT!"

Grasping at the ground for traction, I finally pushed myself up and darted towards the closest wall. Dread filled my gut when a glance over my shoulder revealed my gut wrenching fear. Oxia had learned a new trick since the last time I had seen her. Her diagonal movement beneath the sands pushed and pulled the grains to create a wave that pulsed and moved with her body. As the sound of sand sifting filled the arena, the wave began to pummel towards me, the vibrations of my movement giving her a target.

The only thing that saved me was my proximity to the wall.

As the wave bore down on me, Oxia burst forth from the sand, mouth wide, her venomous fangs glistening with their deadly liquid. Leaping towards the wall, my momentum allowed me to run upwards just enough to launch into a backwards flip. She smashed into the solid surface, making a sound I'd never forget and fell still, dazed. The spectators above us screamed in fear while everyone else yelled in favor of no one in particular, just blood shed. Their shouts were like a bee's buzz in a meadow, ever in the background but only noticeable when it got too close.

Screaming my rage, frustration and pain I lurched forward from where I had landed just off to the left of her. Tears blurred my vision as I heard more than I saw my strike hit its mark. Just at the base of the skull, where the head arched, the plates of her scales had separated just slightly, just enough. My blade slid beneath the tawny hued layers and drove up into her skull with a squealch that made my stomach turn, the 'scchhhhiink' of the metal blade sliding against bone making my teeth clench. Falling to my knees beside her head, I gazed into her eyes as life quickly left them. Leaning forward my forehead pressed against her brow, the muscles in her body still reacting to stimuli so that her body curled in on itself and surrounded me before finally stilling.

Somehow that hurt worst of all.

The arena was an uproar of noise, but I heard none of it. My tears fell freely as I silently cursed these people and this life. I'd see them all burn for what they had taken from me, for what they had cost my soul.

"I am so sorry my sister, be free now. I will tell my mother what became of you."

My voice was hoarse and worn and I barely recognized it.

My mother would already know, she'd feel her magic return to her, but she would need to know what happened. Eventually, I would have to tell her what I had done. My hands shook uncontrollably and it was only then that I realized the announcer was speaking and the handlers and their slaves were approaching me. I rose but nothing registered except the buzzing rhythm of my name being chanted, then a more chaotic cadence. Screams perhaps?

A darkness filled the arena and wrapped around me like a silk cloth. It felt like home, there in the shadows, and it was almost as if someone else was controlling my body as rage fueled me.

Ignoring the spectators, I retrieved both of my blades from my sister's lifeless body. The magic within me popped and sizzled like hot lava and I half expected the sand beneath me to turn into glass from the heat of my anger. A glance down confirmed it had not, though wisps of magic did tickle my toes.

I'd have credited my gorgon mother, except I wasn't made from her blood, it was the Goddess Nemesis who had birthed me and from her blood came my magical gifts. The darkness of shadow and the cold of the underworld numbed me as I danced the dance of death and bathed in the blood of any who dared to enter that arena. The world disappeared in a spray of crimson shadow and when I awoke from my stupor, I stood in a soaked patch of discolored sand, completely whole, with bodies scattered around me like leaves from a tree. For the first time in my life I had channeled the magic of my mother Nemesis. The havoc it left behind would live in my nightmares for decades and stain the pages of history well after.

The crowd erupted into a mass of noise I couldn't decipher. Cheers, anger, excitement, fear, it all melded into the sound the wind makes during a storm as it tears through the trees. My head was light, my vision spotty again. Glancing down at my blood soaked body, I could see more than actually feel that it was trembling. My legs wobbled in place, barely holding me up. It looked as if I had risen up from the earth through the blood pooled around my feet, every inch covered in crimson and sand.

Laughter bubbled up in me, but never spewed out.

My eyes scanned my body and noted that I was visibly wounded, but I felt none of the pain I should.

Instead, I was numb.

A deep inhale disturbed my precarious teetering and my limbs finally gave way beneath exhaustion. Hard cold earth met my hands and knees, then the arena disappeared.

Helheim did not reappear, however, Hel's voice did.

"Quite the unique being you are, daughter of Nemesis and Medusa."

The voice was just behind my ear, the wisp of breath that tickled the side of my neck chilling me to the bone, causing my breath to catch roughly in my throat.

"Of all the memories you must hold at bay, I wonder what it is about this one that haunts you so? I see the life and death of all who walk into my kingdom - yours is not a clean history, Nyx." Hel's voice spoke my name with skepticism.

If only that were the end of it.

A bright light streaked across my face as the shadows were cut away by a bright lamp. A familiar scent filled my nose and my heart soared. In this life Lykos had taken to wearing sandalwood oil and it had quickly become my addiction and soon after, a torture device.

"What happened?" I asked, my lips moving of their own accord, the words sounding hoarse and gravely.

My eyes darted across the room taking in a small bedroom in what must have been an inn. The wood was old and creaky, noise from the hallway drifting in as people walked. It was drafty, but warm enough, with thick decorated canvases over the windows. Average in every detail, but better cared for than I was accustomed to. I suspected it was far from the arenas. That alone should have been a relief, but worry poured through me as I noticed Lykos was keeping at a distance.

"You won. Nyx, you did it - we are free women again. You've been unconscious for a few days," she answered. "I couldn't wait to move you, they only agreed to let you live out your victory if I took you away immediately. An older lady, a healer, has been taking care of you and says you will be well soon. "

Her voice was not one of happiness, instead there was a deep sorrow in the notes, as if she were on the verge of bursting into tears. Her arms were wrapped around her torso, her fingers tapping an erratic beat against her ribcage.

"Then why do you sound so sad, if they kept their word?" I asked.

It was difficult, but I managed to get myself sitting upright, waving off aid when she looked as if she were going to come nearer. Something in the air between us told me I would need the space for whatever came out her mouth next.

"I... I'm sorry Nyx. I've got to go."

Her bright blue eyes were watery and my keen sight spied the tears that broke free and streaked her cheeks. My heart sputtered, something reaching in and grasping it so that it couldn't properly beat. I reached up to my face, pinching the bridge of my nose then moving the pressure up between my eyes.

Everything was once again spiraling out of my control.

"Please, don't do this, just give us time," I sputtered.

The words were pitiful, the notes strained like I'd been pushed underwater and barely had a breath left. My heart shattered into pieces as I watched her eyes avoid me. My mothers had tried to guide her to me sooner, but the Fates had been cruel and put our paths too far apart. This time, when she had stumbled upon me, she was not alone and that had changed everything.

"What choice do I have Nyx? These flashes of the past are just that. The past. I have a life, a home and a partner. There are no words for how thankful I am for everything you've done to protect me, but in this life we just aren't meant to be what we were."

The room spun, the world collapsing all around me. When I could finally focus on more than desperately remembering how to breathe, everything was broken, including me. Words may have fallen from my lips, but when I searched my memory days later, I couldn't recall them. All I could do was pray there was no venom in whatever may have slipped from my lips before Lykos disappeared out the door.

"What did you do after?" Hel asked.

My mind separated from the memories as I stood suspended somewhere in between.

"I disappeared." A sigh followed my words.

"Why did you not pursue her?" Hel's question sounded innocent.

"To have forced anything else would have poisoned my heart and hers for even longer than this heartache would last."

My vision swirled, making me lightheaded for a moment before the world of helheim came back into focus and my mind realigned with the present.

"What was that?" The words came out way more steady than I felt.

"There is a reason many do not dare enter the Underworld without having lost their lives first. Here is where your regrets nest, your failures and guilt, the memories you try hard to bury but cannot escape. It is different for everyone, but none who have come here have done so without at least one." Hel smiled gently, almost remorseful.

"Where is Lykos?"

My mind caught up with the present, casting about frantically for my still missing partner. The fact that she too would have been affected and would be forced to face her demons was not lost upon me. What would haunt my fox? I could not say for certain, there were plenty of possibilities throughout our lives. What I did know,quite intimately, was how horribly she tended to deal with the more traumatic of her memories. For all my bloody retaliations on the world, they were at least controlled chaos comparatively. I needed to be by her side when she came out of it.

"Close by. Safe. You will have to forgive me, I wanted you to myself for a bit. It is not often women like you come willingly into my home." Hel replied.

"Willingly is a bit generous don't you think? What other choice did I have? I will not let the amazons die for nothing when they could be saved."

"This time, you mean?" She grinned, her decaying side somehow less menacing than the healthy one. Her knowing eyes bore into me, seeing far more than what lay on the surface.

My lungs froze and I suddenly felt as if I had been plunged beneath ice cold water. I tried to wash the expression from my face, but she'd landed a blow and knew it. Her cruel smile never wavered even as she reached a hand out to help me to my feet. I said nothing in response. There was no need. We both knew the truth, my motives were purely selfish.

Reaching up, I took the offered hand, puzzled at the way the temperature of her grip shifted, like it was torn between death and life. Rising to my feet I cast my gaze around, hoping to catch a glimpse of Lykos, but a fog had closed in on us so that I couldn't even see the skeletal army I knew must still be nearby.

"There is always a choice, even if we do not like our options. You have shown yourself to be quite aware of this so please, do not play coy." She dropped my hand and although we had no familiarity, it felt like a loss.

A sigh fell from my lips, my soul exhausted and the weight of it seeming to close in around me. The memories were a weight I'd have preferred to forget.

"Every choice I have ever made has been a selfish one, this is no different. I make it not because it is the right thing to do, or the easiest path, but because it is the path which holds the least pain."

"So you fear the pain of losing your friends? Your loved ones?" Her question sounded innocent enough, but I could see the devious shimmer in her eyes. They peered deep into my soul and dared me to lie to her face.

Breathing in deeply, I tried to gather my thoughts. Hel would not be satisfied with pieces of the truth, but could I truly put to words the turmoil within?

The path of least resistance had presented itself on more than one occasion in my lifetimes, but never had I tread down it. Always, the fork in the road presented a sunshine path, with wildflowers and cute bunnies hopping alongside in the grass, opposite a dreary shaded trail with glowing eyes hiding in the shadows. As much as I loved the warmth of the sun on my skin, the darker path called, ever beckoning - promising a beauty that people seldom tried to understand and fewer still succeeded.

My mothers said acceptance was the difference between those who feared the night and those who played beneath the stars and called it home. One feared what might lurk in the shadows, while the other knew full well what awaited them and embraced it all the same. I had always been the latter; Ever pulled into the light but always longing to dance beneath the moon.

Acceptance of such a fate had come to me many lives ago. Afterall, every inch of my life had been drenched in shadows and blood - it was how most of us came into the world and many of us left it. My only worry was that one day Lykos might finally look past the part of me that played in the sun and see the monster hiding in the shadows. That same monster who had thrived in the gladiator rings, until that day when things shifted. She had once seen the darkness and chosen another. I had never questioned her about it in all these years because when it came to those answers, I was nothing more than a coward. The next life we had moved on as if it had never happened and perhaps for her it never did.

Would she once again fear what her gargoyle had become in her absence? What I had become without anything to pull me back into the light?

Could she even fathom just how much I hated myself for what I felt in that coliseum, as much a slave as a masochistic and willing victim. That arena had stained my soul just as much as her choice had all those lifetimes ago.

I finally replied, "Those of us blessed with long life quite often fall into a gray area few like to speak of. In truth, the only danger of living and dancing upon the edge of morality, at least as far as I see it, is forgetting that not everyone does. It is far too easy to get comfortable with those around you and let your nonchalance lead you astray. The moment you forget to pretend, lovers leave, friends become enemies and villages burn to a chorus of 'monster'."

My words were muttered softly, self reflection in their depths that took me by surprise, so much so I cast a suspicious glance to the fog swirling around my feet.

Caring deeply for those closest to me was easy, it was just the rest of the world that I swept beneath the rug. Collateral damage had long been acceptable in times of war, but the moment a woman admitted to indifference, she was regarded as some fiend. Camaraderie that stemmed from having been birthed into the world at the same location had always baffled me, and more often than not estranged me. Villagers could hate their neighbors, but let an outsider move against them and suddenly they were all family.

There was no such love amongst immortals. My mothers had raised me with love and nurturing souls, but without a people to call our own. It had always amazed me how someone could feel a part of something so vast, especially when I had always felt minimalized by the idea. Was I one of many children born of a god? Absolutely. However I was the only child born of the Goddess Nemesis and the gorgon Medusa. That in itself made me a singularity that could not be denied. Amongst a world full of self-righteous, pompous, and self-involved half immortals, I tried my best to make sure I was not piled in with the lot of them.

I was unique, one of a kind and special - yet not special at all. I was just another body walking the earth, selfishly living life to my own fulfillment - or detriment. As was every other person alive, whether they saw it or not. Though I had not always been as I was, I felt no regret towards the legacy I left in my wake. It was to hunt or be hunted and a gorgon was not prey, but that day had triggered something far worse within me.

Hel cocked a brow, her lips curled into a cruel smirk as she gestured with her hand to continue. She was patient, letting my mind wander without so much as a sigh of annoyance. No doubt she was studying me, her voice almost a purr when she spoke.

"Come now darling, dig a little deeper, or else the fogs will be inclined to help."

No, she would not let me get away with half-truths.

"War is one thing, vengeance is the family business - but what I did there, that was for sport, entertainment for the masses. There was no need for any of it and the blood I left in my wake was just as needless. Reconciling that version of myself with this one was hard enough for myself - how could I ever ask that of another? The one time I did, she didn't choose me."

Hel tilted her head ever so slightly, her healthy side closest to me as she asked, "Do you truly fear she might turn away should she discover the truth? Or do you simply believe yourself unworthy of her love because of it?"

My body shifted, the weight moving from one foot to the other as my mind turned the question over, my discomfort growing beneath the weight of the implication.

"I'm not sure." The truth was hard to swallow and stuck in my throat.

"Then tell me little gorgon, has she given you any reason to doubt her? Most of your history has her by your side and just as bloodstained as yourself, do you think she is so fickle as to shy away from what you did on your own?"

I didn't answer her. My heart told me one thing while my brain whispered another. For all that I hoped our love could transcend time, there had been that one single time when it hadn't. Lykos had been my one and only, but without her memories there had always been a slim chance she'd meet someone before finding me. Remembering that moment still soured my stomach.

"Oh sweet Nyx, so loyal. Never has she strayed and too humble to tell her partner so. You two really do need to work on communication."

Hel giggled and gestured to herself, shifting the subject abruptly.

"Many have said that I am both beautiful and haunting. Would you agree?"

The question threw me off balance, but I nodded slightly, assuming she was going somewhere with the question. Something urged me to add to it, so that she did not think I was agreeing just to move the situation along. No need to piss off a goddess of death, after all. The focus finally getting off of me and my memories was also a very welcomed break.

"I would more so say that your beauty is haunting because it is not what humans traditionally count as beautiful. Death is beautiful in a way only some can fathom, most everyone else fears it. For a human to admit that you are beautiful is to deny what they have spent their entire lives convinced is the only form of beauty. You haunt them because you defy their rules and destroy the way they have been taught to see the world." I answered, honestly flowing past my lips far easier than flattery.

"Spoken like a creature who walks the very same line." She smiled.

"Every story has a villain, but who it is depends on the bard's audience. You would not tell a story of a hunt and portray the hunter as a hero to prey." A shrug moved my shoulders half-heartedly.

"You might find hunters who feel the prey is the hero." She casually circled me, the hairs on the back of my neck rising with the uneasy feeling that she was readying herself for a kill strike.

"They are the ones who realize we are all in an endless cycle with no true winners or losers. One cannot exist without the other." Standing taller, I pulled on every ounce of restraint I had in an attempt to appear calm and cool as she walked behind me, into my blindspot.

"Your mothers were right, you have not merely existed in your long life, you have seen the world for what it is. It is a shame that you cannot see what is right in front of your face. Your fox afterall, is a hunter is she not?"

Dumbfounded, I stood there feeling as if my mouth were agape, my brain spiraling as her meaning flew over my head then smacked the back of it. We had traveled the long way, but now I understood her shift in subject for what it was.

"Time moves differently here and your partner is finishing up her own journey - I suggest we discuss what you need to do rather quickly and get you back to the land of the living. This has been fun."

She smiled deviously as she stopped in front of me once again, her expression smug.

The goddess of death then gestured behind me, causing my head to swivel. My vixen looked pissed as she walked forward, her ears would have been pinned if she'd been in her kitsune form, of that I had no doubt. Tension was practically rippling off her, but when her blue eyes met mine, the tremor of anger broke and relief settled her shoulders back.

There was a hint of sadness in her gaze which confused me, but as I reached back a hand her fingers thread through my own as she took it and squeezed. It hurt a little, but I had always liked a balance of pleasure and pain. We had always walked that fine edge between soft and hard; hearth and wildfire.

Squeezing her hand gently in return garnered her attention. I nodded towards the Goddess before us, Lykos' arched brow a silent question that didnt' need answering, though I did for the sake of clarity.

"The Goddess of Death was just about to tell us how we will be bartering for passage."

Hel smirked, her eyes scanning me over as if searching for something.

"Great, the sooner the better, I've had my fill of this place." Lykos' sneer was nothing but genuine, her lips smacking as if she had a bad taste in her mouth.

"Something about my home to your distaste kit?" Hel's lips curled into a wicked smile, but her eyes cut a dangerous line to my fox.

"No, not something - everything." Lykos' words were emphasized with a growl as she used her free hand to waft a stray tendril of mist away from her.

Hel laughed, her glare relenting as her lips curled into a smile.

"The mists do give a rather memorable bad first impression. I assure you the rest of my realm is not nearly as…hostile."

Lykos paused, her head turning as her gaze slowly took in our surroundings. Her gaze landed on me and lingered just long enough for me to give her a warning bulge of the eyes before she decided to reply.

"Hostility I can handle, as long as we don't have to do all that again." She waved her hand behind her towards the fog that had now dissipated almost completely.

"Perhaps I was hasty, not taking a peek into your visions too." Hel looked intrigued but not at all remorseful for her decision to watch mine instead.

Lykos' brow rose, not missing the implication in the goddess' words. For now, I merely gave her a shrug, hoping to avoid another rehashing of the past.

"You will need to find the Hound, Lykos will likely sense her as soon as you're close; She was blessed with magic from the hound that chased the cadmean vixen. This allows her to find anything she seeks, so she can lead you to my father Loki. The Valkyrie transport the dead from battlefields, so they shouldn't be hard to find." Hel smiled, eyes locking with Lykos as she continued, "You will need to leave the way you came, take the first right along the branch and when you get to the very end - jump."

The sickeningly sweet way she said 'jump' made Lykos' lip twitch and all I could do was shake my head. Whether the goddess was truly offended or not was hard to tell, what with her strange mix of demeanor to match her appearance, but Lykos was always game for a bit of banter.

"Is there a soft landing at the end of that jump or should we just cross our fingers and hope for the best?" Lykos' words were dry, her face dead-panned for effect, though I noticed it quirked up into a slight smirk when Hel replied with as much dry playfulness.

"You know, I'm not sure I recall. Suppose you will find out at the bottom." Hel shrugged innocently, her eyes never leaving Lykos.

Shaking my head, I jabbed my dear fox in the ribs with my elbow, forcing her to break her glare with the goddess - who smirked when she won the stare down.

"Always so tactful." My words were teasing as I grumbled softly at Lykos.

"Please, I could have said way worse," Lykos muttered when I caught her eye.

"You know this is why people consider me the smart one right?" My laughter only made her roll her eyes.

"Keeps me out of the boring meetings at least." Lykos' smirk pulled her cheeks up, giving her adorable smile wrinkles near her eyes. My heart caught for a moment, my heart overwhelmed and outpouring with love.

When I managed to look away, Hel was still watching us, her head cocked slightly in the manner of a bird.

"The Fates played a very risky game with you two, things could have so easily gone another way. I daresay it almost did too. I do hope you make it through Ragnarok in one piece."

She seemed genuine, but one never knew with gods.

"Are you as worried you'll die as the other Gods?" My beautiful fox held not an ounce of tact.

"Not at all...Death is inevitable." With that last bit of ominous parting words and no warning whatsoever, Hel disappeared, leaving a waft of fog in her wake.

The thick fog behind Hel had thinned enough for me to see the army of undead that were still guarding the bridge to the other side. They had stilled, leaving the world eerily quiet. A whisper touched my ear, sounding almost like 'ask her', but I couldn't be sure.

"Let's get out of here before we walk another trail down memory lane shall we?" Lykos' words were full of something I couldn't quite place.

"You too huh?" The words were soft, my worry for whatever she might have had to suffer slipping into them.

She nodded.

"When this is over?" I asked tentatively, terrified she might uncharacteristically jump into it instead.

"Yes." She replied, her words heavy and tired.

I was mildly ashamed at my own relief.

It was obvious neither of us would be comfortable discussing what we had seen for a while yet. Lykos had become more open with me in the comforts of our home, but she still struggled when the world could witness it. It was hard to swallow at times, for my own fears could strangle good sense from me, but I did my best not to hold it against her. After all, I'd had consistent years to learn how to be vulnerable while maintaining my own safety. The balance was a precarious one that I'd rather her not risk.

CHAPTER EIGHT
A Fox and a Hound

My head remained on a swivel, glancing behind to be sure the undead would not suddenly rush down upon us as we neared the gateway. The shimmer in the air reacted to our presence. The way it moved was almost nauseating to watch, but it opened up just wide enough to slip in sideways. Once we had stepped through to the other side we found the tree just as we had left it, but not.

The path seemed different this time, though surely the tree had not somehow rearranged its branches. It was so strange, how familiar places could look off merely by changing one's perspective. Settling into a steady pace my tracks followed Lykos'. Silence settled between us as I watched the tension coil within her, my muscles mirroring her own. Our footsteps were light and cautious, though we had left the most dangerous of gods behind us. In the steady rhythm, my mind ran circles - Hel's questions casting a net over me, threatening to drown me in residual thoughts.

Never had I let myself be deluded about who and what I was. History might have painted me in varying shades of light, but I always knew the true colors that stained the pages I occupied. They weren't the beautiful rainbows associated with light and love.

Those who were left to record the past either survived it, or were far enough from it to have no clue what was true. Histories were written by the victors and they often portrayed me as a heroine, turning the tide to assure victory. Occasionally they named me only as a beast let loose of its leash to do another's bidding. This was more accurate. Those who survived the battles I bloodied trembled when speaking of my presence, a name left unuttered for fear it would conjure the monster it belonged to.

It was not that I thought myself a bad person, all things considered, but I was not a hero of some ballad. No, I was the nightmare that tore through the battlefields and only those who never saw me dared to put into words what I had left in my wake. When the world was calm and quiet, I was like any other person living my life, but when the world was chaotic I was a force to change the outcome of great battles.

The Fates had manipulated my life easily by knowing one simple fact; I would always choose Lykos.It was for her that I did everything. Her light was what guided me. Long ago I had lost sight of the trees amongst the expanse of forests, but I always saw the fox amongst them, much like a shepherd spots the wolf amongst sheep. The side I chose had nothing to do with beliefs, or goodness. All that mattered was which side my fox favored. It was always the same; Tyrants lived off the sweat and blood of their people, sacrificing them for mere ego whilst calling their deaths loyalty.

Silently I wondered, not for the first time, if she really did know me better than I thought. The histories could not have escaped her notice and she had witnessed me blood soaked on more than one occasion. I thought I knew the answer to Hel's question, but what if my selfish mind only thought it did? Was the fear in my heart misguided? Afterall, even with her memories intact, she had chosen me - in every life but one.

The problem was that I could never forget that, the pain of her choice had almost broken me as badly as the first time I lost her. The one time she wasn't amongst the fighting was the only life she hadn't chosen me - surely that was no coincidence. Never had I dared to ask and find out otherwise, instead I let it silently torture me from afar - pushing it away and crowding my mind with everything else.

My train of thought was broken as Lykos' steps faltered, causing my unfocused gaze to take in the world around me. Ahead was the place Hel had told us about. Lykos practically beamed with excitement as she leaned over, peering into the endless depths below as she laughed. Despite her words with the death goddess, she apparently had no qualms about what she was being asked to do.

"Well, suppose it's a good thing you've got those useless wings." She said it so nonchalantly I almost didn't grasp her meaning.

Almost.

"Don't you DARE!" My sharp reply was pointless, I already knew my words would do absolutely nothing to stop her.

She turned towards me and grinned with her teeth on full display, then tilted herself to fall sideways. Her mischievous giggles followed her as she plummeted down.

A groan fell from my lips as I instinctively moved after her, mild panic filling and constricting my chest at the impending sensation.

"Dammit Lykos, you know I HATE FALLING!"

The words were torn out of my lungs as I dove after her, the world rushing by in a blur. She laughed more heartily and opened her arms, her eyes closed as she trusted me wholeheartedly to catch her. My hands grasped hers mid fall and jerked her towards me. Her legs instinctively wrapped around my waist as she buried her face in the crook of my neck, clinging on for dear life as if she hadn't just tipped herself over the edge of an abyss with no clue as to what was waiting at the end.

The overwhelming trust between us consumed my seething annoyance. Her warmth surrounded me, the wild scent that forever followed her clinging to my nose. Hair slapped my face, but I'd learned long ago to just deal with the sting and keep my mouth closed. Instead of trying to wipe it aside, I simply held her closer, her presence like a balm, soothing the nerves within. I might have laughed at the ridiculous way she made me smile, despite my heart being in my throat, if I wasn't focused on making sure we didn't become a splat on the earth.

We fell through the tree's branches until the air below us shimmered and opened, allowing us to fall through another gate. The tingle of magic made my skin itch. The sensation was hard to ignore, despite us plummeting towards what appeared to be a coastline in the middle of nowhere. Strengthening my grip on Lykos, I let my wings burst through their skin prison - the sound reminiscent of the crackling pop of lightning. As their leathery canvas caught the air, our bodies jerked up hard before leveling out and gliding gently to the grassy earth below.

Lykos was still giggling at the rush of the fall and I couldn't help but smirk while she wasn't looking. Her happiness had always been contagious, but I really hated her sense of humor sometimes. Still, we had a job to do, so I smacked her arm a little less than gently with the backs of my fingers, both in reprimand and to get her attention.

"Next time you do that I'm going to let your ass take a stone nap wherever you land."

She rolled her eyes and stuck out her tongue.

"You wouldn't dare. You'd miss me too much," She retorted.

She was right, but it didn't mean I couldn't bluff.

I shook my head and huffed instead, "Well, it should be easy enough to find these Valkyries, the smell of death is hard to miss, even for my nose."

The wind blew in strong, rising from the beach below, the tangy and putrid scent of decaying flesh mingling with smoke and charred wood. Peering down from our grassy cliff that overlooked a beach, everything appeared abandoned. Upon closer inspection of the rocky craigs below, it became very apparent that the area had been inhabited relatively recently.

The Vikings had attacked from the water, the remnants of a few fishing boats bobbing back and forth with the lapping of waves upon the shore. Thankfully, wherever we were, these were not Amazons - their craftwork was easy to recognize. Although no less gruesome to behold, it was easier to be indifferent to the mess when they weren't your own.

"If there are fishermen here, there will be a village nearby. I'd bet lunch that's where the stench is coming from." Lykos' nose was in the air, ever reminiscent of her bestial form.

"Yea and it's our lunch that'll feed the scavengers if this smell gets any worse. You're the one with the sniffer, lead the way." I tried not to breathe too deeply as I spoke.

She snorted but immediately followed the shifting wind until we had wound our way down off the cliff and followed a trail between the outcropping of rocks. When we finally hit open space it was on a flat level of rock looking out over a village that had fared far worse than the fishermen.

"They didn't stand a chance." Lykos' words were hollow, stating fact with a practiced void she'd learned long ago.

The quickest way to end up dead was to let the enemy read your emotions freely. Life had taught us that lesson well. All I could do was nod in agreement, knowing full well her mind was not on the villagers below.

"They did try though. Look there, some of the Vikings fell." Gently I nudged her side with my elbow, pointing to where a few burly vikings lay lifeless upon the earth. That regular villagers might be able to take down a few would hopefully give her hope for her Amazon sisters, who would face the same soon.

It was all the comfort I could spare, anything more would be unrealistic and more harmful than good. The truth was undeniable, the odds low, and our morale as wavering as a new foal's legs. False hope would only set us up for heartache should the worse happen.

The sudden sound of wings shuffling through the air drew my eye across the grassy embankment and sandy beaches.

"Definitely in the right place." My words were whispered as I pointed towards the source of the disruption.

High in the sky, armor clad women glided across the battlefield, a few landing at the sides of the fallen. Their wings shimmered beneath the sun's light, the large span of feathers just as unique and different as each woman. The armor they wore had been fashioned from metal, sunlight glinting off the surface in blinding fashion. Many of the women also carried weapons, though my sharp gaze could not make out all of them - none seemed to have been bloodied by the victims below. If they had participated in the massacre, I needed to ask them how they'd managed to stay so clean. The amount of clothing I'd ruined from battle was absurd, not to mention how long my hair smelled of copper afterwards.

With none but the winged women left alive, it seemed safe enough to stride forward. Afterall, we had a job to do and standing there gaping at the Valkyrie was not going to get us closer to the one we needed.

"Let's introduce ourselves shall we?" At my question Lykos nodded in agreement, though we didn't have to go far.

One of the women who glided through the skies alighted next to the form of a viking who laid just a few yards from our position. As soon as she was near, I felt the magic within me begin to tingle, answering a call from deep in my heritage - magic passed down from my grandmother and namesake. Closing my eyes, I let the magic within me shift my vision so that when they opened once more, the world was painted in a different hue. The colors of the world around me became diluted, but without the distraction a new layer of the planes was revealed. Now, as I peered across the field of battle, I saw the dead, forlorn and awaiting ferrying to the underworld.

The man who the valkyrie approached looked up with sorrow in his gaze. His hands were held out, blood staining them even in death. He looked around, but no words fell from his lips when he tried to speak. He crouched towards the earth, hands going to his face as his body began to shake with silent cries.

It was only when Lykos cocked her head I realized she too could see the interaction, our mingled blood giving each other new perks. The woman reached out a hand and helped the crouched man to his feet, though she said nothing, merely beckoned him back the way she had come. Behind her an arched doorway inlaid around rock shimmered with that telltale magic of a realm tear. The archway spanned the length of a house and its height doubled my own. The gates were made of a black metal opened wide and beckoning. It was through here that the dead were being ushered into Helheim.

Once the man had been guided forward, she moved towards another soul, completely ignoring our presence. She had scanned right over us, as if we were nothing more than a bit of shrubbery.

"A moment if you would?" My voice rose against the billowing wind, not quite a shout, but enough to demand acknowledgement.

Lykos snorted her amusement when the woman balked. The valkyrie stumbled in her step, a baffled expression distorting her face as she whirled around to face us. I smiled to hide my amused smirk, certain she had assumed herself invisible to our eyes. She apparently hadn't met very many magically inclined people.

"I'm looking for one of yours, a woman they call 'The Hound'?" Sometimes the quickest way to information was being direct, especially when interrupting one's work.

"How is it that you can see me, yet you are very much *not* dead?" Her hands propped themselves on her hips, the threat of the weapons strapped there obvious though I couldn't quite take her seriously after watching her bafflement.

"Lucky roulette of grandmothers, as it were. Though to be fair, you aren't exactly dead in the same way they are." Pointing to the spirits of the dead I shrugged nonchalantly. "Do you know the valkyrie we seek?"

She eyed me warily, confusion written on her face followed by an obvious desire not to be bothered further. Undoubtedly it was just as strange to her that I could see the souls as it was that we had spotted her. Impatience rolled off her in waves of attitude expressed in a propped hip and scowl.

"Sure, she's in the village, though I wouldn't count on a warm welcome." At that she thrust her wings downward and took off towards a couple of other valkyries that had paused in flight to observe us from above. Word wouldn't take long to get around.

"Right, we're about to get popular so let's make this quick shall we?" I quirked a brow at Lykos who nodded and shrugged at once. She'd never commit to staying out of trouble, it followed her more closely than her shadow and we both knew it. The valkyrie now knew for sure we had magic of some sort and there was no telling how they'd react.

The path to the village was littered with bodies and blood, the smell strong enough to make me breathe through my mouth until my overloaded senses adjusted. Lykos annoyingly seemed unmoved by the stench, which made absolutely no sense to me.

"Are you purposely acting like it doesn't smell terrible?" I didn't pause my stride, but I did look at her fully, only then noticing that she was barely breathing at all.

"Don't distract me Nyx, I'm trying to filter it out." She muttered through clenched teeth, her nostrils carefully flaring to push the scents away as she sucked in a quick bit of breath through her mouth.

Laughter made me pull a deep breath that I immediately regretted, but thankfully the wafting smell finally met a strong westerly wind that carried it away from us. Still laughing, I drew as deep a breath as possible, taking advantage while it lasted. Lykos scowled at me, my giggles continuing as I watched her whole body relax as she breathed easily again.

The village itself was falling apart, but that seemed more from poor upkeep than the actual attack. Whatever had driven the vikings to attack this place, it must not have been any sort of riches. There was an obvious lack of corpses in this area as well, meaning the whole of the village must have been out tending the docks and boats, their fleeing forms struck down before they could make it back. The lack of winged women in the sky confirmed my thoughts, but also made me wonder where the woman we sought would be.

Distracted by my thoughts, I almost ran right into Lykos, whose head cocked sideways as she stopped in her tracks. A grunt fell from my lips but was quickly replaced by a questionable hum, any curses I'd have spoken dying on my tongue.

Ahead of us a lanky creature who looked mildly like a fox whose legs had been stretched too long paused in its stride. Its legs had moved in sync on each side, mimicking the gaited horses I had seen the vikings riding - their legs staying weirdly beneath them instead of stretching out fully, making them quick and smooth but weird to watch. This creature, however, was something altogether strange and intriguing, but also absolutely ridiculous looking.

Lykos didn't hold back.

"What the hell kind of mutated fox hound is that?" Her laughter echoed as she practically bent over from the peals of laughter falling from her lips. Gods, her laughter was like music to my ears and I felt myself giggling alongside her, though I kept mine far more mild mannered. The creature's ears pinned against its head, teeth bared as it stared daggers at Lykos, ignoring me completely.

Her long legs were black as night but she had the reddish orange fur of a fox as well as huge black ears. Although she stood near the size of a pony, I suspected the species wasn't so large naturally. There was definitely magic wafting off the beast, tinged with the unique human saltiness that I couldn't quite name properly.

"She's not a fox, she is a maned wolf." A tall valkyrie walked out of a nearby house, undoubtedly having heard Lykos' now obnoxious, howling laughter. Her brows were pinched with annoyance, but her bright blue eyes were light, much as the sky they reflected. Her long blonde hair practically floated behind her, a pair of wings folded against her back, their longest feathers dragging nearly a foot behind her. Their hue was a mix of tan and cream, the shadows between holding an almost purple tint.

Lykos, ever a creature of self control, paused for a moment to look between them, laughter falling from her lips as she spoke, barely able to contain it to a modest chuckle.

"That is the weirdest fucking wolf I've ever laid eyes on."

"Lykos, don't be rude," I muttered, brushing my elbow against her arm.

"I'm not being rude, I'm being honest. If I shifted into something that absurd I'd expect the same reaction."

Ah, there it was. The purpose of the taunt. Lykos was reckless at times but she was not foolish, the casual comment was confirmation. We had found a shifter, which meant this was very likely the 'Hound' that we had been sent after. Not a great start for building cooperation though.

The valkyrie at the side of the maned wolf cocked her brow, taking information from the conversation as well.

"How can you tell that from here?" she inquired.

"She smells." Lykos said the words with a mischievous grin, goading the maned wolf who in turn took the bait, though the sound she made was something I had never heard. The loud noise was a strange mix between a bark and a roar, and was, admittedly, a bit intimidating. Despite the potential danger, I couldn't hide my smirk when Lykos once again decided to taunt the other shifter, though I did follow it with an eye roll.

"Sorry I don't speak cat-dog." She showed her teeth as she grinned, every bit the fox - only mildly limited by her human form.

"What has gotten into you?" I whispered, though I was no less amused. My muscles twitched, tense and ready for the inevitable explosion that was building between them.

"Eh, she's a jerk - I can sense it." She merely shrugged, as if that were all the answer in the world I'd need. Hel's statement had been informative on a level I hadn't noticed, the reason Lykos was going to sense her so easily was simply because these two were destined to be at odds even before they'd properly met.

Their magical roots were naturally in conflict.

Sure as anything, the air tingled with the sensation of magic and in just a few blinks the odd beast had become a woman, a very pissed off woman.

The Hound was definitely a viking, her build thicker - more acclimated to the cold weather of her homeland. Similarly she was built for war - muscled but agile, her thighs and legs maybe even more chiseled than my own. Where the black mohawk had run along the back of her canid neck, it was mirrored with a black streak down the center of her red-tinted brunette hair. She had braided the black in one large braid while the rest had been gathered back by smaller braids, all pulled behind her head with a piece of leather.

"I said one more smart ass comment and you're dead, kit!" Her voice was accented, though only ever so slightly, like she'd been away from her people for a while. A hand appeared at her arm, but she rather forcefully jerked out of the grip, a glare aimed at her companion. The tension there was palpable and I felt a stab of sympathy when I caught the hurt in the valkyrie's gaze before she covered it.

Oh how I knew that bitter sting of rejection.

"How about we keep our teeth, claws, and venom to ourselves for now." I looked pointedly at my dear vixen. Lykos at least had the good grace to look mildly sheepish as she closed her mouth, no doubt a mere second away from another insult.

"We actually came seeking the 'Hound', which seems a bit insulting now that I see you. Nevertheless, we were told you could find anything."

"Well you found her, but what makes you think I'd be willing to help you find whatever it is you're looking for? Especially after seeing the company you keep." Her growl was evident, rumbling into her words like rocks in a barrel.

"Honestly, I don't. If you're anything like the rest of your people, a few dead Greeks will mean absolutely nothing to you. Perhaps such a thing would even make life a bit more interesting for you and your brethren." I stepped over a body for emphasis as I drew nearer so that we wouldn't be practically yelling at each other.

"However, Hel thought you could be convinced and I've been educated on the idiocy of underestimating her - so I'm betting somehow we will find a means to work together." It was mostly true. Hel had never said she would help, but the assumption she could be persuaded was there.

The valkyrie at her side seemed skeptical and placed what would have been a comforting hand on her shoulder, had the maned wolf not looked annoyed at her and sidestepped the gesture once more. There was something between them, but whatever it was had been deeply disrupted. They moved around each other as if they had once been in sync and only when the wolf realized it did she jerk away, intentionally disrupting their harmony. Now the question was would this aid or hinder Lykos and I?

"Why don't we start with the basics? I'm Nyx and this is Lykos."

"What care would the Goddess of Death have with whatever it is you two are?" The valkyrie's tone was merely curious, but the glare of her companion was pure skepticism. Obviously it was the former I'd have better luck reasoning with.

"What reason does any God have to care? She wants something from us."

"That's supposed to encourage me to help?" The shifter flared her nostrils, scoffing.

Lykos rolled her eyes, arms crossed as her minimal patience waned. I raised a hand ever so slightly, her gaze flicking to me just long enough to see my silent signal to 'just wait'.

"I understand it is a challenge. If you cannot do it, do not be ashamed to admit it. We will find another way if we must, Lykos' nose ought to do well enough, despite Hel's belief otherwise," I stated.

The bait was set and just as I had predicted, the hot headed creature growled, indignant at the suggestion.

"Yea right, like some meek little fox could possibly track down Loki. Besides, it's not about sniffing them out, my magic just *knows* the way." She snorted as she rolled her shoulders and smirked, not realizing she'd just slipped up.

Looked like our new friends were expecting us then. How interesting.

"Tell you what, if your fox can best me - I'll help you. Otherwise, we have more important shit to do than get tangled up in whatever mess you're in." The woman frowned her annoyance, her eyes never even glancing my way. Although her words addressed me, her focus lay entirely on Lykos.

"Oh yes, I can see you are quite consumed with work." I gestured to the dead, all whose souls had already been escorted away. What was with this ruse if they knew we were coming and who had told them? I kept both in my peripherals as I turned towards my Vixen.

"Very well, Lykos, are you game for a little fun?" I arched a brow and wiggled it knowing full well she was dying to take a bite out of this one. Literally.

Lykos grinned like a fiend and even in her human form I could imagine her tails waving and flicking with anticipation. The energy rolling off her was potent, stirring my blood with all the ways my mind could think to burn it off. A sharp chill ran down my spine, her eyes widening as her grin grew marginally. She knew damn well what she did to me, my body betraying me with scent even when I controlled myself physically.

"I thought you'd never ask." She licked her lips subtly and winked at me before setting her sights back on the Hound.

"Alright pup, let's see what you've got." Lykos was already cracking her knuckles and preparing to shift, her weight moving from one foot to the other, the tingle of her magic reaching out and tickling my own.

"No broken bones Lykos, keep control and end this quickly, we don't have the time to dawdle this time round." I had no doubt that my love could handle herself just fine, but I didn't want her to lose herself in the moment and damage the woman more than was necessary. Even if she was hiding something, we did need their help.

Lykos smiled and I could feel my heart leap in my chest, the look in her eyes breathtaking as she absorbed my confidence in her and let pride glow across her face. The love that lived alongside that carnal look of wildness was an intoxicating combination. All I could do was lick my lips and take a step back to watch. Not surprisingly, the Hound's partner moved to stand alongside me.

"I'd apologize for this but something tells me I'll have nothing to say sorry for in a few minutes." She sighed softly.

"So little faith in your partner?" I didn't bother facing her, but I did crook a brow in her direction.

"Not at all, I merely see the faith you have in yours and what it does to her. Ylva would likely just roll her eyes at me." The sadness that flickered across her face made me question if my instincts had been wrong, perhaps it was an unrequited thing between them.

"Are you two not a pair then?" I asked quietly, lest our partners overhear and become distracted as they prepped.

"I wish it were that simple. We are stuck somewhere in between with Ylva unable or unwilling to let go of the only thing standing between us." She watched the other woman with a deep longing that made my heart ache for her. Too often had I seen that same pain in my own reflection. Poor thing likely had no one to confide in either, considering she was admitting this to a stranger.

"Heh. I've been there. Lykos has truly tested the lengths of my patience on more than one occasion. Time solves all problems, though, if given the chance."

"Only if the world doesn't end first," she replied. The scoff of laughter she emitted was barely a breath, but it held the weight of the world.

"Well, that in itself would also be a resolution, though not one you wish for. The end of the world usually makes people reflect a little though."

There was far more beneath this woman's exterior than I could possibly decipher. A deep history lay between the two, like a gaping river between shores. Eventually one would have to cross the rickety bridge between them or brave the waters. From the sound of it, it wouldn't be Ylva. Despite the deception hiding somewhere beneath the surface, a pang of sympathy flickered through me.

"Looks like they are done posturing. I'm Xiomara, by the way," she said offhandedly. She held out her arm in a warrior's greeting. Grasping her forearm I could feel the tension there, well muscled and on guard, despite her friendly smile. Good, they should be wary.

"I'm sure it'll eventually be a pleasure to have met you, for now let's enjoy the show; this should be interesting."

While we had been talking the two women had started shifting after what was certainly a heated moment of shit talk if I knew Lykos at all. From beside me, Xiomara's slight gasp was audible as we observed Lykos' animal form. What they had expected I could not say, but I was certain it wasn't a kitsune the size of a small horse.

Lykos apparently felt like showing off too. The tips of her tails, where the hue shifted to black, were arched up behind her, gently wafting in the air. That wasn't the impressive part though, oh no. The shadow magic Nemesis had created her with spilled off the onyx fur and crept down to the earth to coil back up her paws. They danced across the earth and around her feet like flames, while retaining their smoke-like consistency.

An amused smirk tugged my lips as pride filled me up. The flamboyant display was a tactic I'd taught her to keep her anxious feet from giving away her movements. Predicting her footsteps wasn't nearly as easy when a shroud of shadow hid the entirety of her lower half.

Although Ylva was presumably also over-sized, she only barely met Lykos' height and that was merely because of her stilt-like legs. Mass-wise my dear vixen had the upper hand and was sure to use it to her advantage.

Watching the two puffing up at one another suddenly filled my soul with amusement, giggles bubbling up and off my lips. The Valkyrie at my side looked shocked and confused.

"Who would ever believe us if we described these two, truly?" The words broke out between chuckles.

Xiomara looked over the scene before us and quickly covered her mouth to hide her own giggle. She shook her head, unable to disagree but trying very hard to hold back her laughter as she focused on her partner. Gathering myself, I did the same, though the smile didn't fall from my face. Sometimes it was better to hide your emotions from a potential enemy, but not this time.

Lykos, feeling particularly feisty, held her head low so that it snaked out close to the shadows at her feet, her tails arching up straight behind her, fanning out to be more intimidating. She was absolutely toying with her opponent, overtly exaggerating her fox tendencies so it was easy to forget she was anything else.

I might have rolled my eyes if she weren't so mesmerizing to watch.

Opposite her, Ylva's black fur stood on edge along the back of her neck, the barking roar she released was odd but powerful. Her long lanky limbs still looked awkward, though she stood crouched just a hair, ready to break whichever direction would yield the best evasion.

It only took a few blinks of the eye and they lunged.

They collided chest to chest, Ylva's long front legs reaching out to try and brace the giant fox and keep her snapping jaws at bay. It only worked for a moment, one of my vixen's paws quickly batting the hound's foot away as she nipped at the side of her neck. Throwing her body sideways, Lykos used her weight to her advantage, pivoting so that her tails could try and coil around the vulnerable limbs.

To her credit, Ylva was swift to leap back, her large ears folding against her head in disapproval of the tactic, though she didn't get long to scowl. She was once again forced to dance backwards and off to the side. Lykos was relentless in her assault, targeting the limber legs of her lanky opponent, trusting her thick coat to protect her against any toothy repercussions.

Lykos was as quick and nimble, her teeth snapping mere centimeters away from flesh as she darted in and out of proximity, her high pitched yaps giving warning of her movements. Shaking my head, I ran my fingers along the bridge of my nose to pinch between my eyes. She was toying with the maned wolf and we didn't have time for that. Nor did I wish her to use up all her stamina in case these two were some kind of trap in waiting. Despite how easy the task at hand seemed, luck was never on our side -

we'd surely find more troubled waters than smooth sailing.

"Don't pussy foot around Lykos." My voice was purposefully tight, almost scolding in a tone I hoped she would recognize. If she did, I couldn't tell.

She sneezed her annoyance, properly ignoring me as she continued to dance around the long legged canine before her. Not to say Ylva was not skilled. Now thoroughly tired of her antics, as Lykos leapt and nipped she now met her with full fury, their teeth almost clacking as they lunged together. More than once a growl turned snarl as someone got flesh. Round and round they went, back and forth with each gaining what the other lost and then the tables turning again and again. Red and black fur mingled and merged so that it was hard to tell where one began and the other ended when they crashed together.

This was going to be a problem. Two sides of the same coin, their brethren in the sky had been banished there out of mercy. Lykos would always dance away and Ylva would be on her heels, always able to find where my beautiful fox would be, but never able to grasp her.

Ylva fought like the viking she was, using her opponent's momentum and strength to her advantage. The only problem was Lykos was doing the same. I wasn't sure who would win in hand to hand, for it would be a game of stamina and luck. In her fox form however, Lykos had a few more tricks up her sleeve.

The back and forth continued until Ylva managed to nip Lykos' heel as she slammed her butt into Ylva's side. The crimson that marred her coat was finally enough to piss her off. The dance they'd been in ended as the shadows that had retracted now reached out and engulfed the maned wolf. She was done playing.

Ylva's yelp of surprise heralded the giant fox's movement. Lykos lunged and when the shadows dissolved back into her coat, Ylva lay on her side, Lykos' mouth firmly latched onto her throat, though her teeth did not pierce flesh - yet. The maned wolf's ears were flat against her skull, but her short tail stubbornly slid between her legs. A low whine was her official admonition to defeat. Lykos didn't immediately let go, her jaws tightening ever so slightly - a warning. Although the silent conversation between them was indiscernible to me at this distance, it was clear my beautiful fox had made her point as she gave a soft shake of the flesh she had and promptly let go. Like a parent scolding a pup.

Xiomara had remained in my peripheral vision, but as she released a loud breath I took her in fully. Her entire body was rigid, her face pale and her hand lingering on the weapon at her hip. She'd taken a few steps forward at the beginning and I watched as the tension slowly loosened only to draw taunt again. Indecision and fear of another sort gleaming in her eyes.

"Even if she refuses, at least she cannot say you weren't there." My words were only for us, the decision of whether or not to go to her partner's side was her own and I didn't wait to see which she chose.

"Don't you dare come sauntering over here smelling like dog and saliva expecting a kiss." The laugh in my voice was unmistakable even to my own ears and it warmed my heart to watch her proudly trotting towards me, her foxy grin mischievous as she panted her own laughter.

"What if I just kiss you?" Her ears perked forward and she lunged towards me, my reflexes barely quick enough to grab her muzzle as a wet slobbery tongue attempted to coat my face in a protective layer of gross.

"Lykos don't you DARE!" My words were fruitless and a deep groan filled and left my lungs as her sloppy fox kiss met the entire left side of my face. Defeated, I merely dropped my arms, my face shifting to a completely empty void while I stared at her bright cerulean eyes in disdain. "I really don't like you right now."

She danced around me like a kit, her tails wagging as she trotted a full circle, her adrenaline making her extra spunky.

"That's just because you love me all the time." Her words vibrated in my mind, translated from body language after years and lifetimes lived together. I couldn't even be mad that she was right.

"You are a nuisance my love." The grumbled words were emphasized with a clear swipe across my face to clear the residue of her lick. She let her tongue dangle out, threatening more saliva as she panted more laughter.

"Alright fox. Fair is fair, I'll show you the way." The words were Ylva's, her scowl strong enough that I could hear it clearly even at a distance. She'd wasted no time getting back into her human skin, crimson spotted her neck and a few places on her legs and arms.

"Keep a sharp eye Lykos, they know more than they let on." I whispered the words, careful to make sure my mouth was out of their line of sight. Lykos nuzzled me gently, her furry nose tickling my neck as I hugged her face. When she moved away I kissed the tip of her nose before turning back towards our new companions.

"Let us make haste then, we have people relying on us."

The two of them shared a look, a subtle nod of agreement to something I couldn't guess. Xiomara's face had slid into a neutral expression but Yvla had no problem keeping her annoyed look planted on her now human features. She rolled her shoulders and led the way to who knew where. Her braids swayed behind her, reminding me of Medusa's except for their silence. Medusa always had bits braided in her locks, the soft jingle a comfort I hadn't realized I'd missed. That of course was where any familiarity ended, but it was enough to shoot a pang of longing through me.

It didn't surprise me when Lykos let her magic pull back within her, the air tingling as her body popped, shifted, and shrunk back into her human form. I did, however, wonder about her motivation. Surely it would have been wiser for her to stay in her stronger form just in case their secrets were dangerous to us. Perhaps she was thinking about not drawing undue attention to ourselves. Conserving energy might explain the shifting back as well, but something in the way she walked told me it was for far more devious devices that she had returned to her human form.

My darling fox was rather good at jabbing open wounds, though it wasn't often she did it intentionally. The moment Ylva looked back at her the scowl in her features deepened and her body grew more tense. Lykos was noticeably shorter and extremely scrawny by comparison. That she'd been bested by her must have stung and my mischievous fox only grinned when she noticed the maned wolf's reaction.

Pride was a dangerous companion and I'd have bet money it was whispering dark things into Ylva's ear. She was so distracted by her mind she didn't even shrug off the subtle hand Xiomara pressed against her back as they maneuvered down a rocky path leading back towards the ocean. Hopefully we wouldn't need their company for long - the matter of who was better was far from resolved between them. There was no reason they should be in competition and yet the rivalry there had sprung up the second they had sniffed eachother out.

Living constellations, destined to be rivals and here they stood proving it true. A sigh escaped my lips as my heart ached for the implications. Could we ever truly escape the fate the world set out before us? Had any of our so-called 'defiance' even been real, or was it merely an illusion the Fates had let us keep in order to keep us on track? Were the footprints I left behind even of my own making?

Lykos bumped my hip, her head tilting in question, those beautiful pools of cerulean casting me out to sea without a lifeline. How could they erase all of my worry and doubt so effortlessly? With her by my side I could take on the entire world, but the whispers of the past kept me fearful she'd leave it.

Bumping her back I couldn't help but smile as she slid her fingers through my outstretched hand. Her calloused hand was smaller but she squeezed with a strength I wasn't sure I'd ever held. How easily I'd break beneath her touch if ever it lost the love radiating through. For her I would tear the world apart and nearly had once or twice. Hel had seen my deepest fear and practically laughed. Could she be right? Were my fears unfounded? No, she wasn't there, hadn't seen the look in Lykos' eyes. My hand unconsciously squeezed hers tighter, a quiet yelp falling from her lips.

"Nyx?" Her words were whispered, cautious of our companions listening in.

"Sorry, it's nothing." A lie that wouldn't hold up under pressure, but she thankfully didn't push for more.

We bunked down for the night with the reassurance that the next day would be a few hours of travel and then our destination, but the path was dangerous at night. The argument might have been made that three out of the four of us had night vision, but our trek had not been an easy one and Lykos and I were both yawning by the time camp was made. The tension between us had only worn down a bit. We had all been warriors at one time or another and so marching along in silence had been comfortable, but didn't exactly mend fences or bridge cliffs. Of course, before that could happen there was one major question that needed to be answered.

"Now that we have spent a day together and we've played nice - for the most part - how about you share who it is that told you we were coming?"

To their credit, they hid their surprise quite well, though their teeth both clenched hard enough for their sharp jaws to round out. Lykos snorted as she watched their faces contort, her smirk predatory in a way that made my insides squirm in the best way. Ignoring that, I casually kept myself nonchalant, forcing my body and face to stay relaxed. Pride filled my chest as Lykos mirrored my actions, licking her fingers clean of the salt left behind from the jerky she'd been munching.

"What are you talking about?" Xiomara asked, her tone forced.

"We never told you what we were looking for, nevertheless, whom." My neck popped as I rolled my head back and around, trying to work a kink out.

Ylva shook her head, a growl in her chest. "No, you did. You said you were looking for Loki." Panic flickered across her face as she avoided Xiomara's gaze. She knew she'd fucked up.

"Afraid not pup." The waiting game wouldn't take long, people were notoriously uncomfortable with silence, especially when they were caught in a lie. Lykos and I sat casually, purposefully relaxed as we watched the two fidget uncomfortably, the quiet quickly eroding their resolve.

Xiomara sighed, her head shaking before she shrugged.

"Well, it's not like we were told not to say anything, just to make sure it couldn't be linked to her." The valkyrie rolled her shoulders, the tension fading from her body by slivers.

Yvla refused to meet her partner's gaze, embarrassment or shame reddening her face.

"Freya instructed us that you'd likely seek us out for help and that we were to lead you to Loki when you did." Xiomara's hands spread out before her, a shrug emphasizing her helplessness in the matter.

"Why would she do that? Doesn't she hate him?" Pieces of their history had crept into the continent the moment the vikings had shown up, stories and lore coming across the oceans just as soon as the sea creatures disappeared. The amazons hadn't been keen on finding out more, but I had gathered much from the centaurs, whose contact with them had been peaceful.

"She did, but that was a long time ago. Anger fades eventually and what are you left with then but emptiness? As for the why - well that is simple. Odin takes most of the dead to fill the halls of Val Halla, but the rest Freya shields in Vanaheim. Ragnarok is coming and it will start a chain reaction, triggering a civil war amongst the Gods as each tries to be amongst the survivors. Freya sees what the others do not."

"What is that?" Lykos' question held a scoff that caused Xiomara's brows to furrow.

"That Ragnarok is a self-fulfilling prophecy. Everything that will happen is only due to what the Gods are doing in order to try and prevent it. Ragnarok is what they will call it, but the fruits of civil war have already spoiled in the barrel."

"Where do we factor in?" I quietly prompted.

"Only half the Valkyrie owe fealty to Freya, the rest have been bribed into Odin's service. Simply put, she needs numbers. The amazons you strive to protect are the trick up her sleeve she hopes will keep her people alive, but even she can't get around the rules of Helheim." Ylva shrugged as if in apology.

When we didn't say anything Xiomara picked up the narrative.

"Helheim is the gateway to the other realms, as all who die must pass through its grounds. So, in order to get the amazons to Vaneheim they must have a clear passage. If they were our people it'd be simple enough for the Valkyrie to claim their souls first, but they are not and so it is only by Hel's bidding that they will pass through and to Vaneheim."

"Which is where we come in, seeing as Gods are notorious for not working well together." A groan slipped past my lips.

Xiomara continued, "Plus, Freya cannot be linked to anything revolving around Loki. Odin will use any excuse he has to make a move against her - he has become paranoid and sees enemies in every shadow. So she must be an ignorant bystander." The Valkyrie looked troubled, as if she had witnessed the events and felt their shadow on her shoulder.

"So we get thrown under the lightning bolt instead huh?" Lykos' low growl was audible in her words, but I merely shrugged.

"Better two than hundreds," I replied.

The logic was clear and if Freya was a more benevolent goddess, then it would be the best course of action available to her. I didn't have to like it, to agree it was the logical choice.

Xiomara and Ylva both nodded in agreement and that was the end of it. What more could be asked or argued? We were yet again pawns in someone else's game. Today's game would benefit the amazons, so we would play to win. Tomorrow? Who knew what it would bring by the day's end. When we finally laid ourselves down to sleep, Lykos changed into her kitsune form, curling protectively around me and providing quite the comfy bed.

As it turned out, Ylva's gift was quite impressive. She led us across the wilderness to another portal, but this time we were somewhere higher in the branches of the giant tree. The glowing limbs overlapped in many areas and often we had to stop and carefully vault or crawl between them, their width far more narrow and precarious here.

The maned wolf stopped more than once to feel for the threads of magic she followed. Whatever she sensed I could not feel or see it, which meant it was either quite specific or innate. She had finally relaxed a bit, a job seeming to ease the tension that had her drawn so tight she looked ready to snap. Her grumbling attitude remained, however.

It was surely no small encouragement that the sooner she got us there, the quicker she'd be rid of my dear vixen's company. Lykos had eased off the taunting, but she couldn't help the smirk that graced her lips every time she caught the woman's eye. It was all I could do not to laugh at how much she looked like a puffed out bird, showing off its feathers. We were likely tangled in the limbs of the tree for close to an hour before Ylva stopped at an archway and beamed back at us, satisfied and surely victorious.

"This is it. Loki is through here." She stepped aside and gestured towards the shimmering air, the feeling radiating off it reminded me of something that I just couldn't quite place. More than just a tear in the world, there seemed an extra layer in the depths, though no one else seemed to notice.

Lykos chuffed, but playfully held her hands out, gesturing to the portal.

"Guess we shall see huh? I'll try to remember to say 'good job' if you are right."

Ylva merely rolled her eyes. "As if I need your praise."

I was forced to jog forward to catch up with Lykos before she recklessly walked right through alone. I would be glad to get away from this ridiculous unspoken rivalry, primarily for how well it fed Lykos' already reckless spirit. She paused just long enough to offer a toothy grin before grabbing my hand and pulling me alongside her.

The world shifted much more smoothly this time, the earth beneath our feet only dropping about an inch. Soft grass folded beneath my feet, a false sense of comfort coming over me before it was swept away by a blast of ocean air to the face that made a groan fall from my lips.

"How on earth do these Gods always have random islands on standby for these weird ass punishments they like to bestow?" There was no way I'd be able to get all the sand and salt off my body at this point, my skin already itchy at the thought of it.

Lykos shrugged, unphased by the sand and oblivious to the salt thanks to her shifting. She basically lost the top layer of skin each time, and all the accumulating irritants with it.

"I stopped asking 'why' a while ago." She took a deep breath and held it, relishing the fresh air.

"I'll remember that the next time you question any of my decisions." My lips curled into a smile as she quickly turned towards me, her hand held up and her face pinched in a wince.

"I'll take it back." She pouted sheepishly.

"Too late." The words slipped from my lips as I danced away from her, playfully batting away her hands as they attempted to catch my hips.

Shortly after Ylva and Xiomara followed through, Ylva's scrunched up face showing her displeasure.

"If its not that far then it won't hurt to make sure they get there," Xiomara grumbled, practically pushing Ylva forward.

Lykos and I didn't let it phase us. Our laughter followed us as we made our way down the hillside we'd found ourselves on. Lykos gave me a gentle bump with her hips when she finally drew close enough, the energy dissipating into a soft seriousness. There was much to be said about having to be on guard all the time and with the company we were keeping, the tension had definitely built enough for us to need a moment to shake it away. As much as we were remiss to leave our playfulness behind, the sound of voices meant we had to sober up and focus on the task at hand.

"So what is it Loki did to earn this punishment we are helping him to escape from?" Lykos had withheld her questions until now, though I wasn't sure why. Perhaps she had merely held no interest until it was relevant.

"Freya's son Baldur was killed by an arrow Loki engineered to be used. Apparently it was made of the one thing the god was vulnerable to," I replied. There hadn't been much more information than that in the stories I'd heard from the centaurs.

"It was made of mistletoe." Xiomara offered up.

That made me tilt my head.

"Seriously?" I asked, bewildered.

Xiomara simply nodded, a shrug all the explanation she could offer.

"Do we really believe Freya won't be pissed if he is freed?" Lykos whispered, her head cocked in question. I couldn't help but smile at the motion - she never seemed to notice she did it.

"No, but even if what they said about her is true, acting outraged is exactly what she will need to do in order to keep up appearances," I whispered back, allowing some space between our companions who now led the way.

"What about the other gods? Think we will add a few more to the list of gods who hate us?" She didn't sound very worried, despite the questions.

"Oh, have you been keeping a tally?" I asked, amused. "Odin is the one who ordered his punishment so it is very likely we will piss off him and more to satisfy Hel's request."

Lykos paused, then asked, "Is it worth the risk?"

Her forehead wrinkled with her concern.

"Would you have us abandon the amazons?" My feet stopped in their tracks, turning back and closing the short distance between us.

"Of course not, but."

I placed a finger against her full lips, their edges pulled down into a pout.

"Then it's worth it. Love, I would not leave them to their fate just to save us some trouble. Besides, of all the things I have feared, gods have never been amongst them," I scoffed.

"Well sure, but look who your mothers are. I wouldn't fear gods either if I'd been raised by Medusa and Nemesis." She snorted ever so slightly in the cutest manner.

"You've got more of my mother's magic than I do, sweet Vixen. Together, I do not doubt we could burn the world down if we really tried." My tone remained flat and serious, I didn't want her thinking I was simply teasing her.

"That might be a bit much though, don't you think?" She laughed, but I simply shrugged.

"Depends on how foolish they are. I came close once, I could come close again."

She looked at me with a renewed curiosity and skepticism. I wondered if she was unsure whether I was being serious or not. I had no intention of saying more and she was thankfully distracted from asking any follow up questions when we heard what sounded like a man's scream of pain.

Ylva motioned for us to stay low as we rushed forward to catch up with them. Following echoes of the sound and Ylva's sixth sense, we reached a patch of trees that circled halfway around a large clearing with a stream cutting through it. The earth dipped down here like we were on a hill, then leveled out smoothly amongst some larger more ancient trees clustered around several boulders. The rocks looked out of place, as if some god had thrown them in a fit and this was where they had landed. Debris had scattered from them, undoubtedly having struck each other before settling into the earth.

The weather, or perhaps people had carved out the earth so that the roots of the trees were visible, the earth dipping down to create a cavern of sorts. Huddling close, we all knelt amongst the brush and peered around a bundle of trees just in time to watch a woman exiting the odd formation, a shaky bowl in her hand.

The woman carefully took the bowl and emptied its contents into what appeared to be a small well. It was easy to miss, barely discernible from the loose rocks scattered around it. She carefully wiped the edges in the dirt then hurriedly sprinted back into the alcove's entrance beneath the largest tree. A few moments after she disappeared the screams finally ceased.

"Loki is there," Ylva stated, waving her hand towards the cavern.

Lykos scoffed, "Bailing out already?"

"Don't worry kit, you'll see me when the real fighting starts," Ylva growled, her eyes narrowed in warning.

"Until we meet again," Xiomara stated, rising from her position and spreading her wings wide. Ylva followed her lead, the sound of wings announcing their full departure just moments later.

"Typical," Lykos growled, rolling her eyes as she rose and headed down the slope.

We picked our way along a path and cautiously entered the area where the woman had disappeared. There was not much to it, but the roots had grown closely clustered so that the sunlight only dappled the earth. I had to duck under the entrance but the space above me opened up so that even my wings would have had plenty of room to stretch out had I not kept them furled in. Lykos slipped in alongside me, a soft growl rumbling deep in her chest.

In the center of the room a man had been bound to a large rock by an odd array of materials that looked less and less like ropes the longer I stared. The smell, when it wafted towards us, was so strong and awful I heard Lykos audibly gag, thus bringing the attention to us. Thankfully my nose was not as sensitive, but it was apparent that whatever bound the man to his stone had once belonged to something alive and it had been magicked to stay in a perpetual state of decay.

The woman stood near the man's head, carefully monitoring a bowl that sat precariously perched on the lip of a rock above, capturing a liquid that fell from amongst the tree roots overhead, threatening to hit the man's head. As I cast my gaze to the roof my chest closed in on itself and a hiss of anger slipped between my sharpened canines.

That this man had wronged the Gods no longer mattered.

"Is that?" Lykos asked without needing to specify further. The growl deep in her throat was now vibrating against the room's edges.

"They will regret every single ounce of their disregard," I seethed.

Lykos flinched at my tone, but nodded with understanding. She knew my sisters, had met them early in our lives, and so she recognized the one held captive above us.

Nemesis had long ago pulled Medusa into her meddling, rescuing abused women from the wrath of jealous and angry gods. A handful had become like family and eventually asked to join Medusa as a gorgon. She had accepted, eventually and so a dozen or so women had become 'sisters' to me over the years. Their presence helped to protect Medusa just as much as her magic had protected them.

Angrily, I pulled out a knife at my hip, the blade sharp enough to gleam. The woman next to the man I presumed to be Loki, gasped and threw herself in my path. I only just caught myself from pushing her aside. I was vaguely aware of Lykos' eyes on me and that was enough. I forced myself to contain my beast just as I had lectured her to do so on so many other occasions. Pausing, I glanced over to the bound man.

"Are you Loki?" I snapped.

The man had merely watched, resigned to his fate as I had approached, but he quirked a brow and nodded his head as much as he was able, a strand of intestine wrapped around his neck.

"Hel has sent us. I will set you free, but first I must free this snake."

The woman who had placed herself between us looked up in confusion, but didn't move to stop me when I went around her. My heart felt like it was being stabbed as I climbed up a thick root to reach where one of my mother's snakes had been tied into the tree's wiry roots. Her head had been ensnared with vines that prevented her from closing her mouth, her fangs forced into a yawning position so that her venom dripped down upon the man's head. Her once vibrant red and orange scales were dull and her eyes were completely blinded by shedding that couldn't be removed.

"Sweet sister, what have they done to you?" I reached a hand up only to find her cold as ice. There would be no reaching her until she was warmed up.

"Lykos help me to cut her out, we need to get her free and warm so I can find out how this happened and which god will be made to suffer for it."

She didn't say a word, merely went to work, pulling out her own knife and slicing away at the foliage that didn't seem to want to budge.

Loki's companion shook her head, hopelessly.

"It won't work," She muttered. "I have tried already and the roots will not give to any ordinary blade."

I smirked, though it felt more like a grimace, my muscles taunt with rage.

"Good thing we aren't ordinary then huh?" My scoff sent her back to her companion's side, eyes wide and wary.

I reached within and focused on the soft hum that ran through my blood, magic that spilled through every pore on my body in miniscule measure and willed it towards my hands. A deep purple mist shimmered around my fingertips before becoming a more solid tendril of shadow that slithered along the blade and consumed its edge. The shadow hardened and one strike slid clean through the roots.

Silently I apologized to the mother for the desecration of her tree, but it had to be done. I saw Lykos move out the corner of my eye, the shadows that sprang from her were stronger and more wild, but they eventually mirrored my own efforts. Our blades slid through the wood like butter and soon the snake was free.

Carefully, I pulled the coiled snake from her perch, Lykos helping me to carry her out of the shade and into the sunlight. Kneeling down, I drew myself up close to her head and pressed my forehead against her own, my words but a whisper.

"Come back to me dear sister, I know not how long you have been contained, but come back, please."

Silently, I prayed to my mother, though for a split second I'd almost sent it to the goddess of death instead. It wasn't a plea for mercy or pity, instead simply an acknowledgement, a whispered word to warn that another sister lay at the mercy of cruel fates with gods for pawns.

My mother's magic would do nothing to aid the warming of my sister, but I hoped the echo of it might help pull her back to consciousness. While I waited for her hibernating body to thaw, I returned to the man inside - Lykos staying to guard her without needing to be asked.

"Who are you?" My words were sharper than necessary but I didn't care.

"I am his wife." The woman at his side responded, her head held high and proud despite their position.

"How long has that snake been here?" A glare was the only warning she'd get not to lie.

"She was brought here when they took Loki." She folded her hands over themselves, nervously trying to maintain her composure.

I looked at the man, who confirmed with a nod of his head, he had not yet spoken and I didn't know if it was of his own choosing or not. Those who spoke the least quite often knew more than the rest.

"Can you speak for yourself, or will your wife tell your truth?"

"If I must, though she is more reliable for some of it." He was weary, his voice gravelly from disuse.

I dared to take a chance.

"Hel has asked me to release you and I will, but I need answers first. Do I need to ask them before you're freed or will the God of Mischief keep put until I'm done asking?"

"It will take me some time to regain my strength enough to leave. I will stay for your questions, my body will not allow me to do otherwise," he responded.

An honest reply.

With one smooth motion I sliced his bindings straight up his chest, my blade still covered in shadow. As my knife broke the magic preserving them, the innards instantly dried and crumbled away. Unfortunately the stench of them didn't fade as quickly. His wife cried out in relief and helped him to put his body back in order. One last warning look was shot their way before I walked back out to join Lykos who now stood a few yards away from the now waking viper.

The creature's eyes were blinded, but it did not stop her from tracking my movement as I approached. Her words came out as a hiss, slow and forced as if she didn't quite have total control of her mouth yet.

"I taste a sister..." Her tongue darted out to taste the air a few more times before adding, "...and a fox. Is that Nyx?"

There was a confused but hopeful note to her words.

"I wish I could say it was good to see you Dahlia but I'd have preferred it to be under better circumstances. Will you recover from this?" I almost didn't dare to ask.

Shamefully, my feet hesitated to draw me nearer, the recent reminders of loss striking my soul with a cold blade. She had recognized my scent, but was it enough?

"That makes two of us." There was a long pause as she drew a deep breath, as if contemplating the question herself. "Yes, with time I will be fine - it was just a forced hibernation, my body will need time to wake up before I can shift, though that may be for the best."

She began to unfurl her body slowly, carefully testing her ability to move before she raised her head roughly level to my Lykos, her tongue darting out again to taste the air around her.

"Lykos, be a dear and guide me to the water and bring a knife for my eyes please, I would like to look upon those beautiful faces. Nyx my dear, take your time." Her voice was a balm to wounds I hadn't acknowledged in a long time.

She was herself, she would be okay.

Lykos nodded and let her scent be the snake's guide as she walked towards the small stream we had passed. A smile broke my lips, both happy and relieved. Dahlia had always been good at reading me, even from afar and even blind it seemed. She'd always known when I needed to be left alone or when I needed comfort, giving it appropriately when others couldn't see past my mask.

I was concerned for Dahlia, but I was also vastly overwhelmed with conflicting emotions. Drawing in a deep breath I tried to center myself the best I could. There would be a time to feel it all, but now was not it.

I needed to get this business with Loki out of the way first and with as little information about myself given away as possible. Hel may have bartered for his freedom, but that didn't mean I trusted him any further than an ant could throw him. As I made my way back towards the cavern, I could hear Lykos teasing Dahlia, as if it hadn't been several lives since she had seen her.

"Just don't get any ideas about making a snack out of me yea? I promise that after every place we've been in the last few days, I'd taste horrible," she paused and then added, "plus Nyx would miss me."

Dahlia chuckled in response, but gave no promises.

Returning to Loki, I knelt down, so that neither would take me as a threat, though they were smart enough to know I was one. His wife was polite enough to try and hide the blade at her side and I could only admire her courage.

"I have no desire to hurt either of you," I stated. "I've made a deal with Hel that is now satisfied, all I ask from you is information. Who imprisoned that snake?"

"Odin called for Vidar to bring it once they'd caught us." She paused, as if trying to remember it all. "His men bragged about finally catching it in an invasion of some continent Poseidon had hidden out in the middle of nowhere. Odin wasn't happy when he saw it though. I don't think it was what he had hoped it would be."

Loki nodded in agreement, confirming his wife's words.

"Whatever you plan to do, be careful. Odin is one nasty rat bastard. The only reason he even caught me was because he used my children to lure me out. Bastard even took one of Freya's valkyries and held her hostage in order to threaten my hound into tracking them down." Loki sighed, his face haggard and hollowed out.

No wonder Ylva had been eager to leave, she was the reason Loki was caught.

"I'd bet anything they used her to find that snake too. Once she knows what she is looking for she can find anything." He was a broken man, but there was pride behind his frown as he spoke of Ylva.

How heartbreaking that someone who betrayed you could still bring such pride about. Perhaps that had been what created that weird friction between her and Xiomara as well. Forcing a betrayal to save a life was certainly a move favored by gods. The maned wolf was lucky my sister had survived the ordeal, otherwise I might have had a grudge to remedy myself.

"He has been searching for magical creatures to use against his enemies when Ragnorak starts. He hopes it will prevent my son Fenrir from devouring him as the Norn have foretold," Loki continued.

"Devouring?" I asked, confused.

"He is a giant wolf," his wife answered.

The image of a giant wolf's tail trying to take me out flashed across my memory. Couldn't be too many of those around, right?

"A woman did come for her though," Loki said, grabbing my attention back. "Odd sort of snake woman who was scarier than Hel if I'm honest."

Loki shuddered and his wife nodded in agreement, though her face was grim. My heart constricted with anxiety, unsure which of my sisters I'd be adding to the list of heartaches tucked in my soul.

"Odin himself ordered her to be struck down when she told him he was just another Zeus - one more amongst many other horrid men who didn't deserve their power. Wouldn't do it himself though, had his lapdog Vidar do it. When she was beheaded, her blood seared both of their skin like nothing else has ever done. Now that truly scared Odin. The times he came to gloat or prod me for information, he had the scars covered."

My gut ran cold and my blood felt like it had frozen in my veins, needle-like pain rippling through my body before anger surged through hot like lava. There was no doubt in my mind, it had been my mother Medusa. Her blood was like acid to those who wished her harm, a gift from the goddess who had changed her long ago.

That was how she had died? At the hands of another power hungry man trying to take what wasn't his? My heart broke all over for the misery she had suffered at the hands of the gods, and now the death she'd succumbed to.

I felt the warm trickle of blood as my nails turned to talons and sliced into my palms. I twisted them so that they were facing behind me, hopefully out of view of my company.

"That will be all," I growled. "Take yourselves somewhere safe - I'd suggest Helheim if you can make it, no doubt Hel will be waiting."

Loki nodded, his hand giving a wave that caused a portal to open next to him.

"Give them only as much mercy as they have shown you." It was not he who spoke, but his wife - her face cold and understanding.

I nodded briefly before heading back to where Lykos was, my hands clenched as my temper fumed. The list of gods I wanted dead was growing rather quickly.

As soon as Loki and his wife disappeared, a dark bundle of clouds rolled forward at an uncanny speed. Static danced across their surface, lighting their insides until the sky broke with a streak of lightning that charred the tree all the way to the roots, the slabs of rock Loki had been imprisoned upon shattering to pieces just as the clap of thunder caught up.

The static in the air made my hair stand out, the blast knocking me flat on my ass. My temper was lost as I rolled back onto my feet, urgency in my movements. Running the remaining distance to Lykos, my face turned into a grimace, a horrid sense of repetition saddling up alongside me.

"I don't think we will be alone for long and I'm not sure we are ready for what's coming," I admitted, at great cost to my pride.

The large snake had finally been freed of her shed, her large eyes wide, their slitted pupils taking me in carefully before a long tongue darted out, tasting the air in my direction. She seemed unbothered by the world, almost contemplative as she bobbed her head.

"What do you make of me now that you can see?" Despite the time crunch, I couldn't help but offer a smile to a sister who had been absent for far too long.

"You've looked better, but then again - so have I. The Fates are cruel, we will not have long together. I saw the lightning, Odin, or at least one of his henchmen, will be on his way soon. You must not be here when he arrives." She lowered her head, her movements slow and tight from disuse.

"Don't suppose you remember a way to get outta here?" Lykos asked, her fingers dancing across her ribs, fidgeting. The static in the air increased, her hair standing on end, giving her a wispy sort of halo around her head.

"The earth opens to her children and this land has not changed since I first was brought here after my capture. The water lets out to the ocean, there is a place there that will allow us to slip away." Dahlia's dull scales still managed to shimmer a little as she dipped beneath the water, leading the way.

It wasn't a far trek, though it was an uncomfortably wet one as we ended up dredging through the water to get to where Dahlia was talking about. She was able to move smoothly through the water' s surface, while my steps became clunky and by all means ungraceful. Lykos was far more comfortable, making it a game of sorts as she splashed through like a kid in a puddle, exerting her nervous energy into something calming and productive.

She laughed before offering me her arm the few times I slipped on the rocks underfoot.

"Oh you really do hate it when you're not the most graceful or badass in the room don't you?" Her foxy grin was broad, teasing and serious all at once.

I rolled my eyes as I replied, "I merely hate being wet in any capacity that doesn't involve, bathing, fun, or a flood between my legs."

Two could play this teasing game.

She choked on her own laugh when I added the last bit but collected herself when my sister snickered ahead. For all that Lykos could dish it out, it never failed to turn her scarlett when I said something dirty in earshot of others. It was one of the most precious things about her.

Another loud crack of lightning made us all jerk, ruining the light moment. Our pace doubled, silence settling over us as we all moved forward with our heads on a swivel. We finally reached a point where two rocks sat in the middle of the stream, the space between them shimmering. Behind it the stream spread out to meet the ocean, our way out was clear.

My sister hesitated as we approached it. A soft tension rose between us and my gut gurgled, an uneasy understanding flowing over me.

"I don't know if it's guarded on the other side or not, so be careful." She said softly. "I am unsure how long I was asleep but I have people I need to check on. When you see her, tell Medusa I am sorry and that I love her. I wish we had more time, Nyx, but know that we will see eachother again."

Her body wrapped around me, her tongue darting out across my face briefly before she quickly uncoiled and took off. I had no chance to argue with her before she slipped into the ocean and disappeared.

The question of whether or not she knew Medusa had died lay unasked on the tip of my tongue, but why else would she want to tell her she was sorry? If she didn't know, perhaps it was best not answered anyways.

As we took a step into the tear, a flash of light blinded me only a moment before fire laced every inch of my body. A yelp rose from somewhere behind me, but the moment I made to turn, a shock of magic slammed into my chest, every nerve in my body lit with pain as the world went dark.

This day was just a gift that kept on giving in the worst of ways.

Chapter Nine
Big Holes and Bigger Wolves

Groggily, my mind cleared and the world woke up around me, a distinctly sweet and tangy scent heavy in the air. There was only one thing that I knew to have that particular aroma. No matter where it was sourced or what magic tainted it, blood always smelled the same despite always being different.

My muscles screamed in protest as I tried to rise, pain lacing through my body in waves that threatened to take my consciousness once more. Attempting again and failing, my hand slid against something warm and slick. My face stung as it coiled up in a cringe, cuts stretched and burned, the space behind my eyes throbbing with a headache reminiscent of drums being banged.

My third attempt was finally successful, my hands finally finding purchase and balancing my weight enough for me to sit upright and scramble to my feet, though I had to stay in a crouched position. The world spun for a moment, spots dotting my vision before it went black and then settled into colored detail.

As my eyes adjusted to the shadows it became very apparent I wasn't the sole source of the crimson liquid covering my backside. Although shallow, a 'pool' was the only word I could use to describe the sheer volume of what lay around me. The smell was intoxicating and overwhelming, but even more so than that was the warmth that covered every inch of my skin. Now that my mind was clearing, I could pinpoint the warmth of fresh blood that covered my legs and splattered up my torso. The stuff around me had begun to coagulate, the rubbery surface layer grotesque in the way it wrinkled and split, oozing a fresher layer underneath.

Stretching my body as I slowly stood up, a groan fell from my lips. My body throbbed from abuse, bruises marring what flesh I could see beneath the blood. Far from squeamish, I let the blood stay, far more concerned with what on earth had happened. Twisting around in place, my head swam as I tried to spot Lykos, but came up empty. My gut dropped as I realized she was not with me and I couldn't decipher between the scents surrounding me; they were far too muddled for my foggy brain and poor sense of smell.

Panic struck my heart, its rhythm sporadic as my mind spiraled at the thought of her being the primary donor of this display. I had to find her.

The space was just broad enough that I could not stretch and reach the other side even if I was stretched horizontally, and just narrow enough that I couldn't use my wings to launch myself out. The planning of this moment had apparently been meticulous, for even the walls were smooth, a sheer drop with no cliffed edges. There had been a time I would have appreciated the effort to keep me contained; today was not that day.

The sound of taunting laughter surrounded me, echoing off rocky walls that now kept me prisoner. I twirled in place, trying to catch an angle in which I might see something beyond the rim of my earthy prison. The world spun with me, then away from me, forcing me to lean against the cold wall to keep my balance. Steadying myself, my gaze shifted to the opening above, trying to spy my taunter, but when I craned my head back and peered up my stomach twisted and almost expelled its contents.

Lykos' form stood unnaturally still at the top lip of the pit I'd been thrown into. There were bindings around her, that much I could tell from the lines leading away from her body towards the earth. Narrowing my gaze I focused my magic so that I could see further and instantly regretted it. My beautiful Vixen had lost all her color, her wild fur smooth and lifeless - nothing more than a painstakingly detailed statue perched over a hole. Her head and mouth had been bound and from the dark stains that splattered the wall above me, it was apparent some of what lay across my skin was her blood, likely the freshest bit. Tears sprung unbidden from my eyes as a gasp slipped from my lips, all the air vacating my lungs and refusing to come back.

My legs gave out as I stumbled backwards and away from the wall. Pain flared up my spine as I landed flat on my ass, but I couldn't' even be bothered to wince from the pain, my eyes never leaving my beloved. Anger began to bubble beneath the heartache, every heartbeat fueling it until a fountain burst through. My jaw throbbed from the pressure of clenching as I willed my feelings into something I could use.

As I stared up the pit, a tall man appeared behind Lykos. He was stocky, his muscles bulging against his leather body armor, the hue matching the brown of his long hair and beard. He was exuberant in his bellowing humor, his laughter a roar in the depths of the pit as he celebrated his apparent victory.

He was a fool. This was just the beginning.

An all too familiar hawk sat upon his shoulder, the wispy green hue a tell-tale sign of a soul bound to life by magic. Tereus' soul was once again trapped in his hawk form, but now it looked as if he had made a friend. The cruel son of Aries had once sought godhood through means of killing Lykos and I. Although he succeeded in the latter, he had made one simple mistake that had changed the tides completely; he had assumed the prophecy was for him. Lykos and I had merged, our souls becoming entangled and as one, leaving Tereus with no option but to escape by any means necessary; including the death of his host body.

Vidar was meant to be the Norse god of Vengeance, was it Tereus' he fed off now?

My nails buried themselves into my palms as I drug a deep breath into my lungs, willing myself to remain calm with nothing more than a hope and prayer. I'd be damned if he saw how much I wanted to scream and cry - he didn't deserve that kind of vulnerability. Another deep breath and I managed to force my face to relax, glad of our distance so he couldn't see the tracks left by my previous tears.

A shiver ran through my spine and the emotional mess that I was slipped behind a curtain of annoyance. A well chiseled mask shielded my heart, as Nyx the woman disappeared and in her place the gargoyle stood.

"Oh Nyx, let me introduce myself properly - I am Vidar, though you probably have guessed that by now. I do hope you'll forgive me, but my little friend was feeling a bit nostalgic and his thirst for vengeance is quite divine. Turns out there is a lot more to your history than the Norn were willing to divulge. I have quite the respect for you. I find it curious though, that even after all that bloodshed you still delude yourself into thinking you're the good guy. Just look at you, galavanting along trying to save a group of people you hardly even know," he chuckled humorlessly.

His slimy gaze met mine and it took everything in my power to remain calm. My muscles twitched with the urge to lash out, but I managed to roll my eyes instead, my breathing short as I struggled to maintain my composure.

Who was he to speak as if he knew anything about me? Who the hell was he but another god on a power trip? Who was Tereus but a coward using others to try and elevate himself?

"With that leech on your shoulder I doubt you even know what 'good' is. You say words and have no clue their meaning. You wouldn't know respect if it slapped your ass and called you daddy," I spit.

My vision spun as I tried to move too fast and had to draw a deep breath to stabilize myself. Chuckling, I covered it up with a shake of my head, my vision once again spotting from whatever magical charge had incapacitated me.

"Stop acting like you know anything about me or my life, especially coming from the brute on your shoulder. The only thing that ever put us at odds was his daddy's lies and his own idiocy. I have never deluded myself. I have never and likely will never be the good guy. The good guy chooses forgiveness over revenge and I can guarantee you that once I'm free, it will not be the former I pick," I seethed, teeth bared like an animal.

"So arrogant! There you stand, at the bottom of a hole with your foxy partner dead above you and you still think you'll win this. You are so deluded you don't even realize you have already lost. You will die down there, with only the guilt of your failure for company. Rest assured you will join your sister, your mother, your lover and soon your people." he chuckled.

His words struck me hard in the gut, my jaw clenching in an effort to ground myself in the present. He knew only half the truth, only what he cared to know. My mother may have been dead, but she was at least with Nemesis again. The only sister I knew he'd had contact with was still alive, her gorgon magic preserving her, despite his assumptions. The amazons were alive still, there was time remaining to save them. All was not lost yet, he had not won. Not yet.

That only left Lykos. My beautiful, feisty fox, who stood above, out of reach and turned to stone by the magic we now shared because of Tereus' actions. Even when our enemies had thought they won, they had not. This was no different. This was not the end, it was just the beginning. It had to be.

The thought of losing Lykos constricted my heart as panic flared within, my soul screaming out against the possibility that she was lost to me again. My heartbeat sped up, the pounding increasing in my ears so that whatever Vidar was saying came through muffled and inaudible.

"She's not dead," I whispered, "She can't die. She's healing, just like you do. It's the gorgon magic working, don't panic Nyx. He only thinks he has won. There is still time."

My mind screamed the words over and over even after I had spoken them, until I could once again focus on the brute above me. He may have been a god, but he was one whose skin had already been branded by my bloodline.

He laughed from his belly, genuinely amused, the sound grating against my nerves so badly I wanted to scratch them off. Tereus let loose a shrill chwirk of what I assumed to be laughter, the sound clashing with Vidar's so much that the god side-eyed him into silence.

As my brain emerged from blind panic and anger, my thoughts leveled out and confusion settled over me. Why he was so confident, so certain of his future success? Afterall, we were as close to immortal as one could get without being goddesses, it didn't make sense for him to assume success without my lifeless body in his grasp.

What did he have up his sleeve? Why was he so tickled with himself?

My confusion must have shown on my face, his gaze moving from me to Lykos before he smiled broadly and addressed me further.

"I suppose you can't see it from way down there, what I used to kill Lykos, so I'll let you know what it is I had prepared for your dear fox. Can't have all this work going unappreciated just because you won't live to see it up close," he snickered.

My hands clenched so hard my nails pierced the skin -again, fresh blood smearing my palms.

"Just a little souvenir I acquired from a place buried out in the ruins of Rome. That was probably my favorite place to observe before my warriors brought it down. The air is chock full of vengeful longing. Such a sweet and delicate nectar. Shame I wasn't around for your bout in the arena. The histories paint it a fearsome thing to have seen," he stated longingly.

My chest tightened as memories long buried and recently dug up, flickered across the back of my mind. The one I had re-lived in Helheim was too close to the surface. No, I couldn't go back there again, couldn't revisit those dark places and all the emotions drenched in memory. I needed to focus, stay alert and above all keep my composure. Yet as he spoke, the memories flittered forward and I knew, before he finished, what he had brought back. Somehow I managed not to instinctively look at Lykos.

"Quite the unique device. I read that it was commissioned by a king just for you, to keep you docile enough to be controlled. Truly barbaric, the details they described of those first few experiments with it. Took them a while to get the measurements just right didn't they? Still, I am intrigued to see its results. No doubt it made you quite vengeful in the end. Oh I do wish you'd been born in my age dear gargoyle, we'd have had a riot of a time. Instead, all that chaotic energy was wasted on avenging the innocent. Your mother's specialty, I understand. Personally, petty differences are where I thrive. So many wars started over the smallest of things."

He talked way too much.

My jaws clenched so hard my bones felt like they were about to break. I swallowed hard and took a deep breath. I couldn't let him get to me, couldn't let the words I wanted to scream at him fall off my tongue. That's what he was looking for, what he craved. Instead, I forced myself to wear a mask, as I had trained myself to do.

Disassociating, my face relaxed, the tension in my face resolving into a blank expression I had practiced many times before. Leaning against the cavern wall, I mimicked a yawn, feigning boredom as I gave my shaking body something to stabilize against. He was too far away to see the way my hands had begun to tremble, so my bluff was protected just as much as my pride. The insult of his pity would have been too much.

"What you should really concern yourself with is that it didn't work and all that happened afterwards," I commented casually. "I freed myself and lived to fight another day. Tell me, how long do you think they lasted? Tereus was not there, nor were those who wrote the histories. Do you want to know what I did to them?" I practically snarled the words, despite my best efforts to control my tone.

He chuckled, his joyous face shimmering with a magic that was too strong to contain. He had no fear, not even a thread of it sifted through his body.

I'd have to change that.

"Oh that doesn't matter," he said, grinning broadly. "What does matter is whether or not you told your lover how you did it. If not, her turn in it won't end quite as well, what with her champion of blood and ichor, stuck in a hole below."

Vidar leaned casually across Lykos' back, forcing my gaze to her. His eyes met mine with a wicked glee as he played with the leather straps attached to her head and neck. His blue eyes practically glowed, but they were not the beautiful oceans that Lykos claimed, instead they were a hazy sky-blue that reminded me of bad weather. He leaned close to Lykos' ear, his lips moving to speak words I couldn't hear before he pressed a kiss to the top of her head.

Oh how I'd have loved to carve his flesh from his bones.

Tereus' hawk form screeched, reminding me of his presence. A few moments later a crow suddenly dove from the sky, cawing intelligently as he landed on the shoulder opposite Tereus. Vidar sighed dramatically as if he'd heard words instead of shrill shrieks, which perhaps he had. Gods never did care to waste time with written word, preferring messengers to speak for them.

"Pity, it seems our time is up. I'd love to stay and enjoy the show but such a waste of potential is terribly hard to look at. Plus, I've got loose ends to tie up, amazons to kill, and of course Ragnorak to stop," he stated matter-of-factly.

The crow took flight again, circling around Vidar in a climbing spiral, cawing the whole time. Then, without warning, a crash of lighting sent static through the air and a hot blast of wind that drew me forward then slammed me back against the wall. My lungs stuttered for a moment, my eyes closed against the heat. When I looked back up, Vidar had blinked out of existence, teleported it seemed, by the lightning.

I completely lost my shit.

My legs screamed from pain, the nerves still lit up from Vidar's attack, but up the walls of my prison I leapt, searching the smooth rock for any kind of notch or divot. There had to be something to hold on to, nothing was without flaws. A variety of rocks littered the ground around me, doing nothing to help my attempts as I slid on their blood splattered surfaces. Hardening my fingernails, I launched myself up the walls but found them no match for the earth around me, they simply glanced off and chipped. Frustration boiled within me as I hung suspended for a moment and nothing more. Just as hope filled me, I found myself falling back to the ground with not even a trace of grace or humility. More than once a rock tripped me as I landed, leaving me sprawled out with new bruises on both my body and pride. My claws weren't enough.

I was not enough.

A scream ripped from my throat as I futility clawed the wall, my legs scrambling as my wings arched above me, trying desperately to push the air beneath me to give me any kind of leverage.

Nothing.

I bore shallow scratches into the walls but nothing deeper. Tears streamed down my face, not from the pain which pulsed through my hands and feet, but from fear. Every moment I wasted here, struggling in vain against walls too hard and too smooth to maneuver, Lykos drew closer to the insufferable cycle of life and death.

Attached to the leather straps and aligned with Lykos' neck arteries would be a pair of hollow arrows, their heads curved so that when the points pierced the flesh, the blood would flow down into the hollow reeds that were the shafts. This would prevent the blood from being blocked, the flow staying constant until the victim bled to death. For a creature such as Lykos and I, it was not a death sentence, but instead an eternal torture. The magic in the collar would tighten it with even the slightest of movements from the head and there was no end to it. When I had been attached to it, long ago, as soon as I had begun to turn to stone the magic in it would loosen the collar. As soon as I awoke from my brief sleep, recovering whilst stone, it began all over again. Lykos has never seen the device, but she'd been kept close enough that I would always awaken as soon as I had recovered.

For a creature who healed as quickly as Lykos, it would be twice as bad and happen three times more quickly.

There was only one way to stop the magic. The crystal which fueled the collar's magic had to be removed. In order to do that though, I had to get out of this damnable hole. Time slipped away as I tried and tried again to find somewhere in the wall where they had messed up, missed a ledge - something. My usually level head began to spiral, knowing our torture would be eternal if we didn't get free from this mess. We were close enough to one another that even if I starved to death or broke my neck, I'd awaken as soon as my body healed. We would live only to watch the other die. The irony made me squirm and gag.

A groggy groan and then a snarl of pain registered between the ear jarring screech of my talons against stone. Lykos was awake, but the pain in her voice suggested that wouldn't last long. Even from such a height above me, the scent of blood trickled down on a stale breeze.

"Lykos hold on!" I yelled desperately.

"Nyx?" There was relief in her voice, though it sounded faint and tired.

"Yes my Vixen, I'm here." I tried to throw all my strength into my words, willing her to just hold on long enough for me to figure something out.

"I'm so sorry Nyx, I think I messed up." My heart broke as her voice wavered, fear slipping into the undertones.

"It's okay, we will get out of this mess, we always do," I replied.

I just needed time to figure out a way to get to her, then I could destroy that blasted collar once and for all.

"What is this thing?" Lykos' question sounded rhetorical, but I couldn't brush this off like so many other things, not when it was literally around her neck.

"Something I should have destroyed a long time ago," I stated sourly. There was no need to yell, her sharp ears heard me just fine.

"What do you mean?" Her ears flattened against her head and I could see her tails flicking with annoyance, their tips fluttering into my view sporadically.

"I'll explain later, right now I need you to look around, is there anything up there that you can reach with your feet?"

"No, there is nothing and they've bound my legs with hobbles. I can't move much, these damn sticks at my neck are-" Her scream cut off her words. I couldn't see what happened, but I could imagine it. The device had certainly been set off when she wiggled and the arrows had been pushed in deeper.

Rage and fear flooded my body as I desperately shot up the smooth wall, all that was left of my self control lost as I screamed Lykos' name. The pain of my fingernails ripping out against the hard surface barely made me wince, it was just one more thing to add to my list of injuries and just a little more blood on my already drenched body.

The ways my past had slipped into the present were really starting to piss me off. The sticky feeling and the claustrophobic space was sending my mind to tortures of the past, though at least this time I could breathe. Wet dirt was far less forgiving. We had certainly gotten out of tougher spots.

Again and again I leapt and tried and failed. A scream of frustration shifted into a cry of fear until I felt a gentle push from within. A more feral voice whispered, "One more time."

Closing my eyes, my lungs expanded to their max, drawing in a stabilizing breath as I grasped onto that feeling of certainty, welcoming whatever it was if it would just get me out of here.

Slowly my body began to tingle until every inch was lit up as if something were burning white hot inside me. My magic exploded from within, pain searing through my body, but when everything inside screamed to move, I listened. Running from one side of my prison towards the other, I gained every bit of momentum I could before leaping upwards, my intention to try and run up it's surface.

Mid-jump my body convulsed, my muscles and bones shifting in a way that made the burning pain feel like a pinprick. A scream of pain echoed off the walls, my ears filled with the vibrations of my own voice and the awful popping sounds that traveled through my skull as things moved into unnatural positions. My entire body shook in agony as I crashed to the earth, reaching for my face to try and stop the lightning jolts running through my temples, only to find my hands were not the same.

My vision blurred from the pain, but I repeatedly drug myself into the present, refusing to lose consciousness. The cold chill of my prison disappeared and a warmth spread across my bare body. When I looked down a yelp of surprise fell from my lips, a snout now marring my view in the center as the head splitting pain across my temples subsided.

Holding my hands out, each finger flexed in response to my direction, despite being unrecognizable to my eyes. My hands were stuck somewhere between human and animal, the bones extended and tipped with claws that made my previously magicked nails look like thorns. As I followed the changes down my arms and to my torso I stared in awe at the fur now covering my entire body. The soft coat was onyx hued with patches of the same bright red that Lykos claimed, not at all typical for any fox I had encountered, though I could tell it was indeed her magic that had changed me.

Three tails had sprouted from my tailbone, their movements seemingly their own, the motion of them deeply troubling as I flexed around and watched their dance. When I focused on them they stilled, only moving again when I turned back. How on earth did Lykos control nine?

Lykos.

With no time to contemplate the new body I controlled, I had to let my instincts lead the way, trusting the newly amped up muscles to respond just as the tails eventually had. Pushing down the ache of pain radiating from just about every inch of my body, my canine hands pushed off the earth and I shakily rose to my feet.

Once again I launched myself at the smooth wall, but this time I didn't fall.

My legs, which were now even longer and more muscled, had launched me double the height my human limbs had managed. My claws, now hard as metal, easily cut thick grooves into the rock face before finally catching, allowing me to draw up my feet and plant them into the earth as well.

My wings had also shifted, their leathery texture was the same, but the webbing's hue had shifted to a reddish orange and their structure had become smaller and more compact. They were now less for gliding the skies and more for powerful bursts of momentum and balance. This allowed me to use my feet to push me upwards while my wings allowed me to hover just long enough to grip a higher section with my hands.

With some quick adjustments to my approach I continued to launch myself up the side of my would-be grave. The sound of my claws cutting through the rock felt like it was going to cause my ears to bleed, the new triangles folding tightly against my skull, but I was making progress. Eventually I finally reached the lip of the hole and pulled myself out. Ignoring the screaming pain of my new body, I quickly got to my feet and bounded over to where Lykos stood, hobbled and depleted.

The smell of her blood threatened to distract me, my snout way more sensitive to the intoxicating mix of magic and blood. It pulled my senses from me and clouded my mind until I heard a moan. Lykos was still conscious, though barely. I set my eyes on the device that had held me prisoner for close to a year and channeled every ounce of rage within me into my strike.

My claws, which were far harder than any normal beast's, slashed through the leather as if it were butter, a clean cut that couldn't have been made by a simple blade. Lykos' fur protected her skin, though bits of it were shorn off with the strike. The crystal that had been set into the fixture fell free, splitting and rolling in opposite directions, a small light bursting forth as its magic slipped away.

Lykos' body was limp and still hobbled, but her healing was remarkable and wouldn't take long to seal her wounds. For the bindings on her legs I used my feet, mindful of her flesh but far more concerned for the neck wounds than anything else. What were a few scratches compared to holes?

"Hold on for me Lykos, please, don't leave me again." I whispered the words, their notes shaky.

The primal fear of living without her constricted my heart as she shifted back into her human form before I laid her limp body upon the earth, my hands desperately applying pressure to the wounds at her neck. It didn't matter that I had just seen her wake up from becoming a gargoyle; there were far too many memories of these situations turning for the worst.

"Come on my love, you can do this," I whispered.

Leaning forward to gently press my lips to her cheeks, my nose poked her, reminding me that my face was not the one I knew. Instead of a kiss, I rubbed my furry cheek against hers, hoping it was enough to draw her consciousness back, to keep her from changing to stone once more.

Our magic had woven together like the threads of a tapestry, painting beautiful images of our love, but the fear that one tug would unravel it all would probably never leave me. There had never been a time when I hadn't loved Lykos and there never would be - but that did not mean I had not spent most of my lifetimes alone. I couldn't do it any more.

"Please Lykos, I know you won't die, but I can't keep doing this alone. Don't leave me again." My words were a tearful plea both to her and the universe bearing witness.

Leaning over her with my hands still pressed into her neck, I tried to find that connection between us, but there was so much magic coursing through my veins I couldn't navigate the waves. I was lost at sea with no view of the stars. All I could do was close my eyes and pray that she found her way back to me. Shamelessly my prayers were not aimed towards my own gods, but the newest ally amongst the new ones, Hel.

"If she beckons at your door, please, send her back to me, I will not do this alone," I prayed.

Time seemed to pass painstakingly slowly, my body becoming stiff in its position while I waited for my love to come back to me. A soft shift of her body fluttered against my skin and I bolted upright, joints popping in protest. Her bright cerulean eyes fluttered open and stared up at me, a small smile starting then stopping. Frozen, I watched dumbly as she lifted her hands to mine and moved them away so that she could get a better look at them. She smirked as raspy words left her lips.

"Trying to copy me now?" she asked.

Relieved laughter poured out my body, my stiff muscles finally relaxing just a bit as I settled back upon my haunches.

"More like improving on the design," I retorted.

"Heh, we will see about that," she groaned, readjusting her grip to my biceps to help pull herself up. Stubborn as always.

"Easy Lykos, you lost a lot of blood."

She looked down at her body which was soaked in crimson.

"You don't say," she retorted. She snorted softly, but didn't try to do anything more than sit up.

"I'm so sorry Lykos." The words barely left my lips before she shook her head, dismissing my words.

"Last I checked you didn't summon a god to come torture us. Did you?" she asked, "Cause if you did I'm going to need a safe word and we gotta set some ground rules okay? Kinky is fine but I think this crossed a very heavily drawn line in the sand."

Laughter erupted from my lips, the only weapon I had to combat the tears blurring my vision. It didn't work. In the end I did both, grateful for her undying sense of humor even in the worst of situations. If I hadn't had a fox's face I'd have kissed her.

"Even I am not *that* kinky," I muttered. "Though it is my fault he used this particular form of torture."

She pressed a finger to my muzzle, though it was with effort, her body still working on getting enough oxygen everywhere.

"You can tell me when you're ready," she whispered, eyes full of adoration and understanding.

For all that she praised me for my patience and love, I saw it reflected right back at me in moments like these. My tears fell, though I wiped them away before gently swooping her up, her arms instinctively wrapping around my neck.

"Let's get back to Helheim," I sighed, "we seriously need to regroup."

She nodded as I carried her forward, my movements a bit awkward as I figured out how to balance with three tails in addition to my wings and her weight. In the moment my body had done all the work, but now my brain had to work out the mechanics as the adrenaline slowly fizzled away.

A strong ocean breeze cooled my face, but everywhere else was kept warm by my new layer of fur. Lykos snuggled in close, burrowing into the long hair before she began to fully take me in.

"So, this is new," Lykos chuckled, grabbing my fur and tugging gently.

"To say the least," I replied, my eyes rolling. "I shouldn't fall on my face so long as I'm holding you, but I need to figure out how to change back as soon as we are somewhere safe. This is not an easy adaptation to make, we are too vulnerable as we are curently."

Lykos scowled, the implication that she would be useless striking her pride.

"Follow the magic, you'll feel the thread of the fox, just coax her back in her cage," she shrugged, as if it were the simplest of things.

Sure, that wasn't going to be hard at all.

"I'll be sure to try that. Good thing I've got practice wrangling foxes," I said, looking down into her blue eyes pointedly. She gave me a sheepish grin before nestling in further and closing her eyes.

Lykos dozed on and off, still recouping blood as I carried her in the only direction that looked promising. The trail was overgrown, but at one point had been well worn, the indention still apparent in the earth. As I followed it up a grassy hill dotted with wildflowers, a very distinctly, very large animal sound carried across the open air.

"Do you hear that?" Lykos asked, waking at the slowing of my footsteps and tilting her head as growling rose from a few hundred feet away, accompanied by the rustle of chains.

"No, I've suddenly grown deaf," I retorted back, earning me a scowl.

"Let me walk," she demanded, tapping my chest to make me oblige quicker. Her scowl had disappeared but I could feel the tantrum just beneath the surface, so I obliged.

Moving uphill, I braced her against my side as we walked, though only after she stubbornly tried to do it alone and teetered over. At the top of the hill the earth around us opened up and we peered down the slope to a ridge that opened to a giant crater in the earth. Billowing grass filled with wildflowers and heather sweetened the air, but it wasn't enough to mask the distinctive canine musk when the wind shifted directions.

"I think we found that tail you almost died of." Lykos muttered as we neared, the growling sounds becoming more and more frustrated and pained.

On the other side of the grassy hill was a steep drop into what was inevitably a self-made prison. The earth had been shorn unevenly around the perimeter, long indents marring the walls where nails had obviously struck the earth. Below us stood a wolf whose size I had nothing to compare to, except perhaps a castle.

His whines came between attempts to gnaw at his foot, or rather the binding that seemed to shrink in on itself much the way the leather collar from Rome had. He was so focused that he didn't even notice us as we perched upon the edge of his cratered prison, the interior worn down to nothing but sand from his constant movement.

"Poor beast. This must be the son Loki spoke of. The wolf that will devour Odin." I muttered, Lykos' affirming grip tightening on my still weirdly furry arm. I was definitely not used to this change in dynamics. I was not supposed to be the furry one.

"Perhaps we can find a way to help him?" Lykos' asked.

Her inquiry was one to which I had no immediate answer for.

"If he will even let us get close enough to aid him. I'll try love, but only if you stay here and recover your strength."

She started to argue, but as I gently detached from her side, she slid down to the earth; the weight of her own body humbling her as she tried and failed to rise.

"You know," she muttered, "a rest sounds pretty good actually, I'll just leave this one to you."

She started to laugh but it turned into a coughing fit, her lungs still adjusting to the change from stone to flesh. I knelt beside her, rubbing her back until she settled and the fit ceased. It was only then that I noticed just how quiet it had gotten.

Turning slowly, like a dog caught in the kitchen, I looked up to find a giant pair of deep, crimson rimmed, amber eyes staring at us. The dark gray of his face blended smoothly into the obsidian of his ears but the exposed skin there was rough, wind chapped and sunburned. His whiskers pushed forward as the dry nose flared, taking in our scents as he continued to stare with his ears pricked up curiously.

"You smell of my kin; my sister and father. You look like a fox, yet smell of snake, and she smells more fox than human. Quite strange," he growled.

His voice was deep, vibrating in his chest like falling boulders rattle the earth as they fall. It was pleasant, even if his appearance was not. The poor brute was starved, the godly blood in his veins all that sustained him. There wasn't even a source of water for him to drink from - perhaps the only reason it didn't smell of urine and feces. His ribs showed and his muscled form was wiry, his coat dull and thin from lack of care. There were also rubs his poor legs were subjected to, his bindings causing sores that bled and oozed.

It hurt to see it, for I did prefer animals to people, but also because it was not so far from what they had tried to do to us, more times than not. Although I had been born with a human appearance, I was treated no more like a person than Lykos was when caught by our enemies. To many we had been lower than the street dogs they kicked away from scraps they'd thrown out. If I could not free him, I had to at least try to soothe the aches.

"We have had quite the time dealing with your Norse gods," I stated.

He snorted, perhaps as close to laughter as he was capable.

"Cowards most of them. Locked me up for what the Norn say I will do in the future. Well, if ever there had been a chance I wouldn't, it is gone now. Years of imprisonment will see their words true the second my bindings break and Ragnorak begins," he rumbled.

"The end of the world, I am told," I replied. His gaze peered into mine as he nodded his head slightly, ever aware of his size.

"Whose world though?" he asked, his head tilting as he blinked his giant eyes. "Life will go on, it is foretold, so it must not be the end of all things, just those things we know now."

My new tails swept out behind me, surprising me as I had forgotten this new body of mine. Time was ticking away with all that had happened. Like water in my hands, it was slipping away faster than I could track. I prayed we had enough of it to save our friends, but how long had we been out before awakening here?

"Do you know a way out of this place?" My tongue suddenly felt strange now that I was more aware of the weirdness of my mouth.

He raised his lips in a snarl, though only words followed.

"Of course I do," he scoffed. "Odin is cruelest in the ways he holds what you want most before you."

He leaned forward just enough to reveal a crevice in the earth behind him, a shimmering tear in the world. Beside me, Lykos sighed in relief, though I could see she was struggling to focus on what was happening.

"Would you let us through? My partner has been wounded and I fear those who did it will return here." To prove my point I gestured towards Lykos, who had now drifted off with her head settled upon her knees.

"Since you smell of my kin, I will consider it, but what might you offer me in return? Why should I lose the only company I've had for years? You are the first I've seen since they took my father away." He snorted, the wet hot air making my fur ruffle.

"What if I could ease the pain from your bindings?" I asked tentatively, not at all certain of success with such an endeavor.

He leaned back against the breach in the earth, a heavy sigh falling from his scraggly form as his haunches shifted uncomfortably. "If you could perform such a miracle, I would be indebted enough, surely, to let you through."

"Both of us?" I knew far too well how slippery those amongst Gods could be and if his father was truly the God of mischief, I'd best tread carefully.

He laughed then, fully and without regard, his hot panting laughter sending a wave of sticky, hot and smelly breath my way. I covered my face with a furry arm and leaned into the gusts until he recovered.

"Smart one, you. Alright then, all four feet for both of your safe passage. I also promise not to eat you when you are near," he amended with a panting smile.

That he felt the need to specify that small detail did not make me feel great. Looking down upon Lykos, who had tipped over, curled up and passed back out in the grass at my feet, I found I had no choice but to trust his word. For better or worse, this was our best option, and at least she would be safe here, out of his reach.

"Well, at least the foliage here will be helpful," I muttered to myself as I cast a searching gaze around me. Heather, as I recalled from my time shadowing a healer many lives before, had healing properties and the way it grew in a matted form would provide as comfortable of a barrier as it was a bed for Lykos.

Bending down I nuzzled her hair, my foxy mouth still a bit too weird to maneuver how I'd like, but she murmured in her sleep and settled again. My new ears swiveled too and fro, sure to keep an ear out for her, should she awake and need me, as I started work on culling as much heather as I could.

As I worked, I felt Fenrir's eyes following me, but he said nothing else. His silence was comfortable, his gaze - when I caught it - merely intrigued. A few times he sniffed the air in my direction, but he stayed stoic otherwise.

After what felt like hours of actively practicing the use of my new claws, legs and tails, I had mostly gotten the hang of moving smoothly. The result of my efforts was a huge pile of plants and grasses, purposely placed precariously close to the edge of the ridge. Now I merely faced the task of actually putting them to use.

"If you would, could you grab this pile and place it by your feet?" I asked, hoping he wouldn't make me tip it over and gather it all back up again.

He blinked slowly at the request but obliged, though he snarled his lips back at the taste as he used his mouth to do so. Thankfully my wings were part of this new shape and they worked well enough to glide me down to the earth, albeit not nearly as smoothly as usual.

Despite my bravado in front of Lykos, I was exhausted, running on fumes and in need of a solid meal and a long nap. Thankfully, what I had in mind was less strenuous in nature, though it would be tedious. Settling in aside the beast's foreleg I started work threading the grassy fibers between his skin and the binding first. Once there was a thin layer all the way around, I worked on separating the flowers from the heather plants, grinding them up between a couple of rocks and mixing it with the wolf's saliva. It was not a complete liniment, but it would do well enough to soothe the ache, at least for a short time.

With a mindless task of slipping the now soaked heather greens between the shoots of grass keeping my hands busy, I decided it was worth a shot to see how much he would share.

"So what is it the Norn have proclaimed you will do?" My tongue moved against the elongated mouth oddly, but the words were smooth despite my discomfort. It was always best practice to compare facts given freely with those coerced, especially when dealing with gods. Afterall, they had no qualms about lying.

"The greatest sin of all. I will kill Odin, the king of the Gods, amongst a few other things. I highly doubt if they prophesied anyone else I'd have ended up here. My father tried to help me, but all who have tried have been punished. Vidar himself is said to take my head by the end. Worth it, to see the smug smile fall off Odin's face. Plus, I'm sure I'll get a few good bites first."

I cringed at the name, Vidar's cruelty too fresh to swallow. That he was prophesied to kill this massive, beautiful beast did not surprise me. He was just as all the others had been - deluded in thinking he was the hero of the stories, when really it was just that he was writing the tales. How ironic for him to accuse me of what he himself was doing.

Lykos woke before I finished. I felt her gaze before I heard her movements, though I glanced back to check on her when I felt the giant wolf's attention shift. Fenrir regarded her gently, his ears pricking forward as a soft whine slipped from his muzzle.

"Your partner smells strong, but looks weak." His rumble vibrated the earth beneath me, making my hands pause.

"Vidar's doing," I replied. "She will recover quickly though, she is blessed with healing."

"That is fortunate if you've made an enemy of the gods."

"Just the one so far, though I'm sure I'll add to the count by the end." I spoke dryly, but the beast caught my humor and rewarded me with a rumble of laughter that jarred my body, but warmed my soul.

"At least you've made some friends too then," He replied with a raised brow, his words as much a statement as a question. When I nodded slightly he seemed content.

"What are you doing down there?" Lykos' voice sounded stronger, but tired.

"Just playing with some flowers, would you like to join me?" I couldn't help but smile, knowing the look she'd give me well before she'd decided to make it.

As predicted, her cute nose scrunched up with an eye roll. What did surprise me was when Fenrir's large muzzle extended out to her and, without much consideration, she none too gently leapt onto it. She lay sprawled across the top holding on to his whiskers for balance.

"What a nuisance you are," I teased, laughter echoing in my ears as my giggle came unbidden at the sight before me.

Fenrir laid his head down so she could dismount, which was more along the lines of sliding off the side. As she steadied herself, she pressed a kiss to his dried nose, causing his ears to flatten and his head to tilt ever so slightly as he watched her walk to me.

"Do I get one of those as well?" Silently I held my breath, nervous she might reject this new form of mine now that she was lucid.

She didn't even hesitate. Leaning over my kneeling form from the back, she planted a kiss on the top of my nose, her wavy locks shielding us from the world.

"You know that's not what I meant," I grumbled.

I tried to pretend to scold her, but she only continued to pepper my face with kisses until I giggled so much I couldn't breathe. Batting her away carefully, I finally turned on my butt, catching her face with a long slobbery tongue, just as she always did to me. Her cheek tasted like the wildberries she'd eaten that morning and smelled like wilderness. She was intoxicating.

My soul split open as she squealed in protest then was consumed with laughter. Her joy filled my soul, my heart fluttering as the sound healed something within.

Our lips couldn't lock in a desperate plea to reassure each other, not with me stuck as I was. However, the laughter shared between us was enough reassurance that we were still there, still surviving all that had come for us and whatever awaited around the corner. When we both finally calmed enough to stop giggling, the world was spinning, only righting itself when I breathed in a deep gulp of fresh air, letting my shaking body settle.

She smiled at me and with that look, that depth of love, I knew I'd defy every God that stood against us, for as long as we lived. Which was now, theoretically, forever.

"Nyx?" Her tone said she'd spoken my name more than once.

"Huh? Yes?" My head tilted as I tried to focus.

"I said what can I do to help?" She chuffed lightly, pretending to flick my nose but catching only air, her strength returning with every breath.

I shook myself slightly, lost to the euphoria that came from knowing such a love as hers. Focusing, I cleared my mind enough to actually respond coherently.

"Oh. Thread the grass through his cuffs, then the heather between that, its already been soaked with his saliva and the flowers, so don't worry if it's wet."

She grimaced at that, but moved to start on his last paw while I finished the one I was working on. By the time we finished, Fenrir seemed relieved, his tense body relaxing so much that he seemed larger than before. When we stepped away he rose, testing his limbs. The wet mixture clung to his fur, the tight fit ensuring even pacing would not shake it loose.

"You've offered a great beast a bit of comfort in a most uncomfortable situation - you have my gratitude and my end of the bargain."

He moved aside so that the gap in the rock was clear.

"I wish we could do more," I replied, Lykos nodding in agreement.

"You've done more than you know. When I break free of these chains and devour Odin, I hope you are able to witness my glory. I would hate to die knowing you remembered me as I am now."

His words were ominous. I wasn't sure if he believed the Norn's words to be true, or simply knew that if he succeeded in killing Odin, the others would not allow him to live. Either way, I silently hoped I would see him again before his end, triumphant and whole. One could only imagine what a fearsome and majestic creature he had been before his capture.

Lykos and I approached the tear cautiously, our bodies rigid with nervous anticipation. My beautiful vixen willingly grasped my oddly furry hand as I held it aloft to her. With fingers threaded, we strode through. On the other side I released a nervous breath I hadn't realized I was holding, thankful that only the tree of life awaited us.

After a moment of reorienting ourselves we found the archway that would lead us back to Helhiem. Without much thought we passed through, certain that this passage was safe, since we had traversed it before. Only, we forgot one small detail; Helhiem's fog.

CHAPTER TEN
LOSING MY MIND AND FUR

Shhhhhzzzziiinck.

The sound of my sword gliding along the steel of another's cut through the ringing in my ears. As the vibrations spread up along my arm and into my shoulder, the muscles tightened on instinct, bracing against the movement and pushing back. Liquid fire poured through me, sticking to every fiber of my being like stove warmed molasses, until my body was nothing but a hot ember aching to burst forth and consume the world.

I was determined to get damn close.

Stepping into the next movement, my blade sparked along its edges as I drew it down towards the hands that braced its opponent. The metal was strong and well crafted, but the hands which wielded it had long since tired. A scream of pain barely registered in my mind as a twisting motion tore the weapon from the man's hand, separating a few fingers and continuing forward into the flesh of his arm and chest. There was no plating to protect him -whether he had been relinquished of it or never had it, I couldn't say- but the spray of blood that followed the deep slash added its warmth to my already sticky flesh.

My clothing was sparse and no armor protected me as I danced between bodies, my sword ever searching for its next quarry. If there had ever been a side I had stood with, I no longer knew the difference, nor did I care to look for one. They were all men of war, bloodied and guilty of all the same travesties, many of which I now committed amongst them. They merely blurred into bodies, no 'this side' or 'that side' to be discovered, only soft flesh beneath my sharp blade and the smell of copper rising from pools of blood at my feet.

The sounds of the dying faded into the background, a constant ringing in my ears preventing the horror from truly penetrating into my mind's foreground. The air was cool, so much so that the fresh blood created steam that mixed with the early morning fog, creating hazy lines across the battlefield. When the sun eventually rose, it would be a gruesome sight that would inevitably be accompanied by a worse smell. I didn't plan to stick around long enough to remember it.

One by one the bodies piled up around me as my nasty bare feet squished in puddles of all sorts of bodily fluids I didn't dare to examine. The smell might have made me gag, if it had been able to reach me. My skin was warm from movement and adrenaline, sticky hot where fresh crimson was splattered and flaky black and brown where the older stuff had dried. To gaze upon me might make one fear the underworld had let loose a monstrosity of Tartarus'. Perhaps that was all I was now, some creature worthy of nothing more than a pit of despair. Oh but it was too late to bury me beneath the earth, this world had become my pit and my rage was a creature with unquenchable thirst, forced to drink sea water.

Played a fool by a God, whose status kept him from my reach, I became a beast of vengeance with a seemingly unattainable target. The most dangerous monsters in the world were not those who sought to kill their enemies, but those who could no longer tell who was friend and who was foe. The world had turned me into the latter, at least so far as the battlefield was concerned. The rest of the world moved along without my involvement - there could be no attachments formed out there, for I had laid my heart in the same hole as my lover and didn't dare to look back.

My movements finally stilled as the world around me did the same. After a while, I stared down at a puddle between my feet and saw nothing but darkness with two violet eyes peering out from beneath a pair of leathery wings. The air was cleaner here, detached somehow from the massacre just beyond the entrance and it slowly dawned on me that I had followed the last of the fighters into what might have been a temple. The stone beneath me didn't give, it's cold surface strong and sturdy despite centuries of abuse beneath the feet of supplicants. Something about it felt familiar, though I was certain I had never graced these halls. Then again, what was my memory these days but a cruel and distorted reminder of all I had lost.

I had long since fallen from any grace I might have held and knew retribution would come for me. I didn't care. My heart was shattered and my body unbearably able - a horrible combination for the daughter of the goddess of vengeance. Oh but wouldn't mother be proud?

Silence. Blissful silence beyond that awful ringing in my ears. Slowly it too faded just as my muscles finally relaxed enough to scream in protest for the brutality I had subjected them to. My body ached and hurt, but the battle had pushed that aside. Now, as I stood with no more enemies to strike down, it began to creep in with a vengeance not unfamiliar to me. My blissful detachment from the world slid like sand through my fingers and the thumping of my own beating heart mocked me. The pain would return as it ever did and I would find no rest in sleep, for I always woke in the morning from dreams too sweet and a reality too cruel.

The sword fell from my fingers and I to my knees, a cold laughter falling from my lips as the soft sound of footsteps approached from my front. The gait was one I'd know anywhere, ever instilled in the memories of my mother Nemesis, whose short stride was always marked by the sharp tap of her heels. If that hadn't been enough of a telltale sign of the absolute shit I was about to be in, the soft sigh of scales moving the earth around them would have. My dear momma, Medusa, was with her.

Medusa's slithering snake half started at her hips, though minute scales covered her entire body. The woman I called momma was more beautiful than even the Goddess of Love in my eyes, her shimmering blue scales shifting in hue to teal, purple and pink in the light. She wore clothing on her torso only for modesty's sake, the scales protecting her from the elements with ease. It was a wonder I hadn't been born with them, but then again it had been Medusa's magic and Nemesis' blood which had been used in my conception, not the other way around.

Perhaps this was all just pieces of the Fates' work, they did so love manipulating a dramatic entrance. As I glanced around, it dawned on me that perhaps my cynicism was more accurate than I thought. There was nothing more bitter sweet than realizing that I now knelt in a temple to the Goddess of Vengeance - who stood before me with a disapproving stare.

Oh the irony. It was a true shame the bards would never know about this bit - it would have been pure poetry.

I had no delusions of myself. My actions were nothing more than a fit of defiance and pain, a violent one that had been twisted and manipulated to play a part in the history books. But what was my tantrum compared to that of a king, whose position allowed wars to be started in the name of petty grievances? I would not harm innocents, but there was always a battlefield to be found and some nasty brute willing to let me do as I pleased so long as his side won.

Technically the triumphant side was the one who'd held me in their ranks - even if I was the cause of their own men's fall. I did not discriminate here, why should I? None cared whom they were killing, they merely did so at the whim of one they called leader. The price of victory never seemed to bother those whose men died so eagerly for them. Why should I feel the sting of victory where others did not?

Monster. That's what some had whispered, having heard my reputation these past few years. If that was true, so be it. There were far worse things I could be, complacent being one of them. Never again.

Once I had been ever so complacent, just as the other immortal blooded were, in the face of the gods' cruelty for could they not also be merciful and generous? That was until they all turned their heads towards me, took in the spectacle of my heartbreak and outrage, then immediately turned a blind eye to my suffering. None cared what their own had done and if they did, they remained unforthcoming with aid. Even my own mother had abandoned me to mend my wounds with false reassurances.

They all thought that without their aid I'd let time mend the wound and forget about it. What was a few years in the life of the long-lived immortals, after all?

They'd know better next time wouldn't they? Even if they didn't - she would.

"What do you think, Goddess of Vengeance? Has your daughter done your work proud?" The laugh that fell from my lips was one I didn't recognize, but the scorn on my mother's was intimately familiar. The years had slipped away from me, but it seemed like a lifetime ago that I saw her last, disappearing into the shadows as I mourned my lost love.

Medusa was another story. For all the scorn I had for the rest of the world, I couldn't even look at momma, whose beautiful scales shimmered even with the dullest of starlight. There was no question what I'd have seen had I dared - her eyes sad and her heart ever visible upon her sleeve. She'd at least tried. She had failed, but it had meant the world that she had at least attempted to help me.

Hades was unreachable they said - locked away in the underworld where they couldn't dare try to go. Medusa had lost years of her life trying, she being long-lived but inevitably mortal. There had been no godly blood in her serpentine veins to save her years when her foot slipped. When she'd told me of her attempt, of the path she had found to gain entrance without crossing the Styx, I had not hesitated. The underworld would never hold me, Lykos had guaranteed that, so I had walked the paths for weeks searching. Hades had been nowhere to be found - the other gods were hiding him amongst themselves.

Grandmother Nyx, my namesake, had bade me welcome, let me rest and continue my search, but she herself said the words. *"He is the god of what gods fear most little one. I wish there was more I could do, but the Fates and other Gods will shield him from you."* Those words had been true, for I had never caught scent or sight of him in all my years of looking, and so I sought relief through other means. Let the message of my grudge be delivered by those destined to cross the River Styx, their dying prayers a warning to their favored Gods. If they feared the God of Death, then surely they would grow wary of the woman who came and went through his domain unscathed.

Even now I could feel the shudder of their fear mirrored in the faces of their dead followers the few times any of them dared answer those calls.

"You have done nothing but disgrace your name and smear mine for doing so. This is not vengeance child." Nemesis' words sounded exhausted, the sharp edge on her words forced.

"Is it not? How so? Do I not avenge those these fellows have killed on their march here? The brethren they'd lose regardless if it were my hand or the enemy? Do I not avenge those who toil in fields to fill wagons for a marching army set to fight a fruitless battle so that their lords can boast victory over some squabble while they starve? Who decides mother? You? You should feel lucky that I love you enough not to smear your name intentionally."

She moved forward, as if she wanted to strike me, but Medusa's hand stilled her so that all she did was sneer. Her face was a mix of emotions I could not read, but something inside me stirred, warning caution. Too bad I never listened to that something anymore.

"What is that? Anger for your daughter who you left to suffer, all because you could not be bothered to stand up for her?"

"The girl is dead but will not stay so, why do you go on this rampage for something so temporary?" Nemesis' concern almost seemed genuine, her eyes softening to what might have been a motherly fondness. I would have none of that. All the love between us had been stained scarlett. Still, she tried to justify herself.

"Yes I could have stepped in sooner, but if you think it'd have saved her you are wrong. The Fates wanted her dead so that she could be reborn again when they needed. I would have only delayed the inevitable."

"Then you should have delayed it instead of merely handing the task to another!" My voice shook with emotion.

My teeth clenched so hard I could feel the muscles in my jaw screaming, pain jolting up behind my eyes from the pressure of it. In that moment I hated how keen my eyes were, for I saw the doubt in my mother Nemesis' eyes and the heartache in Medusa's. All the subtleties that might have, for another, been lost amongst the dizzying scene around me, remained stark and clear. Sweat steamed off my skin, the smell tangible and causing my lungs to constrict like a fist. All the world had burned around me, even without a single flame and all I wanted was to curl up in the center of it and forget.

"Every night my memories consume me and then I wake in the morning and for a split second, I forget. I forget that Hades' betrayed us, that you stood lingering at a distance capable of stopping it and that Lykos died in my arms." My breath shook, my lip trembling with each rattling intake.

"For a split second I can smell her beside me, feel her weight against my chest or back. For a quick moment my mind and heart are at peace. Then that moment ends and all the heartache rushes back for me to face alone." My nails dug into my palms as my own hopelessness overwhelmed and angered me.

"Sleep offers me no respite and so I am left to wander this world alone until the *Fates* will it otherwise? Fuck that! If they cannot be swayed by pretty words, perhaps enough action will change their minds. I will turn the earth crimson if I must, but they will all think twice the next time I cross their paths, the next time they deem it necessary to part us."

A sigh fell from Medusa's lips, but it was not impatience. Her scales shifted, the light refracting off in a rainbow sheen that had fascinated me as a child and brought comfort as an adult.

"My sweet child, we have failed you in so many ways. Please know that I have tried everything in my power, but all we could do is find a way for you to wait in peace, rather than live in agony."

Her words didn't make sense, but I was so tired and delirious from exhaustion stemming from adrenaline rushes that not much of anything did. My mind reeled between reality and memory more often than not. I moved mostly on instinct, waking into consciousness having traveled distances I couldn't measure or recant. Even now, the only reason I knew what side I had started on was for the strip of fabric tied around my arm. Though I might have snagged that to staunch a wound - I wasn't sure.

Medusa came to me with no hesitation or apprehension. She held her arms out wide as Nemesis stood back and I couldn't help but fall into them. She had been the closest thing to comfort I had found, but it hadn't been enough. The sound of her hair was soothing, the pieces of bone and beads rattling together like a cottonmouth's tail. Her skin was cool to the touch, her strength surprising to those who did not know her and consistent to those who did. Although her lower half was of a powerful snake, she had lean muscle hidden beneath smooth scales of iridescent hues. She smelled of her favorite perfumed oil, one she had always swore had helped her win my mother over.

"I hope one day you will understand my beautiful girl. Until then, know this gift is yours alone and we will guide her back to you best we can while you sleep." My eyelids drooped as I listened to her words, ever so soft -like a lullaby. Something inside me wished she'd sing, perhaps it would finally override that ever present ringing.

Everything inside of me screamed that something was wrong, but hadn't it all felt that way ever since I had lost Lykos? What was one more wrong amongst an endless sea of them? The world could not deny me this brief moment of comfort, so why should I deny myself?

Her arms tensed for a moment, her hypersensitive skin no doubt feeling my muscles flexing, but I made myself relax. What could they do to me that hadn't been done? What were her words but sound formed into shapes we named? My body and soul were both filthy, but my mother held me tight anyways. Laughter began bubbling from my lips, only for it to break after a moment and turn to sobs and tears.

"Mom, everything hurts." My whispered confession made the shadow of my other mother pause only for a second as she shifted around behind me.

"I know, my love. Just stay with me, focus only on my voice." Her characteristic 'sss' was gone, the exaggeration saved only for those she wished to intimidate. I felt her tail wrap around behind me, holding me steady and offering comfort. She didn't mind the blood or grime, her lips pressing a kiss to my forehead.

The energy changed when Nemesis finally reached my back. It was like the world suddenly held its breath, much like before a snake's fatal strike. Despite her part in what I knew was coming, I did not blame Medusa. She tightened her hold when she felt me flex, but all I did was lean into it. The inevitable time had come for me to be curbed, it was a comfort knowing my enemies would get no such satisfaction.

That didn't mean I wasn't going to make Nemesis regret it though.

"Fitting that it's you who stabs me in the back. Wouldn't be the first time though, would it mother?" There was no need to look up at Nemesis, the energy in the air behind me changed enough for me to know my words struck a chord. Laughter once again fell from my lips, the sound foreign to me as it cracked and charred with an electricity I could only half feel.

"Make sure you don't miss, turns out I'm pretty good at creating rivers in my wake," I hissed.

Medusa's voice chided me, though there was nothing but love in her tone. "We do this for you, know that and try to find forgiveness for what your mother hasn't done. Even Gods make mistakes my darling."

Confusion filled my mind, but I didn't fight her when her fangs extended and disappeared into my shoulder. I barely even registered the sting, or the fire that her venom lit in my veins. A gorgon's blood would not hurt those who would do them no harm, so I was curious about its purpose. Had she grown concerned I had become her enemy as well? Surely she knew my love for her remained pure.

"Let the venom of my blood do no harm, but give peace to she who bears it. Living stone is beautiful and will remain unbreakable until the world has changed. When death no longer appeals to you more than living, you shall awake. Until then, let time mend your broken heart and heal the wounds we cannot see." Medusa whispered.

Pretty words, my mother spoke, but it was not the words I paid heed to, but the magic that danced upon her lips. She had pulled back to arm's length, magic in the air swirling between her lips and the marks upon my shoulder. Blood magic. Distracted, my body remained relaxed until a sharp pain shot through my back and exploded out of my chest. A gasp stole any words I might have uttered and a whine of pain followed.

She actually did it.

The pulse that pounded angrily between my temples slowed and then stopped.

A giggle bubbled with blood as I lifted my fingers to the bloodied edge only to watch it disappear as she seared more pain through me with its extraction. Oh, but to be in pain was to be alive and if I was living, the cycle would never end. How I longed to sleep it all away, tomorrow this might even be funny. Tonight however, it was another strike to my already mutilated heart.

My limbs began to feel heavy, so surely my blood loss was enough to put me unconscious soon. At least, that's what I thought at first. Medusa slowly unwound from around me, though her hands held me aloft still. Nemesis joined her, pain and sadness in a face I only wanted to scowl at.

"I'm sorry, my child. It was either by my hand or theirs and I would not let them touch you," she murmured. "Never. You will not die, but you will sleep. If you cannot stand to simply be a Goddess' daughter- if you insist on becoming a monster in the eyes of all who would see -then so be it. Let you be a gargoyle and maybe after a few centuries you will look upon the world with fresh eyes that see the true realities."

Nemesis kissed my forehead, despite my attempts to lunge forward and hit her with my head. The effort would have been half-hearted but I could not even accomplish that much. Glancing down, the reason I couldn't move was apparent. It was not the heaviness of death that had come forth to cradle me and throw me back, but instead all that I was was slowly turning to stone.

"The gorgon's curse," I whispered, fear finally registering in my mind as I looked to the one who had the power to petrify. "Mom?"

"It's not permanent my love. Please do not be scared. Simply rest," she answered.

There were tears streaming down her face as she leaned forward, her hands softly holding my jaw as she pressed scarlet kisses to my cheeks. "I promise," she continued, "you will wake up, but you are in pain and tired. Rest my sweet daughter and know I love you more than anything else in this world."

Panic filled me as my body refused to move, but the blood was out of me and darkness quickly enveloped my mind - an old friend come to embrace me once more. The warmth of my mother's love penetrated the depths of my soul, a small stitch to the gaping wound in my heart.

The world shifted strangely, a bright light erupted behind my eyelids before settling behind darkness. When my eyes fluttered open, I was in Helheim once more, but Medusa was still there, tears streaming down her face as she held my crumpled form as the fog slowly rolled away.

Confused, I glanced around, searching for Lykos, for some sign I was not still trapped in a twisted version of the memory I had experienced. She wasn't far, just a few feet from myself with her arms wrapped around herself and Nemesis grasping her at arms length.

With confirmation of Lykos' safety, the warmth from my mother finally settled in. Her arms held me with a gentle, but firm grip. Her beautiful purple gaze was practically onyx as I gazed up into them, tears spilling from their corners to streak down her face.

"Momma," I whispered.

"I'm here my darling, its okay, that was just a memory - you're safe," she uttered softly, her grip drawing me in closer.

"I- I'm so sorry momma," I cried, the memories and events leading up to this moment overwhelming me.

Her hand caressed the back of my head as I leaned in, snuggling close as one only does a mother. Slowly, my sorrow slipped away and happiness warmed me from within. To smell and feel my mother so close after so many years stitched a part of me I hadn't remembered was torn. To have felt my life fade at her hands had haunted me for a long time and for too many years I had held a grudge against them both. Now, looking back with a clearer head, it was plain to see how much my mothers loved me and how difficult a choice it had been - even if I saw how very clearly it was the right one to make. Thanks to them, I had become a gargoyle and been capable of sleeping between Lykos' reincarnations. They had killed my body once, but in doing so they had saved my soul.

We sat with our arms wrapped around one another, my mom's lower, snake half curled around us upon the cold stony ground for a long time. So long that I heard Nemesis and Lykos speaking in the background of my hearing, undoubtedly Lykos was filling her in on what had transpired.

Perhaps I'd have just settled into the scenery and remained in the moment forever, if not for a growing noise at the edge of my hearing.

The chortle of a laugh attempting to be held made my ears swivel atop my head. I had quite forgotten my own weirdly fox-like form, the sudden movement atop my head making me jerked back suddenly, causing Medusa to release her hold on me. As I reared back to glare at my mother and darling vixen, the two burst out into guttural, full lung capacity laughter. Their voices bounced off the rocky walls and came back as an echo, so that the air was quite literally filled with their humor.

Confused, my growl rose until Lykos' gaze finally peered open long enough to catch my own, their cerulean depths watery with tears.

"Nyx, you'd be laughing too if you could see what you two look like from where we stand," she said between gasping breaths and laughter.

Craning my head back, I peered over to my mother, whose hair jiggled with one beads carved into snake heads, her scales shimmering a gorgeous shift of blue, teal, and purple. She too seemed to take stock of our situation and as I watched her almost obsidian gaze take me in, her lips cracked into a smile. Raising her hand she too started to giggle, until I couldn't help but join in as the humor spread, the ridiculousness of my half-fox form and Medusa's half-snake form finally settling into my mind's eye.

What a mess of a family we were!

Once we had gathered ourselves together and Lykos and I had switched mothers to greet, we set across the long bridge that led into the true city of Helheim. This time there was no army of decaying skeletons guarding the other side.

"Looks like we didn't earn the welcome wagon this time," Lykos teased, her hand shifting in my grip as she tried to find a comfortable way to grasp my enlarged and furry paws.

"Are we not enough?" Nemesis retorted, her tone naturally sharp, even as she smiled with good humor.

"Is that a rhetorical question?" she snarked back.

Medusa chuckled, shaking her head as she slithered alongside Nemesis, "Somethings never change do they?"

A smile pulled at my lips, though I could not form a response, a shimmer in the air catching my attention just before Hel appeared, as if from thin air. Her healthy side looked exhausted, but a smile graced her lips, white teeth gleaming from behind their pink and grey hues.

"Welcome, officially to Helheim. You two have certainly earned it," Hel said, grandly, her gaze lingering over my form, her smile turning into an amused smirk before resolving back into the former.

She continued, "Much has happened and although I am eager to hear of it all, you have earned your rest. Come, let me show you to my home, which is yours as well for as long as you like."

Hel proceeded to lead us to her home, which was a small fortress set in the center of a large city, carved from the stone of her realm by some unknown force. The structure held a unique design; its carved edges looked sharp at a distance, but a hand ran across its surface was left none the worse for it. If they had once been as sharp as they appeared, the strange winds of the underworld had worn them smooth. The rock was deep black like onyx, but without the shine one saw in a naturally split piece. Instead the material absorbed the light, creating a flat look which in turn reduced the dimensions of it from afar. To look upon it long enough might give away its true shape, or just a headache.

The city surrounding it was made of similar materials at the base, but these were clearly blocks of rock that had been man-made. The buildings varied in size and design, but were obviously only crafted for the occupant, as there was no visible design to their placement and indeed, if one looked closely enough, some of the designs were from different eras all together. People came and went as they pleased, some greeting Hel while the rest went about their day as if no one else were around.

It would have been fascinating to study, if exhaustion hadn't hit me so solidly in the face the second I was up and moving again.

Thankfully the room we were sequestered to lay only on the second floor, though when climbing such, it was obvious the staircases went on much further. My sore body screamed as we climbed, but the thought of having to go further humbled my words of complaint back from my lips. Afterall, at least I hadn't lost my entire body's worth of blood several times over again, like Lykos - though she had bounced back far better than I had.

Much to my chagrin, Hel did not depart after escorting the four of us to the rooms we would be occupying.

"I've put your mothers on the opposite end of the floor, so do not fret for overhearing eachother, there are half a dozen rooms between and the walls do not allow sound to travel easily." She smiled knowingly between us all, though it didn't seem to quite reach her eyes. Silently, I wondered if she might be lonely. Surely a goddess, even one of the underworld, would not be short volunteers to warm her bed.

Casting the question aside, I ignored the implications of her statement and refocused back into the conversations being had around me.

"Perhaps you can help too, since you are a shapeshifter as well," Lykos stated, clearly discussing my current situation with Medusa.

"She wouldn't be the first to struggle with it. Most of my Snakes have a hard time with the change the first few times, I can't imagine this will be much different," she replied, her smile genuine and filled with pride as she turned her gaze to me.

Subconsciously catching up to the conversation, I nodded my consent, completely out of my depths. To shift my eyes or nails was one thing, but to change my entire body? None of the times my body had completely shifted had been of my own manipulation, which was both quite impressive and deeply unnerving. There had never been a time I hadn't been in control of my magic or my body, yet just within the span of months I found myself at the mercy of my magic's whims.

Not that I could complain about the results.

"Yes, please. I would very much like to have my human body back before bed tonight," I said, my tongue lolling out ever so slightly as I raised and lowered my eyebrows at Lykos. Medusa joined my laughter as Lykos immediately turned scarlet at the implications.

"No time like the present," Medusa replied as she followed Hel and Nemesis into a common area between the bedrooms.

The large stained glass windows showered us with Helheim's unnatural light as I stood in the middle of a large rug and tried to follow Medusa and Lykos' instructions. Breathing in deeply I tried to do as Lykos said and find the fox within, but everytime I drew close to that thread of magic, the beast slipped through my fingers and disappeared again. Growing frustrated only made her leap more wildly, my patience waning to the point Medusa stepped in to try and guide me instead, but I couldn't focus. After close to an hour, all I had managed to shift back were my hands and a tuft of hair on my head between my fox ears.

To say my pride was thoroughly damaged was an understatement. With the memories of my past and the ordeals we had suffered so fresh, my soul was raw and sensitive. I would have rather walked naked through a crowded village than watch these three powerful women looking upon my pitiful attempts to change back with pity.

Lykos, at least, had no pity to spare. In fact, she seemed to be quite amused with the whole situation now that we were safe. She was now feeling perfectly fine, her healing having done its work, and it seemed she was getting payback for all the times I'd recently embarrassed her.

Her first act of retaliation was to reassure Hel that *we* didn't mind at all if the goddess stuck around to assist - a direct deference to my pleading look to send her out the door. That may not have been so bad, except that she then proceed to chat it up with the goddess as if they were old friends. Their lighthearted conversation passed over my ears without my conscious mind grasping the words, but my irritability rose all the same.

Although my frustration wasn't truly at them, it lashed out all the same.

"You know, I might actually be able to focus better without you two chirping back and forth like love birds over there," I growled, my throat rumbling uncomfortably. The vibrations tickled my mouth as the sound came out stronger than intended, feeling almost like ants marching across my tongue as I tried and failed to shift my face back to human.

In truth I was not jealous of their interaction, just severely tired and short tempered. Lykos simply grinned in response, knowing full well the short list of things that would truly get to me and that their talking wasn't one of them.

"There is no shame in the struggle Nyx," Hel commented, "this is new for you. I wish I could assist you better, but my father didn't pass along his gifts to me." She shrugged nonchalantly, though she did appear mildly remorseful.

"He is a shapeshifter?" Lykos asked curiously, her knowledge of the norse gods limited from pure lack of interest. An interest she was apparently going to shed purely for her own amusement.

"Oh yes, a notorious one at that, he is afterall a God of Mischief they claim. Perhaps when we are all recovered we can sit down for a meal together and discuss it all." She replied. Hel smiled kindly, but there was a glimmer of mischief in her own eyes that sent me over the edge.

"Seriously, you're only distracting me - SHOO!" My growl was more of a whine, my body shaking from the forced effort of trying to change it back.

They didn't move an inch, both with their own form of a smirk plastered on their smug faces. My ears pinned against my skull as I snarled in their direction but Lykos only stuck her tongue out. She knew me too well to take the noise personally, though

Hel did offer a degree of humility as she covered her smile with a hand.

"Okay you two, your silly tactic is obviously not working, so go!" Medusa commanded, her scales shimmering in the light as she rose a bit higher in height.

Nemesis planted a quick kiss on Medusa's cheek, lingering ever so sweetly, before waving towards Lykos and Hel.

"Let us coordinate with the Valkyries. You do remember we have a plan to set into action right? The Amazons will be needing rescuing sooner than expected. Medusa can tend to our daughter." She waved her hands down the hallway, everything in her manner leaving no room for argument.

Despite her annoying teasing, it warmed my heart to see Lykos' face beam at the subtle confirmation that there were still Amazons to save. She paused long enough to send me a rather smug and foxy grin before darting forward to press a kiss to the side of my muzzle, dancing away before I could retaliate with a wet tongue of vengeance. She then stopped before Medusa, hugging my mother on her way out. They squeezed each other tight, my mother whispering something in my fox's ear that made her smile turn soft. Something about it warmed my soul, my tense muscles relaxing just a bit and as they did, the whiskers on my muzzle fell off.

Hel nodded to us both before disappearing, her decaying side winking at me as she skirted down the hallway. She looked proud of herself, as if she had coordinated this whole thing. That they had purposely ramped me up so that all I had left to do was let it all loose. Even if she had, that did not soothe my mood any; they were both still brats that I would get my revenge on at some point.

As I watched, my mother opened her arms and drew near again. My heart burst with mixed emotions that, when tangled with my exhaustion and frustration, resulted in a near instant fit of tears and sobs. Without an audience, my walls crashed to the ground as my mother's arms wrapped around me in a tight embrace. Her cool skin helped to ground me in an old and familiar way. The soft shushing noise of her scales shifting was a balm to my bruised soul and in that moment I was consumed with how dearly I had missed her.

"Shhhhh, its okay darling - you're okay. Let it all out, they will never know," Medusa muttered into my fur, almost completely muffled by the thick coat.

Her words and her strength were enough to make me oblige. I wept until my eyes burned, my heart hammering against my chest as my lungs lost pace and panicked. All the emotions of the past week erupted through my pores as I grew hot with sweat and tears. She rubbed my back gently, her presence unrelenting as I succumbed to all I'd pushed down the last few days.

When I finally took in a deep, calming breath, I felt something change within, a realignment of sorts. My meltdown relieved my tension enough for my body to sag and the magic that had gripped me in the throws of desperation finally relented. The fox within stopped bounding around, her presence settled, curling in my core and resting. As the fox magic calmed, it withdrew, but in a much more dramatic fashion than I could have anticipated.

My bones shifted and the muscles retracted back into a more human size and shape, the taste of blood filling my mouth as I bit my tongue. The pain overloaded my senses, sweat breaking out across my body as my mind blacked out. When my eyes finally fluttered back open I sat upon the floor, a pile of shed black and copper fur surrounding me.

Medusa laughed, her humanoid form ending at the waist where it gave way to a snake body that was larger than any of her snakes' were and twice as beautiful. Her base was a stone blue but her scales were iridescent, the light catching them and turning their surfaces a gradient of blues that shifted across into deep purples. Even the snakes that danced on her head were of that ever shifting hue, though they were nothing more than a trick of her magic. Alone, she let down her guard and the braided locks merely lay flat, their ends adorned with pairs of beads and pieces of bones that looked like eyes and teeth. I had always loved the way they sounded when they clinked against each other.

Her eyes had always been such a deep purple that they appeared black, seemingly endless. The oil she used on her skin and scales smelled like summer blossoms and had soaked into the very memories I held of her. She drew close once more, uncaring of the mounds of fur and hugged me close. I breathed her in deep before letting myself sag against her, relief etched in every inch of my body, which once again felt like my own. The world paused and for a breif moment, I was just a little girl in her mother's arms.

"I'm so sorry mom." My words sounded so pitiful, like I was just a youngling grasping at her waist again.

"For what my darling child?" Her words held confusion, her brow furrowed ever so slightly. She pushed a strand of my hair back behind my ear, the sweat that beaded across my skin making everything sticky, stray bits of fur clinging and itchy.

"You're here and I didn't even know." My body was still shaking, though I wasn't sure if it was from cold, pain, or emotion.

"How could you know, child? You were sleeping when Odin ordered Vidar to strike me down and my Snakes were scattered to the corners of the world well before that. None of this is your doing." She kissed my forehead, a silent promise of truth that had always been our way, our secret.

"I freed Dahlia, when I set Loki free. She wanted me to tell you she was sorry, but she should be safe now." It wasn't much, but perhaps it would comfort her to know her failure to save her had been rectified. The sigh she released said everything even before her reply.

"Good, she will find her sisters and they will keep eachother safe. You have already had quite the adventure in this life. I want to hear everything, but it will have to be later when there is a bit more time." She rose to her full height, hands extending to grasp mine.

"What did we miss while we chased down Loki?" Grabbing her hands I used her strength to help balance while I adjusted to my own body again. How on earth Lykos adjusted so smoothly was nothing short of amazing.

"We will get to that, but first, are you okay?" Her deep eyes refused to let me escape them, knowing that if I did she'd get only a half truth.

"I'm fine." My words were muttered, a tinge of impatience and bitterness evident in their tone. She did not miss it.

"Nyx, truly?" She tipped my chin up, forcing me to face her with honesty.

"I'm as well as can be expected. Vidar tried to kill us, or at least leave us in eternal torture, we still have to try and save the Amazons, and I've had an uncomfortable amount of reminders of my past lately. It's not sitting well with who I've become. Hel has made me question some things I was once certain of, but I'm too afraid to ask the question that would clarify it."

"Ah, Helheim's mists then?" She smiled, understanding scattered across her face like freckles. She purposely sighed, her words spoken as a cringe. "A most pleasant experience for all."

I nodded in agreement, knowing there was more to be added - the most recent blow, at least in linear terms.

"Tereus has been feeding Vadir information about me. You remember how I was when I came back from Rome?" I didn't dare meet her gaze this time, for although she had only been in one memory, I had once told her the story of the first.

"How could I forget?" she asked, her wince saying more than words.

"Well, that damn contraption showed up again today, he put Lykos in it. That's when I shifted into... whatever it is that was." I vaguely waved towards the piles of fur around me.

"It just felt like my outside finally reflected the inner beast I've been trying to hide, most especially from Lykos. I thought I could leave it behind me, be better this lifetime, yet look at what I became." I crossed my arms in front of my chest, as if they could protect me from the internal war within.

"We are all shaped by our pasts, but they do not define us. We react to the world around us as we find it. For those like us, that doesn't always look the same. You've had to adapt to situations most could not even fathom. I'm afraid that the price of your conception was a steep one we didn't see the extent of, not that we would have chosen differently if we had," Medusa said, curling her tail beneath her and arching it so that she sat upon herself. She leaned forward just as she had when I was a child in need of help to work through something.

"I do not regret them, the things I've done," I muttered, "It was the only choice at the time, or at least the only one I was willing to make. I'm just angry at myself." Goddess I felt like a kid again, scuffing my foot against the floor, embarrassed at my own shortcomings.

"For what child?" She tilted her head slightly, genuinely confused.

"Leaving behind loose ends, not telling Lykos everything, not being better than what her leaving reduced me to." A groan fell from my lips as my toe caught on the floor and jammed a little.

"Lykos is far more perceptive than most give her credit for, yourself included. If you think she has not seen the monster within you and loved you all the more fiercely for it, then you are mistaken." She paused, letting her words sink in.

"Not when I was at my worst," I retorted. "She did not choose me after witnessing what I did in Rome mom. Who could even blame her? Even you could barely look upon me when you turned me into a gargoyle." My lip trembled against my will and Medusa gently grasped my chin.

"Ahhh. Still so convinced that it is always about you hmm? I was ashamed that I had failed you so miserably my darling child - never you. As for Lykos, if you never ask her, how will you know her truth? You have assumed much without verifying details." She gave a gentle 'tut tutt' noise.

"I-" Medusa held a hand to stop my words before they could start.

"YOU, you, you. Yes my child you are my priority, but in this? The answer may have nothing to do with you. Your partner will not bring up something so painful - but you have never asked her reasons why, merely assumed to know them," she said laughing gently. "You are more like your mother in that aspect than you'd like to admit."

She smirked at my sneer, but waggled a finger at me, her beads tinkling against one another as shook her head.

"Many of our issues would have been solved much sooner had your mother merely asked me such questions instead of assuming to know the answers. Trust me my child, ask her - it is the only way you will bury these fears that cripple you so." Her hand moved from my chin to caress my cheek before falling back to her side.

"What if I'm right?" I whispered, afraid of the answer even as I asked the question.

"Then you will work through it. She cannot know your fear if you do not address it. I know it is terrifying child, but wouldn't it be worse to be wrong about this and never know? Helheim has its mists for a reason my dear." She smiled gently, trying to make me see reason.

"Do I even deserve to know, after all these years? After all I've done?" The thought of being wrong in my assumptions was almost as terrifying as being right. How could I justify my actions or how much time I had wasted if I were wrong?

"Our actions are like ripples on the surface of water Nyx, we never know how far they spread, or how they affect the rest of the world. Life holds no guarantees so give yourself some grace my love, we are all at the mercy of the Fates' foolish gambles, but how we deal with the residuals is what makes us who we are." Medusa's hair jingled, the bits of bone rattling together as she shifted forward.

"I suppose you are right," I sighed, defeated in that I could not hide from myself anymore. "You know, I think I like it better when I'm the only voice of reason in the room."

She smiled at me, though the expression was a bit sad, as if she could tell there was still so much I needed to say. A chill ran through my body as I tried to shake the emotion from my body, too exhausted to be responsible for my actions if I kept on. I had cried too much already and if I followed through with her advice, I'd likely cry even more before the night was over.

Medusa, always super perceptive, clapped her hands together and gave me a blissful excuse for retreat.

"On that note, let us not keep them waiting, matters with the Amazons are in fact becoming quite dire. We will have more time to talk when this is all settled, but we need to make a plan before you two get some well deserved rest."

There wasn't much to discuss truly, the amazons would need reinforcements but we were not in any position to be of much use until we had some food and sleep. With Hel's reassurance that time moved much more slowly in the underworld, we accepted her hospitality when we were shooed out of the room. We had spent half the meeting yawning back and forth, much to the annoyance of Artemis' envoy and my mother Nemesis.

The undead soldier who escorted us back to our room was more skeleton than soldier, his clothes hanging off him in tatters, a symbol unfamiliar to me patched onto his shoulder. His skull was held together by magic, that much was clear just by watching the way his form moved without any rattling of bone against bone. That eerie silence was perhaps what made him so off-putting. Lykos seemed particularly keen on his construction, her curiosity apparent as she reached out a hand to touch him. More precisely, she aimed to poke him between his joints.

Batting her hand away I couldn't help but giggle, the skeleton swiveling his head all the way around in what I assumed was the closest thing to a glare he could form. She shrugged sheepishly before heading into our room, leaving me to nod politely and wave an apology to his retreating form - his head still swiveled backwards to make sure Lykos didn't try anything else.

Laughter filled the room when I finally shut the door, my dear fox falling backwards onto the bed in a far corner while I leaned against the door frame. The press of the engraved wood was a solid presence I needed as I slowly spiraled.

Again.

It was unclear how long it took before my laughter turned to sobs, but in an instant Lykos was darting across the small room, her arms grasping my shoulder as she tried to catch my eye, worry-wrinkles scrunching her face.

"Stop, stop, I'm fine," I said, drawing in a deep breath to calm my nerves. I tried in vain to wave her off, but she remained stubbornly persistent.

"In case you didn't notice, you're crying and shaking Nyx. Please, talk to me. These past few days haven't been the easiest, what is going on? Are you hurt?" she asked, concern etched into every note.

Her cerulean eyes finally captured me in the depths of their sea, trapping me on the island at their center. Oh how I wished I could run away from them, but hiding would do neither of us any good. I had never thought myself a coward, no reason to start acting like one now.

"It's just - everything. The mists, the hole, you turning to stone, that damned device and that fucking memory that haunts every movement I make! I'm exhausted, mentally and physically." I muttered, the certainty I had felt in Medusa's arms slipping away like sand.

Embarrassment filled me up as my own lack of control became evident in the way I was beginning to unravel before her. It consumed me until I couldn't face her anymore. Breaking away from her eyes, I fled to the bathing room, secretly hoping she'd follow, if only to know she was near.

The bathing room was as large as the living space, its floors a lighter shade of stone, smoothed over so that one wouldn't risk stubbing a toe while traversing it. The ceiling was high, steam accumulating in the air above as the heat from the water rose. The large bathing tub that had been built into the floor, the bath prepared ahead of us. We had been assured that, in Helheim, it would always stay warm. The gross accumulation of grime on my body certainly needed a good scrubbing and my sore muscles would appreciate the hot soak. If only I could drown my problems along with the dirt.

"What?" Lykos asked, confused. "I mean, some of that I got, but Nyx-"

She followed me, her hand reaching out and grasping my bicep, pausing my actions. My heart thrummed with relief, her touch everything I needed and yet everything that would tear me apart. My gaze stayed focused on the steaming water, unable to meet her gaze.

She growled, "Stop and explain to me what is going on. You can't preach to me about sharing my feelings if you are going to try and hide yours."

A groan fell from my lips as she turned my words against me. She was right. A hypocrite was not what I wanted to be, though truly my strength to resist was practically non-existant tonight. Twisting around I met her eyes, a desperate plea in my words.

"You're right." I muttered, my heart leaping in my chest, anxiety bubbling up alongside my fear. "First though, promise me that no matter what, when it's all said and done we can crawl into this lovely bath and pretend the world isn't falling apart around us. At least for tonight."

My words scared her, I could see it in the way her pupils dilated and then constricted back, but her fear was nothing compared to what grasped my heart and strangled my lungs.

Despite her fear, she didn't hesitate to agree. What a strange shift of roles today.

"I promise Nyx, just please my love, talk to me." She slid her hand down my arm and interlocked our fingers, standing in front of me as I sat on the wide edge of the bath. Her warmth enveloped me, the scent of her consuming and intoxicating me to the point I felt in a stupor. All tact went out the door, wafting away like a hair on the wind. It was now or never.

"Why did you leave me?" I finally choked out.

Lykos' face contorted into a look of shock, confusion and then hurt. Her brow furrowed and her head cocked ever so slight as she stared at me, trying to garner my meaning. Before she could get a word across her lips, I hurried on.

"It is foolish, that I let it shape me so, but there has only been one lifetime amongst them all where you didn't choose me." I blurted, unable to stop my words once they had started. "Why? Was it the monster I had become? Did you truly love her more than me? We have fought alongside each other, but the one time you saw me without the bloodlust of war surrounding us, you chose another and now I'm scared you will see whatever it was you saw that day again and leave me once more."

The wind left me as I barrelled through it all in one breath that verged on the edge of a breakdown. Despite myself, I dared to look into those blue eyes, the ones whose depths could never lie to me. What I saw completely threw me, so much so I almost lost my balance.

Lykos looked confused only for the briefest of moments, before a horrified expression consumed her features. Her lower lip quivered as she bit the edge of it, a habit she had when she was trying to figure out where to begin with her feelings. Fear still held my heart hostage, but a glimmer of hope beamed through as she looked down into my eyes, love shining through above all else.

"Oh Nyx, you've got it all wrong." She knelt in front of me, her hands now resting on my knees as she shifted our perspectives. Looking up at me as if in supplication, her eyes brimmed with tears.

"What and who you are has never frightened me Nyx. Never. Nor has any woman ever held my heart the way you do and always will." A sigh slipped from her lips and she shook her head at herself. "I thought I *was* choosing you. When I left, it wasn't because of anything you'd done or hadn't done. My memories had returned and there was one theme that replayed in every life we lived. Every ounce of pain you suffered was always because of me. The wars we fought, you fought because I did. The vengeance we sought in your mothers name, the death that caught me and caused you to suffer; everything that hurt you could be linked back to me. I thought that perhaps that one time, if I simply chose to leave..." She shook her head despairingly. "...I thought that maybe you would not be sucked into the chaos that follows me."

Frozen, my mind desperately sought to absorb all that she was saying while my heart hammered against its cage, begging to be set free to join hers. Joy and heartache fought for dominance, the battle within akin to being battered with a tree limb. My already frazzled mind struggled to accept her truth, the reality of my ignorance proving both Hel and Medusa correct. My haunting had been of my own creation, perpetuated by fear alone.

"When you never made mention of it, I was relieved, thinking perhaps you had forgotten -

especially when you didn't hesitate to love me once more. Then, in the mists I had to relieve it all and by the goddess Nyx, I am so ashamed of myself. I left you when you needed me most, you who have never strayed from my side, no matter how horrid our situation."

She bowed her head ever so slightly, though I saw the tears in her eyes as she looked down, her hands squeezing my knees gently.

What a pair we were, insufferable idiots the both of us.

"Lykos, everything I have done has been a choice, MY choice, no matter how those choices were influenced and guided by the world around us." That she had blamed herself stung, but it also held relief. All this time, I thought it was that darkness within me that had sent her running, when it had been her love for me instead. Just like my mothers.

Helheim's mists had shown me just how short sighted I had been.

"I know that now." She gazed up at me, a soft smile turning her lips in a sad way. "I just couldn't bear to see you choose me over a peaceful life again, so I took the choice away from you. It was easier to live with the guilt of leaving than that of you suffering or dying because of me." She pressed her forehead into my lap, her shoulders sagging as if a weight had finally slipped free from them.

Humorless laughter rose from my lips as I realized just how easily I had become a self fulfilling prophecy of all my loved ones fears without even knowing it. Everything she and my mothers had done to keep me from danger and heartache had only ever set me on a path right into it.

"Then I went ahead and got myself killed anyway doing exactly what you had hoped to save me from." Bitterness fell from my words, but there were blocks slowly falling into place, painting a whole image much contrary to the one I'd imagined up. How awful it must have been, for her and my mothers, to see all their efforts to protect me be in vain.

What a fool I had been to ever doubt their motivations.

"Yes." Lykos sighed. "You died and I wasn't there to hold you when you changed as you had always been there for me when I'd fallen. I hadn't been around to bring you back once you'd healed. When your mother found me after what they'd done, I realized I had simply abandoned you, when I had hoped to save you. I had run away like a coward rather than dealing with what we faced head on." She kept her head lowered, eyes cast to the floor, her dirty locks spilling off her shoulders to shield her face.

"No," I replied, "I see now why you made that choice and what a fool I have been to let my fear keep me from asking you this sooner."

Lykos' face lifted, her watery gaze searching my eyes for falsehood. There would be none there. A clarity like the sky breaking after a storm, settled over me.

The world around me shifted, a weight that had laid heavy upon my heart suddenly lifted for the first time in centuries. All this time there had been so much misunderstanding between us, all because I'd been too afraid to ask such a simple question. Hel and my mother had been right. Lykos' motives had been from such an overwhelmingly loving place that tears fell from my eyes.

I moved to swipe my face, angry with myself for being so sensitive, but a callused hand gently rubbed them away. Lykos leaned up, her lips pressing gentle kisses to each tear until she reached my eyelids. She leaned her forehead against my own, eyelashes fluttering against my face until a giggle slipped away from me.

"Stubbornness and fear have once again led us astray haven't they?" My words were barely a whisper.

"Yes, but love always smacks some sense into us, does it not?" She gave the back of my head a soft tap, then cocked her head to the side, offering her own up for the same.

Instead of smacking her head back, I drew her face to mine, pressing my lips to hers and sealing the wound that had lain gaping and avoided between us. She sighed into it, her heartbeat just as erratic as my own. Despite how tired and worn we were, a search for answers began as our lips and tongue questioned one another. Every inquiry had but one reply, spoken without words.

'I love you'.

We might have stayed balanced on the edge of that tub all night simply enjoying the comforts of kissing away our hurts, but an over eager fox tipped the scales.

A yelp echoed in the room as Lykos forgot our precarious position and made to climb into my lap. My arms wrapped around her before my brain thought better of it and suddenly that heart-wrenching sensation of falling swallowed me whole. As soon as the water wet my back we became a flailing heap of arms and legs. It took a moment for us to untangle enough to part and resurface, but when we did, Lykos' musical laughter filled the room.

"You always did know the quickest ways to get me wet," she half giggled and half gargled as water lapped her face. Her words were playful and loving, a perfect mix to wash away the seriousness clinging to the air.

My grin faltered as my eyes blinked away the water and I got a full view of my beautiful vixen. Her eyes were puffy from where she'd become emotional, but her face was perfect and full of light, life, and love. A coy grin followed a seductive look that made my now wet nethers even more slick. Any laughter in my lungs quickly died as a fire engulfed my entire body.

She cocked a brow at me, as if daring my roving eyes to do more than make promises. A soft anxiousness tightened my chest as she began very carefully peeling her clinging clothes from her body, only breaking eye contact when pieces got in the way. By the time she stood stark naked in the warm waters my mouth was practically salivating with anticipation. Perhaps sensing my sudden uselessness, she reached down and grabbed my hands, guiding me into standing as she worked on my attire.

For all the grace I had in day to day life, there amidst the hot waters in the depths of Helheim, faced with the most beautiful creature I had ever known, I was rendered completely graceless. When my pants caught on my legs I almost sent us both careening back into the water again. Lykos steadied me as I tossed the clothing aside, her small but strong hands guiding me back down into the steaming tub, pressing me back against the sloped end so that she could hover above me.

The waters held nothing to the heat of our bodies as they pressed together, our lips igniting a flame that soared down our lengths and back up again. My hands felt clumsy but somehow ventured their way to the round smoothness of Lykos' ass, my nails clenching just enough to make her groan with pleasure against my mouth. She left little to be desired as she pressed against every aching inch of flesh, somehow knowing every piece of me that yearned desperately for her affection. Always she came back to my mouth, placing kisses in between pleasurable nips and grasps, knowing kissing was by far my favorite thing in the world.

When she finally made her way to my core, she needed little effort to bring me to my peak and I only briefly felt sorry for any who dwelled nearby as my scream of pleasure overtook me and echoed against the walls. Lykos grinned like a fiend as she rocked against me for as long as my sensitive bud could take it, then settled in to receive just as much attentive affection. When she'd been pleased to contentment and we'd come once together, we finally washed properly, barely resisting another round.

By the time we finally left the bathing room, the water was half gone, having spilled onto the floor, which thankfully had been designed for such an event. Every inch of my body was sore and aching but the sleepiness that now wrapped around me was blissful instead of pure exhaustion. I was only vaguely aware of Lykos curling up and laying her head on my chest before sleep stole me.

CHAPTER ELEVEN
AN ELECTRIC EXPERIENCE

Two days later, we departed Helheim, having taken an extra day to get ourselves collected, assured no extra time would pass here.

This time, the tear we traveled through was much closer to the amazon village, but any comfort in knowing we were closer was quickly diminished by what we found waiting for us. The sky was overcast with what seemed like clouds at first glance, but the heavy scent of smoke destroyed that illusion as soon as we took a breath. In the distance a warm glow tainted the treetops, whatever had caught fire was dry and wouldn't take long to spread.

The sounds of the crackling flames were drowned out by screams that echoed against the mountains, bringing the battle to us - despite its true distance. Turning to face my fox, we shared a look of dread, knowing time was not on our side. As Lykos and I jogged one of the trails that would lead to the village, the sound of horse hooves pounding against the earth echoed out against the mountain. A familiar scream rose up amongst a plethora of terrified whinnies and panicked neighs.

"PRINCE?!" Lykos' voice cracked with the smoke inhalation, but it carried well enough for the ears of the herd pummeling towards us to swivel. A few moments passed, then she yelled his name once more and that same neigh sounded out amongst the stampede of hooves. Then they all shifted course, headed straight towards us.

"Oh shit, please tell me they will know to stop Lykos."

She just shrugged, holding far more trust in the lead stallion's control than I did. The only thing that kept me from really panicking was the appearance of my own mare at the head of the herd. Sprite snaked her head out, nipping the horses that dared try to pass her, curbing their blind panic to something more manageable.

"Thank the goddess," I muttered, releasing a sigh I hadn't noticed I was holding.

The horses slowed, easing down into a trot and then into a walk, seemingly grateful for the break, though they were all extremely jittery. Their skin was in a constant state of twitching and their bodies were soaked through with sweat from their fear fueled run. Sprite tossed her head in distress as she trotted up to me, then placed her head low, bumping my chest in greeting.

"Thank goodness you're alright. Are you taking these to safer lands?" My gesture barely engulfed a piece of the herd behind her.

She bobbed her head, her nostrils flaring as she blew out hard, the noise seeming offended, as if she'd be doing anything else. Lykos had taken off, running right through the herd, which parted at her scent. There was no point in trying to stop her as she disappeared in the crowd of horseflesh, she wouldn't have heeded me anyways. It didn't take long for her to return with Prince, both undamaged. The beautiful paint trotted up alongside Sprite, sparing a greeting for me in the form of a fond lipping of my hair.

"The amazons set them loose with instructions to get to the centaurs. Onya's girlfriend sent word ahead by bird. They should be on the roads waiting and ready to care for any injuries the horses might arrive with." Lykos hurried on, " We have to hurry Nyx, Prince says that from the way they were carrying on, the Amazons do not expect to survive the battle. The queen hopes we will show, but they are ready to meet their end as warriors if we do not."

Lykos' eyes were wide, the animal in her feeding off the nervous energy of the horses, which only compounded with our own.

"Then let us say our goodbyes and get going," I replied reluctantly.

How much more could we take in such a short span of time?

She nodded solemnly, her arms wrapping around Prince's neck as he arched it to hug her back. I turned to Sprite, whose head was on a swivel to keep an eye on the less magical of the herd. Taking a deep breath, so as not to lose control of my emotions, I reached out a shaky hand. The gentle mare bypassed my hand, instead pressing her head into my chest as I wrapped my arms around her, pressing a kiss atop her head, just between her ears.

"Keep them safe and stay alive. If there is any place for you with us, I will come back for you. If there isn't, know that it was my honor to serve as your rider, no matter how short our time together." She whickered softly before nudging me away, tossing her head and trotting off to herd a youngster back in.

"She said she will tolerate no other and she will see you on the other side." Lykos translated as she trotted off, her eyes watery and her face red from the strain of trying to keep the tears in. The tracks down her face were proof she had failed. Prince looked back and paused more than once, as if he might change his mind. Eventually they all disappeared over the ridge, following the river downstream so they could cut across safer countryside.

"We will do what we can to bring them with us." I offered, knowing her heart would break to be parted from him.

"I know. I'll be happy so long as he is safe. For now, we have to hurry to the amazons. Will you fly or ride?" She asked with a forced coyness that told me she knew exactly what she was doing.

"You know damn well my wings are for gliding, not flying." Glaring at her did no good, she merely shrugged her shoulders with a snicker. She had gotten good at pushing down her emotions until she could deal with them properly, but knowing she had to do so hurt my soul. Perhaps one day we wouldn't need to.

"Riding it is then," she replied.

Her shifting took only a few moments and just as quickly I was situated astride the large fox, my wings extended and ready to help maintain her stamina. We had practiced it a few times before and, as long as our rhythms matched, it seemed to be quite helpful. It took a few strides for me to get the pace matched, but once I had, I timed the arch of my wings with her front legs. Extending them out and then pulling them backwards, I was able to double the length of her stride without any extra exertion on her end. When we needed to leap across gaps of rock or streams, I maintained my wing's outstretched position; my legs and arms holding Lykos close so that the momentum kept us both suspended. She giggled every time as my hands had to slip into her armpits and my legs stretched out so that my feet hooked into the pit her hip and leg joint formed. Even as a fox she had her tickling spots.

We had been transported closer than the tear we had used to depart Midgard, but it was still a fair distance away and by the time we finally reached the path that would take us into the Amazon village, it was obvious the fighting had already turned for the worse. Lykos slowed to a walk and I hopped off her as we trudged through what could only be described as a massacre. I cringed as I took in the sheer number of amazons who lay lifeless upon the earth, the smell of death strong, the kills no longer fresh.

We hadn't made it in time.

"That bastard Vidar must have moved against them the moment he had us trapped," I snarled.

My fingernails pierced my skin, my own blood added to the crimson splattered across the earth. The subtle pain grounded me as my anger flared, letting it fuel me for what lay ahead.

"They didn't know they were coming." Lykos muttered, her nose flaring as she took in the scene, her ears were on a swivel for any other surprises, but her eyes were focused on the scent markers only she could see.

"What do you see?" Even with my tracking background, there was no comparing it to Lykos' nose.

"This was a group from the coast, joining up with our amazons. That's why there are so many here. Our women would have known better than to bunch like this. It was a greeting party, not a war group," she growled.

"Fuck!" My words left my lips before I could think better of it, but it was the only expression I could allow myself right now. To lose my composure would mean to lose focus and now was not the time for that. My chest clenched, sorrow passing in a wave I forced myself to push aside.

There amongst the bodies, was a familiar face. A sigh fell from my lips as I walked over and knelt beside the woman, her beautiful eyes lifeless as they looked up into the skies. The humor that usually graced her flirtatious face was absent now, her features lacking the bright spirit of her personality. Our friendship had been a slow thing, but a decent one. Pointless, this loss of life.

"Rest well Camilla, I pray that Artemis finds you in Helheim and takes you home." My fingers shook as I brushed her eyelids closed. With the discovery of a friend, I made a point to glance around at the rest of the faces, assuring myself she was the only one I knew. Lykos' energy shifted, a hand upon my back was all she could offer as solace, she too knowing that the emotions brewing within would have to wait.

"I don't think the rest of our friends are here, let's get a move on and make sure they don't join them. We will have to take care of these later." Death had never bothered me on the surface, but the cowardice of this take down lit a fire within me that would not be easily staunched.

The trail of bodies did not end there. Small breaks down the path led to more bloodshed, though it was obvious when the main force of amazons had arrived once we were closer to the scout paths. We held our breath as we trudged through at a swift jog, unwilling to accept a hard truth; that we may have been too late to save anyone.

Close to the village, where the last outcropping of rocks bunched up before the ravine, a familiar sound caught my ear.

"Lykos," I muttered a flutter of hope in the wind.

"I hear it." She growled back, her claws digging into the earth as she doubled her gait.

The ringing of metal and the buzz of arrows filled the air before we could see it and had quieted significantly by the time we arrived at its source. Hope that we would at least be in time to help some of our sisters mingled with the tingle of bloodlust every warrior knew. As Lykos ran harder, I felt my blood grow hot with anticipation, a twisted part of me looking forward to the destruction I'd leave in my wake once we found the proper direction to aim it.

Once upon a time I might have blamed the Roman coliseums for turning me into a battle crazy monster, but the truth was I had become what I was long before the gladiator fights had gotten hold of me. They had been crueler, but I had been no less ruthless when war had been our past time. Peace had been far harder to adapt to than the battlefields ever were and at least then I had an outlet for my anger and sorrow. Though perhaps I'd have done a better job if I'd known the truth of it all.

Lykos must have felt my muscles tense, or perhaps she was feeling the same energy sizzling through the air, as I heard and felt the rumble of a snarl rising through her chest. I couldn't see the whole of where the fighting had started and avoided looking too closely. Sorrow would have to wait, there were still, with any luck, amazons to save.

"Let us show these new gods what happens when they mess with the Norn's Catalyst, shall we?"

We were running so fast now that I had to shout for Lykos to hear me.

"One way or another they are following us to Hel," she snickered wickedly. I couldn't help but to roll my eyes.

"I'm sure they will be *dying* to meet her," I replied.

A smirk flitted across my lips when Lykos snorted, the chittering laughter of a fox falling from her muzzle. The amusement carried us for a few strides longer and then the battle was upon us.

A small group of Amazons had been herded into the rocks, but had found a big enough hollow that they were able to defend the only entrance. This would be the last defense, the last chance to save those in the village who couldn't fight and were undoubtedly hidden deep in the hot springs.

Artemis truly had provided well for the amazons, the land itself becoming a shelter when needed. The thick canopies were barely green, their growth slow from the harsh winter, but their spindly limbs remained spread out and overlapping. It was just enough to deter most of the arrows that the Vikings tried to shoot through. The grumbling of their frustration was matched with the metallic clashing of those alternating attempts to push through the band of warriors guarding the horselength opening.

As we neared, a flash of red and black sent the front line of vikings backwards, that weird but familiar roaring bark echoing down the line. The strange noise made them pause just long enough for the Amazons to regain their footing and send a short volley of arrows into the once again advancing group.

"Looks like part of the cavalry has already arrived," I said more to myself than Lykos, though her ears were pitched forward with interest.

I had no doubt this was only a piece of the forces, but I knew better than to lose focus on the most immediate threat. Ylva could only hold them back so long. If they broke through before we got to them, there would be no one left to rescue, the entirety of the tribe would be lost in one fell swoop. I had learned long ago that sometimes you had the luxury of plans, sometimes you did not. Today was the latter. Today was a 'strike anything that moves that isn't a sister until nothing else remains standing' kind of day.

"No survivors," I muttered to Lykos. She nodded, her anger boiling just beneath the surface, a fire fueling her magic.

Leaping from Lykos' back I just managed to hit the ground before she quite literally ran into the midst of the battle. War cries from the front were now drowned out from screams of surprise and pain as my beautiful vixen went in full fury of fang and claw. Her onyx tipped tails spewed a stream of magic that would make it hard for the vikings to find anything to actually hit as she weaved gracefully between them. The world grew slow and muffled as my mind became numb with the awe that always overwhelmed me when I saw her in action.

I was quickly pulled back to reality, everything converging on me all at once as the fight came to me.

The sound of a sword's swing drew my body into action, muscle memory serving me well as I dodged the blow, stepping into the man's reach only long enough for the sharpened tip of one of my wings to jolt forward and pierce him through the throat.

Ironically it was the only place not covered and protected. He couldn't scream but the men and women around him certainly could and shouts of distress drew more towards us, lightening the load on our amazons up ahead.

A hiss fell from my lips as pain erupted across my arm. Turning with a fanged grin on my face, I narrowed in on the woman who had thrown the spear that grazed me.

"You're going to have to do a lot better than that." My monster chuckled as I let her out to play and the world became a symphony written in blood and performed with the screams of the dying.

They were good, well seasoned warriors who died with glorious snarls of triumph even as their blood splattered bodies fell to the earth, lifeless. The tin of metal against metal slowly disappeared from the world as one by one they dropped like flies swatted out of the air. The world's discomforts slipped away; the bristling fire in my lungs, the sting of cut flesh, all of it was laid aside, a problem for after the battle was won.

The part of me that was not Goddess, but instead a mortal beast created by them, flourished. Medusa's magic, which ran strongest through my blood, narrated my story like a bard in an ale house, pronouncing each word so that every movement hung on its perfection. I twirled across the earth, my clawed feet leaving indentations for those to later witness my trek as I danced like a monster from a child's nightmares.

Dropping to the earth, I grabbed my first victim's sword to glance a second attack away, rising as I pushed my enemy back, my free hand lashing out with fingers that had become talons. My wings pulled in so that I could see more clearly as I twirled around the woman before timing a drop into a crouch as she struck again, this time with a knife. At the last moment, my wing arched out and around to slash the back of her ankle, that oh so famous spot of Achilles' crippling her. As she crumpled towards the earth she dropped the knife she held and in one smooth motion I reached out and snatched it from the air, spun around her on my knees and buried it in the base of her skull.

It was quick and hopefully painless. I was vicious, but not cruel. That was the one line I made sure never to cross into. In wars, life was sacrificed - quite often meaninglessly, but that was the way of it. That reality however, never justified cruelty to another living being. I'd had my vengeance before and knew that justice was not the same. Not when it came to those who were just following orders.

Another came for me, the broad axe undoubtedly heavy, but the man wielding it did so as if it were as light as a play sword. His strokes were quick and before I knew it, he was right on top of me. The air from his strike blew past me as I barely managed to dive away quickly enough to miss the killing blow. The sword I still had in my off hand was all that saved me from the follow-up swing.

The hard metal chipped from the force of impact, then followed his momentum, screeching as I guided the heavier weapon off to the side just long enough for me to dart away again. Diving across the dirt, I went head over feet and rolled behind him, the sharp back edge of his axe slicing a long line in my calf. A snarl of pain fell from my lips, but it was not deep enough to do more than bleed and hurt like hell when dirt promptly made a home in it.

With a grunt I swung my damaged blade round, pivoting on my toes while he hauled his weapon up once more. Sparks skittered across the ground as the metal drug across rock as I rose to my feet, swinging the blade forward so that its arched ascent left a jagged gouge across the viking's back. Crimson blossomed immediately as he staggered forward, so I knew I'd struck true. His clothing was thick enough to protect him from permanent paralysis, but it would at least slow him down.

The sound of Lykos' snarls found their way into my consciousness and I subconsciously tracked where she ought to be in case they turned from aggressive to pained. In the meantime, the man I'd hit had dropped his axe, one side of its edge having cut cleanly into the earth so that it stood erect and gleaming. The brute was snarling and cursing as he tried to reach around to squelch the bleeding from his back, giving me just enough time to act. With a well placed sweep of my leg, my foot snagged his ankle, jerking his leg from beneath him. He went careening towards the earth too quickly to catch himself, landing solidly on the axe's exposed edge.

My jaw tightened at the sound of impact. Cringing, my eyes took in the effect for only a moment before I turned, not caring to examine that one too closely. The distinct squelch it made had painted a clear enough picture without putting the imagery into memory.

"Oof, no one will ever have to remind me not to run with double sided weapons again." I muttered to myself, a shiver running down my spine in sympathy of the gruesome death. What a horrible way to go.

Midstep, the sound of a hawk's cry pierced my ears only moments before the blur of an arrow whizzed past my head. The laughter that followed was far too familiar, instantly igniting a rage within my core.

"Well well well, what do we have here? However, did you manage to get out of that hole? Looks like your little fox managed to survive too. Hmm Tereus, what do you have to say for yourself?" Vidar's disapproval was evident in every word he spoke.

The hawk was tethered to the god's shoulder, the greenish hue of his spirit wafting on the edges of a real hawk's form. It hurt my head to try and focus on the beast, the edges blurring uncomfortably as he shifted in and out of the plane.

The bird danced nervously from foot to foot, but whatever he was saying was nothing more than squalls in my ears. Then, without any warning at all, the God he was tethered to reached up and grasped his spirit, his hands aptly wringing his head, snapping the neck with the ease of cracking a knuckle. The feathered creature flew away, but the spirit of Tereus fell to the earth and dissolved into nothing.

"Not quite as satisfying as watching him splatter at the bottom of a cliff," I commented. My sneer would never do justice to the distaste that filled my mouth at the mere thought of that brute. Though that seemed far more permanent than what he managed on his own.

There was nothing felt for the loss of Tereus' soul except the disappointment of not being able to send him to Hel myself. There was a special place for his sort and Hel did not seem like the type of Goddess to let the time between the crime and death ease the punishment. Hades had been far more lenient than most knew, unwilling to be bothered with the more gruesome parts of his rule. The irony of that made me hate him more for what he'd put me through. Too lazy to make the sinful dead suffer but not too lazy to leave me and mine alone.

Vadir turned his focus back upon me and laughed, his voice full of bravado. "Not even a flinch? You're a cold one aren't you? Perhaps I should get a new pet, that fox of yours would look lovely at the end of a leash." He licked his lips grossly and the rage within me turned to a tidal wave that threatened to devour everything in its path.

My lungs drew in a deep, controlled breath.

Being goaded into rashness was unacceptable, but letting him think I had been? Now that could work in my favor. I might not be able to kill a God, but I could damn sure make certain he thought twice before playing stupid games with me or those I loved.

Scowling, my face scrunched up, pearly whites on display as I lunged blindly, clearly telegraphing my movements so that he could easily evade. His expression shifted to amusement, his ego fed as he effortlessly dodged every blow, even going so far as to pretend to yawn.

His overconfidence would be his undoing.

While he played at boredom, moving without much thought, I put his movements to memory. The way he shifted and adjusted, how he favored his left side over his right, and that while he talked he had a bad habit of looking up at the sky, as if he were invincible. The love of his own voice and his self-indulgent pride kept him from noticing exactly what I was doing; herding and baiting him into a horseshoe of rock.

"Oh I am enjoying this pitiful display of just how overblown your reputation is, but once again, I really do have places to be. I'm afraid I'm going to need to kill you now Nyx, but don't worry, after I finish off the amazons your dear fox will live a life of luxury - at the end of my leash." He made a vulgar stroking motion between his legs near the end of his speech and I decided then and there it would be one of the last things he ever said.

As he strode towards me, my legs bent and jerked as if I'd go left, and when he altered his course, my eyes widened and my arms rose in defense as he drew his sword and struck. His eyes narrowed in confusion when at the last minute I made eye contact and winked, my lips curling into a sinister snarl. Playtime was over.

Diving beneath the arcing sword, metal sparks popped off the rock with the strength of his blow, the fiery flecks unable to follow me as I carefully maneuvered back to my feet behind him. Vidar twisted around, far more agile than I'd have given him credit for, but I was ready and waiting. While he was still mid-turn I set my weight back upon my non-injured leg and slammed my foot into the knee nearest me; the one he was pivoting on. His screams of pain were almost as satisfying as the sound of the bone reversing and jutting out of his flesh.

"Oooh. Bet that one stings a bit huh?" I taunted. My grin was inescapable and unhindered by guilt.

Vadir was mumbling and blubbering but his words were indecipherable from the whimpers in between. He fumbled back into the rock face, balancing himself upright best he could on one leg. There would be no quarter given, gods recovered far too quickly to take that risk. With only that thought and his last words in mind, I picked up a jagged sliver of rock that was longer than my hand and lunged.

The shard sliced my own flesh just as deeply as it pierced the flesh of his shoulder, but it was easy to ignore the pain as I carved a line down his chest, doing as much damage as possible by pushing my weight behind it. He crumbled to the earth in a pitiful and bloody pile, his hands grasping my arms to try and push me away. He was already healing - I could feel his magic stirring in the air.

"Odin." He whispered the words, but I knew the power names held.

"Oh no, not just yet Vadir. You can lick your wounds with daddy when I'm done," I snapped.

Kicking him hard in the gut to distract his defensive arms, I planted my full weight into his groin as I pulled the shard out of his flesh. All these wounds would heal, but there was one way I knew for certain to maim him permanently. The price of ill intent towards Medusa's daughter was a steep one to pay.

"A parting gift to remember me by. Payback for my mother and sister. Consider us marginally closer to even now," I seethed.

He attempted to fight back, his good arm reaching out so that his fingers dug into the slice in my calf. Pain laced through my leg, but instead of crying out in pain I let it fuel my rage. There was nothing he could do that would ever top the worst pain of my life. To someone whose life had been destroyed more than once, in the worst of ways, a flesh wound was easy to bear.

The blood from my sliced hand had oozed down all over the sharp end of the stone, but I made sure to rub it down so that there was no spot left untouched. With my foot still planted in his groin I grabbed his jaw with my free hand and squeezed until his mouth went slack. Fear finally showed in his face as I channeled my mother's gorgon magic - blood magic at its best. The edge of the blade grew sharper, the magic glinting and shifting within my blood. This was why I had been feared amongst the gods - why Hades himself had run and hid. Tereus was the only one foolish enough to cross me.

He was about to learn what the greeks knew all along; I could harm them.

His screams rang out but quickly became gurgles as the blood covered shard sliced through his tongue. His fist collided with my jaw, but a few less than clean slices later and half his tongue bounced out and down his chest, flopping into a puddle of saliva and blood.

"Never piss off a Gorgon." My snarl was emphasized with a kick to his damaged knee, the pain finally enough to make his eyes roll into the back of his head. My jaw throbbed, but damn was it worth it.

As his consciousness left him, his dark hair began to stand up as a charge fell across the air. A small, but too late, warning of what was to come. I'd gotten a little too cocky and taken just a smidge too long.

"Fuck." The words left my lips but their sound remained unheard.

Thunder rumbled only a split second before a jolt of lightning arced across the sky then abruptly exploded at my feet. Too fast to follow with even my keen eyesight, all I could do was close my eyes as the world around me became a blinding light. My wings were thrown wide as my muscles spasmed from the shock. They caught just enough air to soften my fall, but even that wasn't enough to dull the pain that rippled through my back.

My entire body buzzed with pain, fire running through my nerves. Charred black was all that remained where Vidar had crumpled, rescued by his father Odin. Or at least I was fairly certain that was all that remained, my eyesight was mostly spots and shifting flashes at that point. Despite the situation I found myself in, I couldn't stop laughing, even when it had simmered from a full chest heaving laugh to mere giggles. Every sound hurt, each breath agony as my lungs were scorched, my life saved only by my proximity to Vidar.

The lightning bolt hadn't struck me directly, but I had sure as shit been hit with its residuals. From the corner of my eye I could see patterns along my arms that looked like a plant's roots, like my nerves had branded me from the inside out.

That only made me chuckle more, which burned my lungs and throat more from the raw friction. Oh how the heat of battle infused me with something wild and wicked, so much so I could practically hear the cheers of the Roman arenas, the armies of my allies roaring with victory, and most importantly - Lykos yelling my name in triumph.

Everything soon became numb and then the bright spotty world disappeared, replaced by darkness.

Chapter Twelve
Tingling the Bad Way

The depths of night dissipated, though my vision swirled. My entire body jolted upwards and then fell back into paralysis. Panic began to bubble as I feared my stone state had taken hold. Surely the lightning had not done enough damage for that. A groan escaped my lips, a painful tingling sensation spreading through my limbs until at last, there was a small wiggle in my toes.

Still amongst the living and mobile, hopefully.

Sound wasn't quite registering, almost like my head was under bubbling water. Closing my eyes against the nauseating swirls of my vision, I attempted to center myself with a deep breath. Thankfully all my organs were functioning just fine it seemed, though as my lungs expanded and pushed my chest outward a million tiny needles jabbed my insides. Biting the inside of my lip, I held back a scream of pain, but I definitely made some sort of noise.

The vibrations of footfalls registered along my skin, sound struggled to trickle in, so I couldn't hear how close they were. My only hope was that they belonged to someone I knew.

"Nyx!" Was that my name I heard? It was like the ocean was in my ears, crashing against the rocks as someone called out to me.

Focusing past the noise, my hearing cleared just long enough to catch my vixen's voice, my name upon her lips sounding more like a question than an acknowledgement.

"Nyx?" Lykos asked, concern filling her words.

Blinking a few times she finally came into focus, jogging towards me and then slowing when her gaze flitted across the charred earth. Her eyes trailed down my body, no doubt taking note of all the blood splattered there.

"Are you okay?" She asked softly, approaching cautiously with her hand outstretched. It reminded me of when people approached a predator, unsure if it was going to snap at them or not. The darkest part of me was satisfied to know she saw the truth of me, but another part of me was ashamed. Although prudent, it hurt my heart to see her hesitate.

Reaching out, I took her hand, thankful that my body responded. Her energy shifted immediately as she pulled me up from the hard earth and into her arms. Our lips met and fire exploded throughout my body, a deep moan falling from my lips as she deepened the kiss to the point I had to press my core into the thigh she hand placed between my legs. All the damaged nerves in my body flared with a mix of pain and pleasure, my magic rushing to heal the confusion.

"By the Gods you are everything." My words slipped out before I could check them, but when I opened my eyes, hers were alight with a fire I hadn't seen in ages. It reminded me of the many past battles we had won, often ending in a romp that couldn't be matched as the adrenaline and rush of war found a safer outlet in our intimate dance.

She smiled and kissed me more gently, though the look in her eyes remained hungry and in awe. Her words were hoarse with desire. It was a ridiculous time to be hyped with desire, but adrenaline did weird things to the body, better to crave one another than blood.

"We have to help the rest. Can you walk?" she asked.

Who would have thought she'd be the voice of reason. It took every ounce of self control I had to let her go, but soon enough I'd have a different outlet for the wild thing that had awoken within me. Though if I had taken a moment to really feel out my body I'd have realized I was in no shape to be doing anything of that nature.

"Yea, I mean, everything is numb or on fire with pain, but that should all sort out quickly enough. It was just a bit shocking is all." I grinned as she went to slap my arm but then thought better of it.

"Come on then, Xiomara and Ylva will guard this pass, they say Freya is working on delaying the next wave of attacks." She snorted, her eyes rolling to the back of her head before she shook it, her wild hair dancing in the breeze. If ever there were a more beautiful creature gifted life, I had not seen it.

"Oh? So kind of Freya to lend a hand," I commented sarcastically.

We made our way towards the surviving Amazons, though my stride was a bit more akin to a three legged horse's hobble than a run. It got me there nonetheless. At the top of the path the remaining Amazons stood, their exhaustion evident in the way they slouched against their weapons and the rock face. The last of the Vikings had finally retreated, eyes glaring back at us as they shouted obscenities at the maned wolf chasing behind. The vikings would be back, but they would not find us waiting.

A breath I didn't know I was holding washed out of me the second I spotted Xalia standing tall amongst her sisters. She was worn and battered, but the second she caught sight of me her lips pulled into a small smile, relief sagging her shoulders.

"I'd say you were late, but I think you're actually a few days ahead of schedule. It's too bad our enemies didn't keep to the same one." She spoke loudly, as if her hearing had suffered. It was then I noticed she'd taken a blow to the side of the head, a stain of blood running down her neck from her ear.

Shaking my head, I hurried to meet her half way, my uninjured hand stretched out, grasping her arm and pressing tight. She drew me close in a warrior's hug and I could feel her legs shudder. Or perhaps it was mine. We leaned against each other for a moment, foreheads pressed against the other.

"The queen is dead Nyx. They breached the village before your friends showed up and helped us push them back. There is only a small group left, aside from us." Her words were softer now, exhausted and full of grief.

I would have to remember to thank Xiomara and Ylva the next time I saw them. Whether or not by Freya's command, they had likely been the deciding factor in our friend's survival.

"We saw Camilla on our way here," I whispered. It pained me to add to her misery, but surely it was better than guessing. They had been friends since childhood, afterall.

Her eyes were misty when we broke apart, though I kept hold of her arms to brace her against the news. The deep breath she drew in rattled, but she calmed herself quickly.

"I assumed as much when the enemy made it to our doorstep and they did not. I wish we had time for a proper funeral, but I daresay this reprieve will be short. We must gather the survivors and depart. You've cleared a way for us haven't you? The weird fox creature's partner said you were successful." Her words were full of desperation and hope.

All I could do was nod, the sorrow seeping from her threatened to drown me beneath waves of memory. This was a small blow compared to the ones I had felt over my lifetimes, but the sting was never lessened. Mourning would come later, now was simply not the time, though I did stop her long enough to ask the hardest question there was.

"Xalia. Did Serah and Onya make it?" I hadn't tracked Lykos' path, knowing she was seeking out those she loved most and afraid she wouldn't like what she found.

Relief flooded me when Xalia smiled.

"I sent Onya back to the village a while ago, before the viking's second wave came through and forced us back here. Serah stayed behind to attend the wounded." As she spoke she noticed the blood that now smeared her own arm from where I had grabbed and steadied her. Before I could protest she had ripped a strip from her tattered shirt, grabbing my hand and tying it off to staunch the bleeding.

Casting my gaze across the small group I found Lykos' searching gaze, wide eyed and worried. She paused when she noticed my stare, her head cocking to the side like a pup. When I smiled and nodded, her chest stilled in what I knew was her best effort not to sob with relief. She swiped her eyes only once, then moved to help the others along as we silently agreed to start our trek home - destined to leave it just as quickly.

The distance back to the village was not far but it was a long trek for us all. Exhaustion had worn everyone and most had injuries of some sort. Xalia and I walked in the rear, protecting our rear in case any had slipped past the hound and valkyrie, while Lykos had shifted and carried several of the worse for wear at the front.

"How many live?" The words were hard to ask, but knowing what I was going to witness helped me keep my composure under duress.

"Less than a couple dozen of those who stayed. The families with children did not come here, but instead took refuge amongst the centaurs, so they were spared," she stated sadly.

"At least they will know protection." A sigh of relief fell from my lips.

"Is that not what we have acquired?" Xalia's hand touched my arm, slowing our gait so others would not overhear.

"Protection is rarely free amongst humans and when bartering with Gods it is guaranteed to come at a price. Whatever it is we've acquired for you is more akin to enlistment, this was your first trial to join the ranks." The words were far truer now that they were spoken, a reality I'd pushed down in the face of no other options.

"A second chance, all the same. One way or the other we were going to the underworld, at least this way we will be mere visitors going on our own terms," she replied, nodding to herself and posturing her shoulders back with resolve.

"If the Goddess keeps her word. We will see what comes of it, though Ylva and Xiomara's appearance is a good sign." My lips fluttered as I blew out roughly.

"Have you so little faith?" Her tone was merely curious, no skepticism to be found.

"Faith is for those who have not lived amongst gods and seen just how human they are. Perhaps it makes me jaded, but I grew up with their kind and remain unimpressed at best." A shrug was all I could offer her.

Xalia nodded, mulling over my words as she worried her bottom lip with her teeth. I'd long had a habit of the same, but my sharpened canines tended to mutilate the flesh, so Lykos had helped me to mostly stop. The thought made me want to chuckle, but I resisted. Morale was down, best not tempt the fates by laughing amongst their chaos.

If I could have strangled Rhea, I would have. Our relationship had been tumultuous to say the least, but at the end I had thought her more friend than fiend. Suppose it wasn't the first time I'd been so incredibly wrong. She'd had all the power to prevent this, but instead she had taken the coward's way out and left me to do her dirty work, yet again.

The trek was uneventful, my mind drifting off in thought. I didn't even realize we had reached the village until a familiar cry of relief echoed to the back of the line. A happy stream of yips followed it and I couldn't help but let a smile pull at my lips. The happiness of my fox and the enthusiasm of her best friends were contagious. Glancing to my side I saw Xalia matching my sentiment. The rest of the amazons seemed to sigh in relief, their steps which had been dragging picked up in pace as they filtered into their home.

As everyone trickled into the village, it took no time at all for me to spot Serah and Onya, both with their arms wrapped around my love's neck, her whine a familiar note of relief, her tails creating a weird gust behind her as they all wagged out of unison. She yapped when she saw me and Xalia, alerting Serah to her partner's arrival. The look shared between them was one that I felt in my soul, practically tangible for all that it said.

The next half hour was spent catching everyone up on what had happened while we took a well earned break to rest and eat. The shortest version was all we could afford, but it was enough. Questions were held back, though they were poised on the tip of almost every tongue.

Xalia nodded, taking everything as fact and absorbing it, Serah tucked into her side. "Alright then," she said, "we will make ready to leave, you guys just get us the means. If they were going to hesitate before, they surely won't anymore, not now that one of their gods has been brutalized."

Lykos snorted, mildly indignant, but I merely shrugged. The bastard had earned it and I was more than willing to live with whatever the consequences of that were. Knowing all he had done to those I loved, I felt completely justified in all the misery I could wrought upon him.

"Hel has promised a way to her realm through the temple to my mother. We will head there and cross into Helheim. From that point, a new world awaits in Vanaheim with the Goddess Freya, for any who wish it." I waved my arm out to encompass everyone as I spoke.

"Hel has also extended a permanent welcome to all those who do not wish to fight, or serve a foreign Goddess," Lykos added.

Everyone nodded solemnly, the implication clear enough. The only thing that remained was for us to get everyone to the temple.

Every woman was lost in thought or worrying over the decision they had to make, some were so distracted that they almost walked into those in front of them when we slowed. The sound of scuffing feet, boots and weapons were the only noise to come from us.

There was no sympathy left in me for their struggle, we all had to make tough decisions and I had done my part to create a smooth path to whatever they chose. They were alive and had a path forward, my promise was fulfilled.

When we finally reached the temple, I made sure that no one went into the actual building. Rhea's body undoubtedly lay within, the walls and floor still blood crusted with splatters everywhere. Time was funny in the way that it remained fluid in one's mind. For everything that had happened since then, for all that time moved differently in the underworld, it seemed like a year had passed since I'd stood and watched the Fate take her own life. Surely it had only been a month or so though. I had lived so long I rarely kept track of the days, but I was certain the sun was higher, longer.

Lost in thought, I startled at the soft touch of Lykos' hand against my arm. She tilted her head, concern in those deep pools of hers. All I could do was offer a soft smile before my brows quirked up. In her hand she held a bundle of heather, bound in place by a particularly large wolf's thread of fur.

"I found this on the pedestal between the buildings. What was it you said to me then, about why it had to be blood?" Her sly smile curled up half her face, mischief in every line of her crooked brow and cocked head. It wasn't the time or place, but when had that ever stopped me from taking the opportunity to turn her scarlet?

"I do believe I might have insinuated that it was better than wetting the podium with the cream of your pleasure. Though I'd have no problem helping you with that, if you wanted to give it a go. The norse must have a goddess of love or lust we could appeal to," I whispered.

Laughter spilled out of me as she turned pink then crimson, her cheeks flushing with embarrassment as she glanced around to make sure no one had heard me. Of course I had whispered the words, my love and pleasure for her was our business alone, but by the Goddess it was hilarious to watch her panic. Teach her to start something she couldn't finish.

"You're right though," I amended, "it seems I've had an extra helping of my own medicine with that particular bit of wisdom."

Stepping away, fully intending to leave her there to recover, a pressure again my arm halted me. Her grip was firm as she turned me back towards her, her free hand moving across my jawline to bury itself in my hair at the back of my head.

The world shivered and froze, then went up in a blaze of fire as her mouth met mine, wet and hot and full of a desire strong enough to transcend the planes of life and travel through time. Every hair on my body stood at attention as chills ran up and down my spine, my core ignited with such an intensity that my lungs forgot their duty. The kiss was deep and passionate and oh too short. Her tongue caressed mine, her teeth grazing my bottom lip and nipping the tender flesh, then there was nothing. Cold air replaced all the warmth and passion that had radiated around my body as Lykos got bitter sweet revenge.

Oh what a vixen.

When I recovered enough to open my eyes and breathe again, she was grinning and playfully swaying her hips as she looked back at me, walking towards the center of the temple gathering area, calling the amazons together.

"Oh what a fucking tease." My uttered words were emphasized with a shudder of delight as I made my way to where she was. Thank goodness the fried ends of my nerves had all recovered from the lightning fiasco, despite the charming marks along my arms. Though it had never matched Lykos' ability, my own expedited healing was extra appreciated in that moment.

Without words, for I didn't trust myself not to go down that inappropriate road once more, I drew my thumb across my canine until the skin split, then I let three drops spill over the heather she held in her hands. We set the gift down to the earth and waited. In mere seconds the air shimmered with magic and a portal to the underworld appeared, its hue an eerie green.

The amazons muttered, surprise and confusion all present, but they all fell silent after a collective gasp as the shimmering air contorted and a figure walked through. The Goddess of Death stepped halfway through the portal, her healthy side exposed, the other half partially remaining in her realm. She scanned the gathered crowd until her eyes settled upon Lykos and I, a smile spreading across her features.

"I would like to speak to you for a moment, but first - business." She turned her attention back to the amazons, her smile genuine, if a bit terrifying on such an imposing figure.

"You all have a choice. My lands may be traversed only once without the cost of your soul. However, I understand your struggles have been hard and many of you lost loved ones who now dwell in my realm. You are welcome to pass into Vaneheim and join the Goddess Freya and her Valkyrie; to live a new life in a new land. You also have the choice to stay. You will not have to suffer the pain of death, your mortality will slip away on its own and you may call Helheim your home and be with those you have lost," Hel proclaimed, her voice warm and welcoming.

A hum of murmuring rose up, the prospect of being reunited with loved ones a tempting option for many. There were those amongst us who had come to live with the amazons after the death of their families, the loss of their children and friends. Others had lost their partners in the fighting and had yet to cease the tears of heartbreak. Although we had told them there would be a choice, hearing it from the goddess herself made the idea a reality that could no longer be corrupted with denial.

"You do not have to decide now. Walk into my realm and rest a while, protected from those who would see you returned to the earth," she continued, sensing their discomfort.

Whether they believed her intentions to be good or bad, the truth was there was no other option before them. The enemy would return and there would be no surviving their next attack with as few numbers as they had. So, one by one the amazons pulled themselves to their feet, cautiously passing by Hel in order to find their salvation. She offered each a kind and encouraging smile, like a mother fondly looking upon lambs finally coming home from roaming the hillsides.

Xalia and Serah gave us a silent nod before they walked through, looking weary of heart even more so than body. Only Onya and her partner remained with us and I could practically hear Lykos' heart shattering when she realized why.

"I love you Lykos and when our time comes to leave this earth, I hope you will cross the planes and visit us in the underworld." Onya opened her arms and for a moment I thought Lykos would refuse, her cerulean eyes wet with unshed tears, but finally her shaking hands moved and she fell into a tight embrace. They stood that way for a long moment.

I couldn't hear the words mumbled between them after that, but when they parted Onya pressed a quick, soft kiss upon Lykos' cheek, squeezing her hand before hauling herself up onto her partner's back. Her own face was red and tear stained, but as she took a deep breath, she relaxed into the assurance of her decision and offered us a smile.

Onya had only been with the Amazons for a few years, coming to live with them as an ambassador for her people, the centaurs. It was no surprise to me that she would return to them, especially since she had only just reunited with her partner, whose half-horse form twitched eagerly. They would undoubtedly be eager to see that their own people were as safe as they had been told.

I reached out a hand, my sweet vixen taking it in hers with a death grip that told of just how badly she was struggling to contain herself. Stepping closer, I released her hand in order to draw her to me, pressing her shaking body into my side, trying desperately to give her my strength.

The centaur stepped a few strides away before pausing, her hand rising to her heart as she nodded to us both.

"It's been an honor to know you both. We will make sure your names are never forgotten amongst our people for all you have done. Should you find yourselves in need of a home - you will always be welcome where centaurs roam." She then turned towards Hel, nodding respectfully. "We appreciate your offer, but our people await our return. We will not be shy to speak of your kindness either, Goddess of the Underworld."

The goddess nodded her head, silently watching as they disappeared through the brush, taking a path I didn't even realize existed. She was patient enough to wait until Lykos had wiped her face before speaking.

"Do not mourn, young fox, every separation is only ever temporary. Even if you do not return to this world, all return to my realm one day and with what you two have done, you will always find a warm welcome in my realm."

Although it seemed innocent enough, the way she said it made me think there was more happening than we knew.

"Surely we have done nothing more than what was required for passage." My words were a statement, but the goddess saw the question in my gaze and obliged.

"You two have been quite busy. Loki's freedom was all I expected to give passage to your amazons and yet you have done so much more. Vidar has been silenced, which few gods will begrudge. Already they mock him as payback for all his bragging and boasting - now he is the silent god, humbled by a woman of all things," Hel laughed.

She raised her hand to her head in a dramatic display of disbelief. When she turned her smile towards me once more, part of her decaying features met my gaze, turning the sweet smile wicked as it contorted to a toothy grin.

"Most importantly amongst your deeds however," she continued, " is the aid of the wolf Fenrir. Although none other than myself and father know it was you - the tides have turned thanks to a bit of heather and grass. What you did in kindness, allowed the magic in the bindings to be disrupted. When my dear brother realized there was finally a weak point, it was a simple matter to break himself free. He is hiding now, but Odin knows he is free and is rightfully freaking out."

My mind summoned the memory of our conversation, Fenrir had been absolutely certain the norn's words would come true, whether by their doing or his own intentions. He had every intention of swallowing Odin whole, no matter what the prophecy said of his demise because of it.

Was that truly all because of what I had done? Had Rhea truly set this all up through the ages, knowing our actions - even in her absence - well enough to manipulate events? Bitterness soured my mouth, both at her presumptions and that they might be true.

"Do you still not understand?" Hel asked. "The end of the world will begin with an eternal winter."

She laughed and gestured to the sky above which had slowly grown dark gray, blotting out the sun. As we turned our heads to the sky, an unspeakable thing began to happen, as if summoned to life by her words.

Snow.

Thick flakes of snow were slowly but steadily falling to the earth. The first layer melted before it hit the ground, but that it could fall at all was insane. No matter how far off my days might have been, there was no explanation for snow to fall this late int he season.

Hel's laughter turned to giggles as she opened her hand and watched as one or two flakes turned to five or six, then the sky began to haze with it.

"You two have triggered Fimbulwinter, the second sign of Ragnarok," Hel stated.

Oops.

"Well, fuck." Lykos' words were loud in the silence that had grown as we watched the sky, her shiver shifting from emotion to cold as the temperature began to drop suddenly.

"I offer the same to you as your Amazons, but even more so than that. Your immortal souls will be left unclaimed and so long as there are realms to travel, you are free to come and go as you please." She smiled coyly, as if she were offering the most delicious of fruits up for our tasting.

"What is the catch?" I asked. Nothing in this world came for free.

"You were once meant to be your mother's champion," Hel stated with a growing smile. "I would have you now be mine. I will not further disrupt your lives, you can live peacefully in or outside of my realm until the time comes that I will need you."

She leaned back with a hip thrust out to the side, a picture of nonchalance.

"Which will be?" Lykos arched her brow, she too knew better than to take a god's word at face value.

"When the wolves Skoll and Hati devour the sun and moon and the stars disappear. In the darkness the war will truly begin. I will need warriors who can see in the dark. Freya has the Hound, Odin has Sleipner and I will have you." Hel gestured only to myself, which made me pause.

"If this is just for my aid, what of Lykos?" I asked cautiously.

"Lykos is your mother's champion. Since she still lives and is a guest no less, I cannot claim her as I can you - but I have no problem with you being a package deal. I do not foresee your mothers having an issue either." She waved her hand off to the side, as if it were nothing but a wisp of a detail.

"How long do we have to decide?" I asked, making sure Lykos knew I would do nothing without it being a joint decision. The time of us avoiding communication was over, everything forward would be with open eyes and hearts.

"Fimbulwinter was foretold to last three years. When it ends, the skies will clear and that is when the wolves will finally catch their prey. I'm sure you will have given me an answer by then. " Hel replied. "For now, we must go, this tear is temporary and fading."

Three years would fly by in a blink, but it would give me enough time to be sure of my choice, to speak with Lykos on it, and to spend time with my mothers - time I might not have ever had otherwise. Hel knew it was an opportunity I couldn't pass up, she'd have time to try and convince me. Afterall, how could I walk away from freedom and protection all wrapped in a bow with a tag written in death's hand.

Even if I were to say no, I'd end up in the fighting all the same - how could I not with loved ones at risk? Truly the choice had already been made by both Lykos and myself. Rhea had known all along what was to come, she had sealed our fates long ago, but damn it all, Lykos and I had carved the trail to it all on our own.

Nodding to Hel I grabbed Lykos' hand, squeezing it to give her comfort as she peered down the path Onya had disappeared on, barely seeming to notice the conversation being had around her. That she trusted me enough to allow herself to drift meant the world to me, though I'd have to repeat the interaction to her later.

The world we knew was gone. The earth was now covered in half a foot of snow in the beginning of what should have been late spring turning to summer. The white gleam was blinding and we were both shivering as we stepped into the portal and crossed into a whole new world.

The end of an era was coming, a few years time was all we would have before everything changed and if the stories were to be believed, it had all started with us. Who knew the extent of that truth, other than the fates themselves? The crones who had, amongst the chaos, slipped away and out of existence.

Stepping into Helheim, we accepted the possibility that perhaps one day, the chaos might settle and a new world would lay open to us. A new world where gods held no sway, where the hauntings of our past could be laid to rest and the rest of our lives could finally, truly begin. A place for us was guaranteed, we only needed to embrace it. There would be a place not just for me and my fox, but also for the darkness within, the monster who crept at the edge of my soul. My fate had always been laid out before me, though I'd tried to deviate from it as often as possible. Perhaps now was the time to simply embrace it.

All we had to do now was survive Ragnarok.

EPILOGUE
A HOMECOMING

A gentle breeze blew across a small field of grass, the tingle of magic the only true hint that it didn't belong there. Trees lined the edges, their branches low hanging and filled with an array of fruit, many combinations unnatural to the world from which we had come. The underworld had once been a beautiful place all on its own, but now had grown into something else altogether. Life thrived, even after death.

The landscape of the underworld was never ending, so it was a simple thing to ask a goddess to create a place from memory and mold it to the world she controlled. That was how I found myself lying upon a small hillside covered with wildflowers, filled with a nostalgic warmth. The blades tickled my bare feet as I spread my toes wide and reveled in the world around me. A smile fluttered across my lips as a warm hand lay across my own, a gentle squeeze saying all that words could not. Turning my head, I found myself lost in the cerulean gaze of my love.

Lykos' grin was foxy in nature, pulling high at the edges so that her canines were always visible. She beamed love and excitement, practically buzzing with energy, despite how still she lay. We both breathed in deep, a false sun warming our flesh and the scent of nature filling our lungs. This was peace.

Hel had kept her word. When Ragnorak truly began, I would be enlisted to fight for her, but until the fighting started, there was nothing holding me here. She even swore to release me from her service as soon as the wars ended, the first amongst gods who I believed would keep her word to me.

In the meantime, Hel had bid us welcome, kissed our cheeks and opened the way to wherever we chose.

Lykos and I had been free to leave, to truly live. We explored the worlds now open to us, forever leaving the world we had known behind and embracing a freedom that still felt foreign. Along the way a fresh joy I couldn't describe had found us, but there was a lingering hole in my beloved that could not be filled. The other worlds worked differently, so it had taken longer than expected, but I had done everything I could to fix it.

"Although this is lovely, I'm not sure I understand why you wanted to come back here so badly. After all, Hel says we probably have another year before things get bad. Surely there were closer fields like the one we remember?" She crooked her brow at me, skeptical of my motives.

I could only grin, which made her even more curious.

"What are you hiding from me?" Her eyes were narrowed, the brows slanted in mock frustration. She sat up on one elbow and rolled to the side so that she could straddle me, her lips pressing out in her best performance of a pout and puppy dog eyes.

Right on cue, a horn sounded out across the field, Hel's sign that our guest was coming.

"Look down the hill and I'll show you." A grin pulled my lips high, my sharpened canines grazing the skin.

She scowled, now knowing she was right and there had been some nefarious plan about all along. As soon as the tear opened however, she was on her feet, shock skittering across her face before it blossomed into a joy that immediately spilled from her eyes.

Gracelessly she scrambled down the hillside as I quickly followed, the sound of hooves preceding a familiar flash of white and red.

"PRINCE!" Lykos' words were half scream and half sob as she choked midway through. No longer able to see through the tears, she wiped at her face furiously. Disbelief contorted her face as I finally caught up to her, a hand gently touching her back in comfort as my own tears slid down my face.

Prince's ears flicked forward, surprise widening his nostrils so that he could better scent the air. As soon as he had confirmation, his answering cry rang out. He reared high in the air, his forelegs pawing out as he sat back and then launched himself towards us. Slamming his hind legs into the earth he reared up again mere feet from Lykos, who in all her nimble excitement met him midair. She hung off his neck as he gracefully found the earth again, careful not to stomp her feet as she slumped against him.

She cried into his neck for a long while, his head curled inward to hug her close, ears pitched forward as his nostrils flared, soft comforting whickers chuffing out his nose. When she finally had herself composed she stepped away from him and turned back towards me.

"Did you do this?" Her breathing was short and sporadic as she dodged hiccups, but her eyes were wide and earnest.

"No, of course not. I don't know how the oaf got himself unalive," I said, chuckling.

Prince snorted and tossed his head, apparently indignant at the implication it was his own fault. Lykos, however, wasn't looking for a joke and put her hands on her hip as she waited for a real answer.

"Yes, of course. I had Hel get a message to me as soon as she knew he was crossing. You've been missing a part of yourself without him and I couldn't bear to see it." I gently amended, "Time has moved differently in each world we visited, so it was hard to know when he'd come."

Prince snorted and shook his head, as if he might blame me for the circumstances, but I didn't get a chance to ask what was said. Lykos' full weight launched atop me, my instincts kicking in just quickly enough to catch her as she wrapped her entire body around me. Her legs and arms wove together in an indiscernible bundle at my back as she buried her face into my neck. I adjusted my feet to better balance us and just barely heard her whisper.

"Thank you for this, for understanding." She clung to me and I held her back as ferociously as I could.

"My love, I would do anything for your happiness," I whispered lovingly.

She had tried to hide the sorrow, to be whole and hale no matter where we were. Any others might have missed it, but there was nothing she could hide from me, not after all we had been through. The subtle frown when she saw any beast of burden, the way she paused at the scent of leather, all of it had accumulated and confirmed what I'd already known in my heart.

She leaned back and the gentle kiss I received was worth every ounce of bargaining I'd had to do to get this timing perfect. She detached herself and I sat on the hillside watching them catch up, giving them all the privacy the underworld could offer, enchanted just to watch the happiness that radiated off them both.

"She is a lucky woman." Hel's voice was a whisper, her presence a gentle caress of cold and darkness at my back. She sat alongside me, her decaying side facing me. It had taken a while, but slowly I had recognized it as a sign of trust, rather than an attempt at intimidation.

"You can bet she knows it too," I replied laughingly.

A smile pulled my lips as Lykos animatedly retold a story, her hands flailing in the air with big gestures that made the horse she spoke to whicker in what I had assumed was laughter. He occasionally pawed the ground, perhaps impatient, when she grew thoughtful, but bobbed his head encouragingly whenever her excitement grew.

Hel chuckled, the notes almost sad, as if she were missing something long lost. She said nothing more and just as quickly as she'd appeared, her presence slipped away, leaving a cold emptiness at my side. In the grass where she had sat, the illusion withered away and a familiar gleam of rock shone up at me, perfectly matching the stone kitsune hanging around my neck.

Although the worlds had been filled with excitement and adventure, I had been eager to return to Helheim.

In this place, with my love and all those I cared for - perhaps I was truly and finally home.

Author's Note

Thank you so much for continuing this journey with me! If you enjoyed this story, please remember to leave a review, it's the best way to support authors and help others find our work.

If you're interested in keeping up with other projects, updates and artwork from the books, you can find me on insta @l.a.raewrites

Keep an eye out for the third and final installment of Nyx and Lykos' journey as I wrap up their portion of the Sealed Fate series!

Thank you again for your love and support, it means the world.

ABOUT THE AUTHOR

L. A. Rae's love of reading and writing started young, encouraged by her mother who has supported her every step of the way. When her head isn't in the clouds dreaming about future stories, she's most often found gardening, horseback riding, and making weird noises at her dog. She lives with an endless supply of dog glitter generously donated by her pack of corgis.

www.ingramcontent.com/pod-product-compliance
Lightning Source LLC
Chambersburg PA
CBHW031139160726
47991CB00004B/1486